"Have you considered that perhaps you were the intended victim?" Nico said.

Frustration and fear washed over her. "I cannot imagine why anyone would wish to hurt me. But then I do not know why anyone would wish to hurt you either. Why? What has happened?" She realized her voice had risen alarmingly, and made an effort to collect herself.

Nico took a step toward her, the cool arrogance gone. *"Maledezione,"* he muttered. The next thing she knew he had pulled her against him. His lips came down on hers and her mouth parted under his as reality and dream merged into one.

He finally released her; for a moment she had no idea where she was. Her eyes shot open and she stared at him, the blood pounding in her head. He looked equally dazed, and then his expression closed. "As you can see, I pose another danger to you as well. For, if you stay, I have every intention of seducing you."

* * *

The Venetian's Mistress
Harlequin® Historical #796—April 2006

THE VENETIAN'S MISTRESS

ANN ELIZABETH CREE

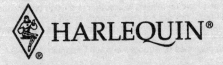

HARLEQUIN®

TORONTO • NEW YORK • LONDON
AMSTERDAM • PARIS • SYDNEY • HAMBURG
STOCKHOLM • ATHENS • TOKYO • MILAN • MADRID
PRAGUE • WARSAW • BUDAPEST • AUCKLAND

ISBN 0-373-29396-8

THE VENETIAN'S MISTRESS

To Linda Kruger, whose encouragement and faith has helped me grow both as a writer and a person. You've been a special friend as well as a wonderful agent.

Chapter One

Lady Thais Margate's long-lashed blue eyes were filled with concern. 'I did not mean to overset you. Perhaps I should not have said anything.'

Cecily Renato took a deep breath and willed herself to remain calm. 'Oh, no, you were quite right to tell me. It is just I am rather surprised.' Actually she was quite shocked, but hardly wanted to tell her companion that. 'I will speak to Mariana straight away.'

'You must not be too hard on them for it was not a very…very improper kiss, but I know you would not want such a thing to happen again. If the wrong persons should come upon them…one would hate for there to be gossip.'

'No. Of course not.'

Lady Margate rose in a rustle of fashionable blue silk. 'I must go for I have an appointment very soon, but I wished to see you the very first thing today. You may be assured that none of this will pass my lips.'

Cecily stood as well. 'I know you will not say anything.' At least she hoped she would not as Cecily hardly knew Lady Margate, who had leased a house in Avezza just over a month ago. But the lovely young widow had already impressed Avezza's residents, both Italian and English, by donating to several charitable causes as well as by heading up a committee to repair the damage done to the church of Santa Sofia during the French occupation.

Lady Margate took Cecily's hand. Although Cecily was not particularly tall, Lady Margate's fine-boned features and delicate build made Cecily feel ungainly next to her. Lady Margate smiled kindly. 'You are such a devoted mother. I have no doubt you will do the right thing, although you must not be too harsh with your stepdaughter or Lord Ballister. The very first time I saw them together I could sense a special sympathy between them. It is most unfortunate that the Duke of Severin is unlikely to allow them to marry. I have heard from Severin himself that he wishes to procure an heiress for his cousin, preferably the daughter of a peer. There is a certain earl's daughter that I have heard…but that is only a rumour.' She regarded Cecily with sympathetic eyes. 'It would not be easy for your stepdaughter to live in England. The society is so very different, as you know.'

'Yes, it is different.' Cecily attempted to suppress the twinge of resentment she felt at Lady Margate's implication that Severin would not consider Mariana suitable for his cousin. 'I will see you out.'

'That will not be necessary. You must give your lovely daughter my regards. And Signora Zanetti.' She pressed Cecily's hand before releasing it, her grip surprisingly strong. Cecily accompanied her across the small salon to the staircase, which led to the ground floor.

She watched Lady Margate depart, her thoughts in turmoil. Mariana and Lord Ballister? How had this happened when she had made certain they never met except in company? Why had she not watched Mariana more closely last night at Lady Margate's *conversazione*?

Because she had been certain that Mariana's *tendre* for Lord Ballister had faded just as she was certain Lord Ballister's initial interest in her stepdaughter had died away. So when Mariana had gone to the garden with her friend, Teresa Carasco, and Teresa's brother, Cecily had not been concerned. Nor had she worried very much when Mariana had been unusually quiet and preoccupied on the carriage ride back home.

'Why was she here? That woman?'

Cecily jumped when her sister-in-law spoke from behind her. Barbarina had the disconcerting habit of suddenly appearing and startling her.

She turned. 'Lady Margate was here to pay a visit, that is all.'

'She is not good. She brings nothing but trouble.'

'Surely not.' When Barbarina merely stared at her, she tried again. 'At least not today. I must speak to Mariana now.'

'She came to tell you that the English lord has kissed Mariana, no? You must hope that she does not tell anyone else. Such as his cousin, the Duke. Or Rafaele.'

'I have no idea why she would want to do so.' Cecily said. 'Please, Barbarina, do not eavesdrop.'

'What can I do when you hold your conversations in the salon where everyone can hear?' She shrugged and fixed her dark gaze on Cecily. 'You must send Mariana away before Rafaele learns of this. It will not please him to discover that you have allowed the cousin of the Duke to kiss Mariana.'

'Rafaele is in Verona so it is unlikely he will hear of this. At any rate, nothing more will happen.'

'You must hope not. For if Rafaele does, he will come and challenge the Lord Ballister to a duel. If that happens, the Duke will come and there will be another fight. In the end, Rafaele will send Mariana to the convent. Where you should have sent her as her mother, Caterina, had wished. Then there would be no need to worry about kisses.'

Cecily quelled the sharp pang of hurt she still felt when Barbarina compared Cecily to her husband Marco's first wife and Mariana's mother. 'I would hope that everyone would behave in a more civilised manner than that. Why do you think that they will fight if they meet? Is it because of something that happened in the past? When the Duke was here?' This was not the first time since Lord Ballister's arrival in Avezza that Barbarina had hinted at some sort of quarrel between Mariana's trustee, Rafaele Vianoli, and the Duke of Severin, who was Lord Ballister's guardian.

'It would be better if you do not ask more questions.'

Cecily bit back her frustration. Barbarina always lapsed into odd, cryptic pronouncements when she no longer wished to answer any questions. 'Very well. I won't. For now, I am going to speak to Mariana.' She walked away before she said something she would later regret. She tried to be patient with Barbarina for, before he died, Marco had asked her to watch over his older widowed half-sister. She reminded herself as well that Barbarina had never really recovered from the discovery that her beloved husband had died while running off with another woman. But sometimes it was all she could do to keep her temper. Particularly at times like this.

Mariana was in her bedchamber. She sat on a chair near the window and when Cecily entered she looked up from the book on her lap. Cecily crossed the room and pulled the small stool near the bed to the chair and sat down. 'I must talk to you.'

'Is something wrong, Mama?' From the anxious look on her daughter's lovely face, she suspected Mariana had a very good idea of why Cecily was there.

'Lady Margate came to tell me that she found you and Lord Ballister in an embrace last night. That he kissed you. Is this true?'

Mariana looked away for an instant before she answered. 'He kissed me and I kissed him back.'

Oh, dear. 'I do not need to remind you that it is most improper for young unmarried girls to be alone with a man. And very improper to exchange a kiss with any

man except a fiancé or a husband. Lord Ballister should
know this. He also must know that he risked your reputation by such behaviour. You are fortunate that Lady
Margate discovered you and not one of the other guests.'

'It is not Si— Lord Ballister's fault. I asked him to
meet me in the garden.'

'Why would you do that?'

'I…I wished to talk to him.'

'Have you met him alone like this before?'

'Only a…a few times.'

Cecily tried to hide her shock. 'Has he ever done anything besides kiss you?'

'No. We only talk. He has not kissed me before last
night.'

Thank God. 'Then I must forbid you to see Lord
Ballister again, except in the presence of others. I will
not allow him to ruin your reputation.'

'He wants to marry me,' Mariana said flatly.

Cecily's heart stopped for a fraction. 'Did he tell you
that?' she asked carefully.

'Yes. But he said he would not ask me until I am seventeen and then he will speak to you.'

Cecily drew in a breath. 'I see.' She felt as if she'd
been hit in the stomach. Did Lord Ballister hope to seduce Mariana by promising marriage? He did not seem
the sort of young man to do so, but then she had not
thought Mariana would ever arrange a rendezvous with
a young man in a dark garden.

'You will approve, will you not?' Mariana asked. A
note of anxiety had crept into her voice.

'You are still young, too young to think of marriage,' she began.

'Mama was seventeen when she married Papa.'

'Yes, but they had known each other since childhood. You have known Lord Ballister scarcely a month.' She hesitated. 'It hardly matters whether I approve or not, for it is unlikely the Duke of Severin will. Or Rafaele.'

'But why not? Because Cousin Raf and the Duke have quarrelled?'

Cecily started. 'How do you know that?'

'Zia told me. But she would not tell me what the quarrel was about.'

A surge of anger shot through Cecily. Barbarina had no business telling Mariana such a thing. 'I am not even certain they did quarrel. There are other reasons, however, why a marriage between you and Lord Ballister is impossible.' Mariana stared at her, her expression stricken. Cecily took her hands. 'I am sorry, but you are scarcely more than a child. Some day you will meet a man whom you can love, someone more suited to you.'

'There will be no one else.' Mariana rose and Cecily could see she was fighting back tears. She walked to the door and stopped her hand on the handle. 'You are wrong. I am not a child.' She left, her pale quietness more alarming than if she had burst into tears and run from the room as she had in the past when angry or upset.

Cecily quelled her impulse to go after Mariana, suspecting she would only make matters worse. Mixed in with her anger and worry was fear. Fear that Lord Ballister was more to her stepdaughter than a young girl's first love; fear that if Mariana was capable of meeting him alone, she was capable of something even more rash.

Surely Lord Ballister must realise he could not marry Mariana without his cousin's consent. He must have some idea that his cousin wished him to marry an heiress; although Mariana was not penniless, she was far from wealthy.

He must know, as well, that Mariana could not marry without Raf's and Cecily's permission. Although Raf was Mariana's trustee, Marco had left Mariana in Cecily's care and had made it clear that both Raf and Cecily were to approve any potential husband for Mariana.

If Raf and the Duke had indeed quarrelled, it was even more unlikely either man would approve, thank goodness.

Then she felt guilty for even thinking such a thing when Mariana was so unhappy. For her own selfish reasons, Cecily did not want Mariana to marry an Englishman. She could not bear to have Mariana go away and live in a country that Cecily could never return to.

Lord Ballister had told Mariana he would wait until she was seventeen before speaking to Cecily. She assumed he would wait until then to speak to his cousin as well. She only hoped that, by that time, Lord Ballister would be long gone and that Mariana would have recovered from her infatuation. What if they did not? What if they decided to run off together? She knew only too well how easy it was to take such a course.

She could not entertain that possibility. She must

speak to Lord Ballister today and tell him in no uncertain terms that he was not to see Mariana alone and he was not to speak of marriage again.

Nico stood in front of the window of the small villa Simon had leased. It stood on one of the hills that gently sloped up from the town providing a clear view of the red tile roofs and green trees against the blue background of the distant Dolomites. To the right he could see the brownish-red roof of the Villa Guiliani, the villa that had once belonged to Angelina's family. He turned away, as an unexpected surge of regret and longing shot through him.

He was not in Avezza to relive the past, but to deal with the present in the form of his cousin and ward, Simon, Viscount Ballister. If Simon's friend, Philip Ashton, was correct and Simon was indeed flirting with Mariana Renato, then Simon needed to be removed from her vicinity as quickly as possible. Before Rafaele Vianoli got wind of this and decided to call Simon out. For according to Ashton, Vianoli was Mariana Renato's guardian, although Ashton had also told him Vianoli had not set foot in Avezza for months.

Vianoli would return quickly enough if he thought Simon was trifling with his ward. It was unlikely he wanted an alliance between the two families any more than Nico did.

He could not fathom why the girl's stepmother did not put a stop to this, although it was possible she did not know of the quarrel between himself and Vianoli.

Perhaps she did not care and hoped to attach herself to a duke's family through her stepdaughter. At any rate, he intended to put a quick halt to any such plans. His first order of business was to call on Signora Renato and make it clear she was to keep her daughter away from Simon. He would deal with Simon after that.

For now, he needed to find the housekeeper and have his trunk taken to his room so he could change out of his dusty travelling clothes. He crossed the room and as he did heard a woman's, *'Buongiorno?'*

He strode into the hall and saw a woman standing near his trunk. The missing housekeeper, undoubtedly. 'I will use the blue bedchamber. Tell Giovanni to take my luggage there directly. I wish to change.'

'I suggest you tell Giovanni yourself, *signor*.'

Her cool voice startled him as much as her words. He looked hard at her. She was much younger than he'd expect for a housekeeper and much too pretty with a pair of large eyes set in a delicate oval face. 'I beg your pardon, *signora*?' he said coldly.

'I said you should tell Giovanni yourself.'

'And who are you, *signora*?' She was not Simon's housekeeper; she carried herself too well and her gown, although worn and unfashionable, was made of good material. Her dark eyes met his despite the flush that stole over her cheeks. He had an impression of quiet dignity.

'I was looking for Lord Ballister. Is he at home?'

'Not at the moment. Perhaps I might help you.' Perhaps it was not Mariana Renato he needed to worry about, but this woman who seemed to be running free in his cousin's home.

'I…I doubt that. My business is with Lord Ballister.'

'Is it? Then I suspect it might be with me as well since I am Lord Ballister's guardian. First you will tell me your name.'

Her eyes widened. 'You are the Duke?'

He allowed a smile to touch his mouth. '*Sì*, and you, *signora*?'

'But why are you not in Venice?'

'Because I am here. Your name, please,

'I am Signora Renato.'

This time he started. Ashton had not mentioned that Signora Renato looked to be a scarce dozen years older than her stepdaughter. He recovered quickly. 'Signora Renato? How convenient. I believe your business is with me after all.'

'I have no idea what you are talking about.' Her slightly apprehensive expression belied her words.

'But I think you do. You have a daughter, I believe.'

'Oh, drat.'

He'd hardly expected that. 'Such a very English expression.'

'But I am English.'

Ashton had said nothing about that either. 'Are you?' He switched to English. 'Then allow me to compliment you on your command of Italian. I would have thought you spoke the language from birth.'

'I might say the same thing for you, your Grace.'

'But I have. My mother is Italian. You may come to

the library with me. I do not wish to continue this discussion here.'

'I do not wish to continue this discussion at all. My business is with Lord Ballister and since he is not here, then I will take my leave.' She turned and started towards the door.

He caught her arm. 'Any business you have with my cousin is with me. And since I came to Avezza particularly to see you, then I've no intention of allowing you to leave before I accomplish the task.'

She turned and looked up, her expressive eyes meeting his. Her soft mouth was parted slightly and he felt the faint stirrings of desire.

She swallowed before she spoke, 'Please let go of my arm. It is not necessary to take me prisoner.' Her voice was calm.

His hand fell away. 'Then you will come with me to the library.'

She eyed him for a moment. 'Very well,' she said coolly.

'Good.'

A short dark, woman bustled into the hall. Her face broke into a smile when she saw Signora Renato. '*Buongiorno, signora.*' Her smile faltered a little when she glanced at Nico. She fidgeted as he gave her brief instructions, then she curtsied and bustled away in obvious relief.

He led Signora Renato to the library, a small room off the grand salon, a pleasant room that faced south towards the green fields beyond. He indicated one of the upholstered chairs. 'You may sit here, *signora.*'

Instead of sitting, he leaned against the marble-topped table near her. Signora Renato sat on the edge of the chair, her hands locked around her reticule. She looked like a young girl herself, although he guessed her to be in her late twenties. 'I assume from the enthusiastic manner in which the housekeeper greeted you that you must be a frequent visitor here.'

'I have never been here before. Flavia's sister is my housekeeper.' She looked insulted that he would even suggest such a thing.

'Is she? Then I will get to the point of this conversation. It has come to my attention that you have been encouraging a match between your daughter and my cousin.'

She stared at him as if he'd run mad. 'I have been encouraging a match? I assure you I have done no such thing!'

Her outraged seemed genuine. Or she was a consummate actress. 'Are you denying that my cousin has an interest in your daughter?'

'I really have no idea whether he does or not. You will have to ask him.'

'I will. But first I wish to ask you.'

'You may ask as much as you wish, but I will still give you the same answer,' she snapped. From the stubborn look on her face, he doubted she'd tell him much more.

'As you wish, *signora*.' He felt his own temper rising. 'However, I will suggest that you curtail any sort of plans you have made that include my cousin.'

She stood, her hand trembling around her reticule. 'I

have no idea who told you such things but your…your informant was quite wrong. Lord Ballister is the last person I would want my daughter to marry. Good day, your Grace.' She stalked to the door. This time he made no move to stop her. At the door, she turned, her eyes blazing. 'There is one more thing. If you do anything to hurt my daughter, I will cheerfully tear you limb from limb.'

He was too taken aback to speak. She left the room, her head high, and he stared after her with the sense he'd lost the round. Tear him limb from limb? He'd hardly expected that from such a mild-looking creature. But then, nothing about the encounter had gone as planned. Certainly he had not expected her to declare in such disdainful tones that Simon was the last man she would want for her daughter.

He frowned. Was it possible Ashton was wrong and there was nothing between Simon and Signorina Renato? If that was the case, why had Signora Renato told him to ask Simon instead of telling him she did not know? He had failed as well to ask her why she had called on Simon today. Not that she would have told him. She would probably look at him with her large disdainful eyes and tell him it was none of his affair.

He was hardly finished with her. Not until he discovered if Simon indeed harboured feelings for Mariana Renato. Particularly if it turned out that Signora Renato knew about it all along.

Cecily did not slow her pace until she had passed through the pillared gates of the Villa. Anger, coupled with the irrational fear that the Duke of Severin might try and stop her from leaving, had driven her steps. Now that she was safe, she realised her legs were shaking. She started down the narrow road that led towards the village, her thoughts in turmoil.

Whoever had told Severin that she was promoting a match between Lord Ballister and Mariana? And how dare he come here and accuse her before he even knew the facts? Just thinking of the cool, arrogant way he had looked at her made her angry all over again. He was not at all what she had expected—if she thought of him at all, she had pictured him as much older, which did not make sense for he must be Raf's age and Raf was two years her senior. Nor had she expected to find him as darkly attractive. If one liked that sort of cool, male look.

Which she did not. In fact, there had been nothing about him she liked. She would never allow Mariana to marry into a family with that man in it. He would ride roughshod over her just as he had attempted to do with Cecily.

She could only hope that, in time, Mariana's infatuation with Lord Ballister would fade. Perhaps she should send Mariana to stay with her mother's cousins in Padua. Vittoria and Serefina were strict but kind, and doted on Mariana. She would send a letter off to Padua tomorrow.

If only she had someone to turn to for advice. Someone to reassure her that she need not worry about Mariana—that her feelings for Lord Ballister were the normal ones any young girl felt for her first *tendre*.

Barbarina was no help. Even if she knew exactly where Raf was, she could hardly write to him if there was any possibility at all he would quarrel with Lord Ballister or his cousin.

Perhaps she should have returned to England a year ago when her grandmother had summoned her, but the bitterness over Lady Telford's rejection of Marco and Mariana still hurt. And, despite her grandmother's adding that, of course, 'the child must come', Cecily could not put aside her pride.

Well, it was too late now. She had dashed off a chilly response, making it quite clear she neither wanted nor needed her grandmother's help and she was doing very well on her own. She was already regretting her rash words before the letter had left Italy, but she had no way of retrieving it.

She was on her own.

Chapter Two

'Nic? What are you doing here? I thought you were in Venice.'

Nico looked up and for a moment was startled to see his cousin in the doorway. Simon moved into the room, a handsome youth with a pair of startling blue eyes, and a charming smile. He was dressed in a riding coat and boots, and carried a crop.

'As you can see, I am not.' His gaze raked over Simon. 'You look well. Italy must agree with you.' In the time Simon had been away from England, he had grown. His shoulders were broader and his face had lost some of its boyishness.

'It does. I cannot imagine returning to another English winter after this. So why are you here?'

'To see you safely to Venice,' Nico said carelessly. 'Since we have not set eyes on you for the past five months, my mother and Eleanora are understandably anxious to see for themselves that you are well. They are in Milan, but will be in Venice by the end of the week.'

Simon hesitated a fraction. 'Then there's no rush. I can stay for a few more days.'

'You are not bored yet? If I recall, Avezza is not exactly filled with the sort of entertainments that you favour. And it is a two-day journey to Venice. I would have expected you would prefer to be closer.'

Simon shrugged. 'Oh, 'tis not so bad. I find I rather like the quiet. I've learned to speak a tolerable Italian and there have been enough *conversaziones*—they are rather like our routs—and the like to keep us entertained. There's going to be some sort of fête at the end of the week—rather like a miniature Vauxhall, I am told. In fact, there is to be a *musicale* tonight I had planned to attend, but since you are here… I know you detest that sort of thing.'

'You do not need to change your plans on my account. I will accompany you, of course. If you wish me to.'

'That would be splendid.' He grinned at Nico. 'You will cause a stir. I must change. Do you have everything you need?'

'Yes. I am quite comfortable. By the way, you had a visitor today. A Signora Renato.'

Simon, who had started towards the door, stopped. 'Signora Renato? Are you certain?'

'Quite. She gave me her name herself. You seem surprised that she would call.'

'I am. I have always had the impression she does not like me above half. Did she say what she wanted?'

'No, she left no message.'

'I see. Most likely nothing of importance.'

Nico thought his voice was a little too casual, but decided not to pursue the matter, at least for now. 'Will you dine here tonight?'

'Yes.' He started to leave the room and then paused. He flashed Nico a boyish grin. 'I am glad you are here.'

Nico watched him go. He'd said nothing about Signorina Renato, but then he had hardly expected him to. So Signora Renato did nòt like him? He wondered why, for most people liked Simon. He hoped Signora Renato and her daughter would attend the *musicale* tonight— he was now very curious to find out exactly what was going on between his cousin and the Renatos.

Cecily glanced down the dinner table, grateful the tense meal was nearly finished. Barbarina ate in her usual silence, speaking only to complain about the food. A thin woman, dressed from head to foot in black, she resembled an underfed crow although her appetite was certainly not lacking. Mariana sat next to Cecily, her eyes slightly swollen, her manner subdued. She answered Cecily politely, but refused to look her in the eye or contribute anything more than necessary to Cecily's efforts at conversation.

'There is something I must tell both of you,' Cecily said finally.

Barbarina continued to pick at her fish without looking up. Mariana said nothing.

'The Duke of Severin, Lord Ballister's cousin, is in Avezza.'

Barbarina paused, her fork in mid-air. Mariana raised her head. 'Why?'

'He should not have come,' Barbarina said before Cecily could answer. 'He brings nothing but trouble.' She forked the bite of fish into her mouth.

'I pray you will not say such things.' Cecily was in no mood to put up with Barbarina's vague, dire predictions.

Mariana's sulks had vanished. She propped her chin upon her hand, her eyes sparkling with interest. 'Because of cousin Raf? Do you suppose if Raf returns they will fight?'

'There will be no fights. I am certain the Duke means to leave very soon.' At least she hoped he would once Mariana was gone.

'If he has any sense, he will leave right away. Before there is more tragedy,' Barbarina said.

It was clearly time for dinner to end before Barbarina said something about Raf and Lord Ballister, which would only serve to upset Mariana. Cecily rose. 'I do not want to hear any more talk of fights and tragedy. We must get ready for Signora Bartolini's salon. Are you certain you do not wish to go, Barbarina? I can order the carriage be brought around.' Barbarina never went to such events, but Cecily always felt obligated to ask her

Barbarina frowned at her. 'I never go out in the evenings.'

'Do you suppose the Duke will be at Signora Bartolini's tonight?' Mariana asked. She now looked worried.

'He might be, which is why I wished to tell you.' Cecily hesitated. Should she hint to Mariana that the

Duke's purpose for coming to Avezza was to quell any romance between her and Simon?

Looking at Mariana's pretty face, she decided it would not be wise. 'Perhaps you should go and make certain the gown I had laid out for you is the one you wish to wear.'

As soon as Mariana left the room, Cecily approached Barbarina. 'Please do not say such things in Mariana's presence. I do not want to worry her.' She tried to keep her voice as reasonable as possible.

Barbarina fixed her small black eyes on Cecily. 'It is a bad sign that they both are in Avezza. That woman and the Duke.'

'You are speaking of Lady Margate?'

'Yes.'

Barbarina's conversation was proving to be more confusing than usual. 'But what does she have to do with the Duke? Why do you say he will bring more tragedy? Are you referring to his quarrel with Raf?'

'Perhaps.'

'But what did they quarrel about? Why has no one ever said a thing about it until now? Not even Marco told me.'

'Why should he? It happened before you came and has nothing to do with you. Why is it your business?'

Because she cared about Mariana and Raf, but she had given up telling Barbarina that. It made no difference that Cecily had been Marco's wife for two years and his widow for the past seven—Barbarina still considered Cecily an outsider. 'Perhaps it is not,' she said quietly, 'but I do not want Mariana upset. I must go and

change. You should let me know if you need anything
before I go.'

She waited a moment, but Barbarina merely grunted.
Cecily left the room. She wished it were possible to
plead a headache and stay home, but she had promised
Signora Bartolini she would attend. She feared it would
be a very long evening.

Cecily glanced around Signora Bartolini's crowded
salon and was relieved that neither Lord Ballister nor
his disturbing cousin seemed to be present. She spotted
her friend, Viola Carasco, and her daughter Teresa sitting nearby. Viola smiled and motioned and Cecily saw
two empty chairs next to her.

Viola moved over a chair so that Mariana and Teresa
could sit together. She was a plump, pretty woman with
a pair of sparkling, dark eyes. She leaned towards Cecily. 'I have heard the most interesting rumour. It is said
that Lord Ballister's cousin has arrived in Avezza. Perhaps you have heard that also?'

'Yes.' Cecily hesitated and then decided against telling Viola about her encounter with him since she had
not told Mariana or Barbarina. 'You met him, did you
not?' She recalled Viola had mentioned that shortly after
Lord Ballister arrived in Avezza.

'Once or twice, but the Conte's family did not spend
as much time at the Villa Guiliani as they did at their
villa near Treviso. They were here so much that summer because of the damage done to their primary villa
when the French occupied it.'

Cecily wanted to ask more, but just then the pianist played the opening measures of an aria and soon the high clear notes of the soprano filled the salon.

The applause had just died down when two latecomers entered. Cecily paid little attention until Viola craned her head around to look. She turned back to Cecily. 'He is here,' she whispered.

She did not need to ask whom Viola referred to. Unable to resist, Cecily looked towards the door. To her chagrin, Severin's eyes fell on her and a cool smile touched his mouth. She quickly looked away. Mariana touched her arm. 'Is that the Duke?'

'Yes, but please do not stare.'

Mariana sniffed and looked indignant. 'I was not.'

Cecily found Viola staring at her. 'He seems to know you.'

Her cheeks heated. 'I did meet him. Quite by accident.' She was grateful when the next piece started. Not that she paid the least heed to it, for she was planning how to convince Mariana to leave during the interval. She certainly did not want Severin and Mariana to meet.

Her plans were thwarted by Lady Margate who appeared almost as soon as Signora Bartolini announced there were refreshments in the adjoining salon. She was charmingly dressed in her favourite shade of pale blue, her fashionable gown overshadowing the made-over and outdated gowns worn by most of the other women in the room, including Cecily. Napoleon was now gone, but nearly a decade and a half of French rule had left many of the residents of Avezza impoverished.

Lady Margate greeted Viola and then turned to Cecily. 'I must speak with you for a moment if Signora Carasco does not mind.'

'Of course not,' Viola said.

Lady Margate waited until they were out of earshot. 'I do not know if you saw the man with Lord Ballister, but that is his cousin, the Duke of Severin. Because of our conversation today, I felt I must warn you.'

'Thank you.' She did not think it prudent to tell Lady Margate her warning was much too late.

'We are old acquaintances so you must tell me if there is any difficulty.'

Out of the corner of her eye, Cecily saw Teresa and Mariana heading towards the refreshment room. She prayed Mariana would stay away from Lord Ballister. And that Lord Ballister would stay away from her.

She smiled politely at Lady Margate. 'I am certain there will be none. You are most kind to offer. I must beg your pardon—I need to speak to Mariana for a moment.'

'I do understand.'

Cecily paused in the doorway of the salon. The table in the centre of the room was filled with trays of cakes. She did not see Mariana or Teresa among the guests, but finally spotted Lord Ballister talking to Paolo Carasco, Viola's son. Thank goodness he was not with Mariana.

'*Buonasera*, Signora Renato.'

She spun around, her relief vanishing. 'What are you doing here?' Severin stood next to her, tall and far too attractive in a well-fitting coat of dark blue over black pantaloons. A small diamond gleamed in the folds of his snowy cravat. Despite his elegant attire, he looked equally as dangerous as he had this afternoon.

'As in this particular spot? Or in the house?' A slight smile touched his mouth. 'Not that it matters at any rate—my sole purpose for coming tonight was to see you. As well as meet Signorina Renato.'

'I cannot think why you would wish to do either.' Heat stole into her cheeks despite her effort to remain cool. 'Nor do I want you to meet my daughter. I will not allow you to frighten her.'

'I would not dare. Not unless I wished to be torn limb from limb. Cheerfully, I believe you said.'

'I still mean it.'

'I have no doubt that you do.'

'Severin! How naughty of you to come to Avezza without telling me!' Lady Margate glided up to them. She glanced at Cecily and arched a brow. 'Signora Renato, you have been naughty as well, for you did not tell me you knew Severin.'

'I do not know him. I met him quite by accident.' Lady Margate's tone was quite playful, but Cecily suspected matters would only be complicated further if Lady Margate discovered they had met earlier.

'Just now? You seemed to be engaged in such serious conversation for meeting so very recently.' She turned to Severin.

'We have not been formally introduced,' he said coolly.

'Then I must set that to rights. Signora Renato, may I present his Grace, the Duke of Severin? Severin, Signora Renato. She is one of the nicest persons in all of Avezza.'

Cecily found herself giving her hand to Severin. He took it, the warm strength of his fingers closing around hers. 'Then you must be if Lady Margate says so. Signora Renato, I am more than delighted to meet you.' His expression was all that was polite.

'As I am to meet you.' She kept her voice equally polite.

He released her hand. Lady Margate smiled. 'Signora Renato has the most lovely daughter. You met her when she was very young, I believe.'

Cecily stared at her, dismayed. Why would she say such a thing?

'Then I hope to become reacquainted with her very soon.' Severin's voice was bland.

'Perhaps.' Cecily gave him a vague smile. 'I am certain you and Lady Margate have much to discuss, so I will leave you. Goodnight, Lady Margate, your Grace.'

'You are not staying for the rest of the concert?' Lady Margate asked.

'No, I promised Barbarina we would return early. She has one of her headaches.'

'The poor thing. Of course you must go.'

'Yes.' Cecily made her escape before something else happened, such as Severin suggesting to Lady Margate that they meet Mariana.

Mariana was neither near the refreshment table nor anywhere else in the room. Cecily left through the door that led to the next small room, intending to return to the salon through it so she wouldn't have to pass Severin. A number of people had drifted to this room. To her consternation, Mariana and Simon stood in one corner, engaged in conversation. Neither Teresa nor Paolo was anywhere in sight.

She crossed the room. 'Good evening, Lord Ballister,' she said. 'Mariana, I have been looking for you.'

Mariana looked decidedly guilty. 'Oh, have you?'

'I fear I detained her,' Simon said in his easy way. His face sobered. 'My cousin said you had wished to speak to me when you called this afternoon.'

Mariana swung around to face Cecily, who managed a smile. 'It was nothing of importance. However, Mariana and I must leave so we will bid you goodnight.'

'But, Mama—' Mariana began.

'We must go.' She gave Mariana a sharp look. Mariana stared back at her, her expression a mixture of defiance and misery.

'Don't,' Lord Ballister said softly. 'Everything will be fine.' The tender look he bestowed upon Mariana made Cecily feel odd and, when Mariana nodded, her heart suddenly felt like lead.

Someone appeared beside her and the skin on her neck prickled. She did not need Lord Ballister's surprised, 'Nic,' to tell her who it was. How had he managed to extract himself from Lady Margate so quickly? She felt rather ill—if he saw the expression on Lord Ballister's face he would never believe the young couple were mere acquaintances.

Mariana looked up and the faint apprehension on her

face made Cecily move closer to her. 'We must go. Goodnight, Lord Ballister.' She glanced at Severin. 'Your Grace.'

'But not before you introduce me to your daughter.' The slight smile at his mouth did not quite reach his eyes.

She could not evade him unless she wanted to be insufferably rude and she knew she was coming close to it. 'Very well.' She looked up; a smile of her own on her lips although she knew it was equally as false as his. She performed the introduction, her eyes never leaving his face.

He took Mariana's hand. 'It is unlikely that you remember, but I met you when you were very young, perhaps only three.' He spoke in Italian, his voice polite, his expression surprisingly kind.

Mariana gave him a tentative smile. 'I am pleased to meet you, your…your Grace.' She glanced at Lord Ballister.

'That is correct.' Lord Ballister looked at his cousin. 'Signorina Renato was not quite certain how one addressed an English duke.'

'You did very well.' Severin released her hand and Mariana flushed, her face shyly pleased. She looked pretty and charming and vulnerable and Cecily wanted nothing more than to protect her.

She took Mariana's arm. She could see the other guests were starting to drift towards the salon. The second half of the concert was about to start. 'Come, we must take our leave of Signora Bartolini.'

'Did you walk?' Lord Ballister asked.

'Yes.'

'Then you will allow us to escort you home,' Severin said.

That was the last thing Cecily desired. 'That is hardly necessary. It is not far and we prefer to walk. Besides, I have no doubt you wish to hear the rest of the concert.'

Lord Ballister laughed. 'You do not know my cousin well. He almost always leaves in the middle of any sort of performance. Claims he does not like to sit for long.'

'Quite true. In addition, I have what I came for tonight so I have no incentive to stay.' He met her gaze, challenging her.

'Indeed. But we would still prefer to walk. I should not want to inconvenience you.'

'It will be no inconvenience.'

'No use arguing with him, Signora Renato,' Lord Ballister interjected. 'He always has his way.'

'I imagine that must be rather annoying at times.' She spoke more tartly than she intended to. Lord Ballister looked rather startled and Mariana now had the expression she always wore when she feared Cecily was about to argue with a shopkeeper and embarrass her.

Severin appeared unaffected. 'Very annoying, I have been told. My cousin will send for the carriage while we bid our hostess farewell.'

Cecily opened her mouth to protest, but Mariana tugged on her arm. 'Mama, please do not say anything more,' she whispered.

'But...' She caught a glimpse of faint amusement in Severin's eyes and suspected he had overheard Mariana's plea.

'Very well,' she said.

Signora Bartolini was quite sympathetic, although she only half-listened to Cecily's explanation. 'Ah, the headache, of course you must go. How kind of the Duke and Lord Ballister to see you home so you do not risk making it worse.' She turned to the Duke before Cecily could correct her impression. 'You have been away from here far too long. How are your dear mama and your sister? They are not with you?'

'They are in Milan visiting cousins. They are both well.'

'Very good. How long will you stay with us?'

'I have not decided.'

She glanced at Cecily and Mariana with a little smile. 'I quite understand.'

What did she understand? Oh, lord, at this rate, he would never be convinced she had not plotted to bring his cousin and Mariana together.

She could hardly wait to escape, but after leaving the salon they were forced to remain in the hall while the footman fetched their shawls. 'I did not realise you had a headache as well,' Severin said, with what she considered false concern.

'I did not earlier, but I most certainly have one now.'

'I wonder why,' he murmured. For the first time she saw genuine amusement in his face. It was quite unnerving. She pulled her gaze away just as the footman returned with their shawls. Severin took them. 'Allow me,' he said. He draped Mariana's around her shoulders with a gentle touch and then turned to Cecily. 'Signora Renato?'

'I prefer to carry my shawl.' She held out her hand.

'As you wish.' He gave it to her, his hand brushing hers. She nearly jumped at the contact and prayed he had not noticed anything amiss.

'The carriage is here,' he said. He was looking at her rather than the door.

She felt rather breathless. 'How do you know? You have not looked.'

'Are you always this argumentative?'

'Goodness, the poor soprano will have no audience if anyone else leaves!'

Lady Margate stood in the hall behind them, her gaze going from one to the other. 'I had no idea you wished to leave as well, Severin. But then I should not be too surprised, for you never do like these things!' She descended the last few steps and smiled at Cecily. 'I hope he is not being too difficult.' She tossed a quick glance in Mariana's direction. Mariana had now drifted towards the door.

'No, he is not.' It was quite apparent to Cecily that Lady Margate and Severin were much more than acquaintances. She suddenly did not want to reveal anything more about Mariana in front of the other woman.

'Then you have no more objections to accepting my offer to take you and Signorina Renato home in my carriage,' Severin said smoothly.

'He is to escort you home?' Lady Margate said. Her look of arch surprise made Cecily cringe. 'I had come out for the sole purpose of offering the very same thing after Signora Bartolini told me you had the headache.

You must allow me to do so since there would only be three of us instead of four and you would be much more comfortable.'

'You are very kind—' Cecily began, only to be cut off.

'I have no doubt Signora Renato appreciates your offer, but my carriage has already been brought around. She will be more comfortable if she does not have to wait any longer.'

Brief discomfiture flitted across Lady Margate's face and then she was smiling again. 'You are always so logical—it is quite appalling. You must not bully Signora Renato too much then, particularly if she has the headache.'

'I have no intention of doing so,' he said coolly. 'Goodnight, Thais.'

'Goodnight. And, dear Signora Renato, I will call on you tomorrow, if I may, to see how you have fared.'

'Thank you. Goodnight, Lady Margate.'

Although Severin's touch was light as he took her arm and then guided her across the hall, Cecily still felt like a prisoner. Worse, Mariana had disappeared outside; when they stepped out, Cecily could see her and Lord Ballister talking together on the steps. They quickly drew apart when Severin and Cecily appeared. She dared not look at Severin's face as he helped her into the carriage after assisting Mariana.

No one said much on the short distance down the hill to her house. Severin escorted Mariana and Cecily to the door. 'Goodnight, Signorina,' he said to Mariana. 'I trust you will not object if I detain Signora Renato for a minute.'

'No, your Grace.' She cast Cecily a hesitant look before going inside.

He waited until Mariana had gone. 'I will call on you tomorrow,' he said to Cecily.

'I cannot imagine why.'

'No? After tonight I think we have a great deal to discuss.' He braced one arm on the wall and looked down at her.

'I believe we agree that neither one of us wants a match between them.'

'Perhaps I have another reason as well.'

'And what would that be?'

'To further our acquaintance.'

Her heart slammed against her ribs. 'I…it is quite unlikely I will be at home.'

'I think you will be. Goodnight, *signora*.' The slight smile at his mouth panicked her more than anything else he'd yet said. He turned and strode towards the carriage before she could answer.

Cecily dashed inside her house and leaned against the door. Of course, he meant nothing by that last enigmatic remark. He undoubtedly wished to intimidate her by implying he had an…an interest in her. She very much feared, however, if that had been his intention, he had quite succeeded.

Reluctant to go inside, Nico leaned against one of the pillars on the portico. The night was pleasant—the sort of night he remembered. He could not fault Simon for flirting with Mariana Renato, for she had grown from a charming small child with a pair of large dark eyes and a sweet smile into a beautiful young girl with large dark eyes and an equally sweet smile. Very much like her mother, Caterina. She had died after he left Italy and he had been sorry to hear of her death for she had been kind as well as lovely. He idly wondered how Marco Renato had come to marry a young Englishwoman. Had they met in England, Italy or elsewhere?

He reluctantly decided he could not blame Marco Renato for choosing her as a second wife, for Cecily Renato was certainly as lovely as Caterina had been although in a quieter way. She was intelligent, and, from the protective, anxious way she regarded her stepdaughter, he did not doubt her devotion to Mariana was genuine.

'What do you think of Signora Renato and her daughter?' Simon asked as he joined Nico. 'But then you knew Signorina Renato when she was very young.'

'I found her a very pleasing child then and I still do. I know very little about her stepmother, however.'

'Her maternal grandmother is the Countess of Telford.'

'The stiff-necked old woman who went to school with Grandmama?'

Simon grinned. 'The very same.'

He was surprised. Not only did Cecily Renato seem an unlikely granddaughter for the cool, aristocratic Countess, he would not have expected the Countess to allow her granddaughter to marry a man such as Marco Renato. Although he was from an old Venetian family, he had not been particularly wealthy and he was not English. 'When did she marry Marco Renato?'

'She has been Mari…Signorina Renato's stepmother since Signorina Renato was seven years of age.'

Nine years if Mariana was now sixteen. Cecily Renato had indeed been young when she married Marco Renato. 'You seem well versed in their affairs. Is Signorina Renato a particular friend of yours?'

'What do you mean by a particular friend?'

'I noticed that you spent a good deal of time with her. I will own I was surprised. She does not seem the sort of girl who usually attracts you,' he said carelessly.

'No, which is why—' Simon stopped. 'Is this why you are here? Because you were informed that I have a *tendre* for Mariana?'

'Do you?'

Simon's eyes narrowed. 'No. I do not have a *tendre* for her. I am in love with her. I plan to marry her. As soon as she reaches her seventeenth birthday.'

'You are too young. So is she.'

'That does not matter.'

'You have a reputation for flirtation, so why is Signorina Renato more than one of your other flirts?'

'She has a kind heart,' he said quietly. 'I can talk to her, tell her anything and she listens. And…' he paused '…the first time I saw her I felt as if I had been waiting for her all of my life.'

'Does Signorina Renato feel the same way?'

'Yes.'

He looked at his cousin's quiet, determined face and

wanted to curse. This was much more than an idle flirtation. His cousin was in love. He should know—he had felt exactly the same way when he first laid eyes on Angelina.

Chapter Three

Cecily tugged the sole weed from the damp dirt and then leaned back on her heels and pushed an escaped tendril of hair from her face. Now she probably had a smear of mud on her cheek. Not that she cared—in light of everything else it was hardly important.

She rose and stood for a moment, looking down at the now tidy patch of flowers. The only thing that seemed tidy about her life at the moment. After seeing Mariana and Simon together last night, she knew she could not expect Severin to believe they were mere acquaintances. She certainly did not. Which was why Mariana could not remain in Avezza. Not as long as Lord Ballister was here.

Or his cousin.

What if Raf heard the same sort of rumour that Severin had and thought Cecily was promoting a match between Lord Ballister and Mariana? And what if Barbarina was right—that Raf and Severin would fight if they met?

She could only surmise that their quarrel had something to do with Angelina Guiliani. Marco had told her very little; only that Angelina had been the daughter of his uncle, the Conte Guiliani. The cousins, Angelina and Marco and Raf, had been playmates since childhood. When she was sixteen she had become engaged to the son of an English duke. Less than a week before the wedding, Angelina had died in a tragic fall. Her mother, heartbroken over the death of her remaining child, had fallen ill and, less than a year later, died. The Conte had sold the lovely old villa shortly after that and had never returned to Avezza.

Until Lord Ballister had come to Avezza a month ago, almost nothing had been said about the young Englishman whom Angelina was to marry. Cecily had been shocked when Viola mentioned Lord Ballister's guardian had been betrothed to Angelina. When Cecily confronted Barbarina, she had merely shrugged and replied it was not Cecily's business. It was only recently that Barbarina had begun hinting at quarrels and fights.

She wished Marco was here. At times like this she missed him terribly. He had not loved her the way she had loved him, but he had always been unfailingly kind and gentle. She missed his strength and the certainty that he would always know the right thing to do, whereas she often felt so much at sea, most particularly when it came to Mariana.

A bee buzzing around her head brought her back to the garden. She bent down to retrieve her basket of cut flowers when she heard footsteps on the path. She looked up and froze. The Duke of Severin stood behind her, regarding her with his dark, slightly sardonic expression. 'Whatever are you doing here?'

'I told you I planned to call on you.'

'And I said I would not be home.' His mere presence made her feel uncomfortable, and, in a faded gown and dirt-smeared apron with her hair escaping beneath an old bonnet, she felt even more at a disadvantage.

'Apparently you did not make that clear to your housekeeper. Signora Zanetti did her best, however, to convince me that not only were you not home, but that my presence in Avezza was likely to prove disastrous.'

'Oh, dear.' She had never even considered the possibility that Severin and Barbarina would meet. 'I am sorry. She sometimes entertains the oddest notions—you must not heed anything she says. She seems to be becoming more and more eccentric.'

'A fearsome thought, for she was eccentric enough thirteen years ago.' He looked down at her, a little frown on his brow. 'How did Barbarina Zanetti end up living with you rather than with the Conte Guiliani? Or Rafaele Vianoli?'

'She came to live with Marco and Mariana after Caterina died. After Marco's death she stayed on. The Conte offered her a home, but she refused. Raf is gone too much, but I am certain she would not go to him anyway. She fears I cannot bring Mariana up properly without her.'

'It is apparent your stepdaughter has been brought up very well and I suspect Signora Zanetti deserves little credit for it.'

His unexpected compliment filled her with pleasure and pride in Mariana. She smiled. 'It is really to Mariana's credit—she has been the sweetest, most loving child imaginable. She means everything to me.'

'She is very fortunate.'

'No, I am.' Her smile faded. 'But you did not come here so that I can praise Mariana.'

'No. We can sit on the bench under the arbour and talk.'

'I was going back to the house.' She bent to retrieve her basket, only to have him reach it first. His hand brushed hers, sending a warm tingle through her gloved hand. She jerked her hand back and straightened. 'It is really not necessary. I can carry it very well on my own.'

'I've no doubt of that, but I wish to do so.'

'It is rather dirty. You might soil your coat.'

He actually looked amused. 'Then you may brush off any stray dirt with your handkerchief.'

'I do not have a handkerchief.'

She felt even more stupid when his mouth quirked. 'Then I will loan you mine.'

She suspected he was teasing her, but instead of coming back with a witty rejoinder she could only make the same sort of silly remarks as a schoolgirl.

'What is it you want, your Grace?' she asked as they started along the path.

The amusement left his face. 'Last night my cousin informed me that he planned to marry your stepdaughter when she turned seventeen.'

'Oh, no.' Mariana had spoken the truth; and if Simon

had gone so far as to tell his cousin, he was indeed serious. 'This is impossible.'

'What is impossible? That he told me?'

'No, that he would even think of such a thing. That they would…. Of course they cannot marry. They are too young and you would never approve and I would never approve and…'

He stopped. 'My cousin is in love with Signorina Renato.'

'He cannot be. She is too young. Both of them are and they have known each other for scarcely a month.'

'Neither of which precludes falling in love. Have you not heard of love at first sight?' His voice was laced with irony. He began walking again.

'I have always considered it ridiculous.'

'You are not a romantic, *signora*?'

'Not at all.' She looked straight ahead. 'I have written to Mariana's cousins in Padua. I will send her there as soon as possible.'

'Have you told her that?'

'No. I wish to put it off until I receive a reply, for I suspect Mariana will not be pleased. Until then I will make certain that she and Lord Ballister have no opportunity to meet.'

'Is she in love with Simon?'

Again, he startled her. 'He is very charming and attentive and I can see why a young girl might develop a *tendre* for him, particularly if she is very sheltered.'

'I am asking about your stepdaughter, not young girls in general.'

'I am certain she considers herself to be.'

By now they had reached the edge of the garden next to the narrow strip of lawn near the steps to the house. He stopped. 'I wonder if one can distinguish between considering oneself to be and the actual thing?' he asked drily. 'I suggest neither one of us makes it too obvious that we wish to separate them, for I would not wish to drive them into each other's arms.'

'No.' She had not expected a man with his cool arrogant demeanour to be quite so understanding. As if he had once been in love. Had what she'd heard been true? Had he loved Angelina? She realised she knew nothing about him at all. 'No, that would never do.'

'Where is Vianoli, by the way?'

She looked quickly up at him, but saw nothing more in his expression than polite curiosity. 'He is in Verona, or at least I think he is. He has undertaken a commission to oversee the restoration of a church.'

'He is not often in Avezza?'

'No, not often.' She held out her hand. 'Thank you for carrying my basket. I…I can take it.'

'There is one more thing.'

'Is there?'

'You have a smudge of dirt on your cheek.'

'Oh!' Her hand flew to her face and then just as quickly fell away as she remembered her gloves were dirtier than her face.

'Now you have dirt on both sides. We will need a handkerchief after all.' He set her basket down on the top step and then reached into his waistcoat pocket and produced a snowy handkerchief. Before she could protest he had tilted her chin. 'Let me do this.'

She froze as he dabbed at her cheeks. His touch was surprisingly gentle, but her entire body prickled with awareness. 'Better,' he murmured. He still cupped her chin. 'Do you always do your own gardening?'

'It is very conducive to mulling over one's concerns.' She felt rather dizzy.

He dropped his hand. 'I did not see many weeds left. You must have a number of concerns.'

'I…yes.' Over his shoulder she saw Lady Margate standing near the corner of the house, watching them. 'Oh, drat.' She backed away from him.

Severin's brow rose but before he could speak, Lady Margate crossed the lawn towards them.

'Dear Severin,' she said with a smile. 'Must I warn Signora Renato about you already?'

'It depends on what you wish to warn her about.'

'That you are quite dangerous. For women. They are far too susceptible to your charm. I would not want Signora Renato to become a victim.'

He glanced at Cecily. 'You need not worry about Signora Renato. She seems quite immune,' he said drily.

'Then she is a rare exception.' Lady Margate smiled at Cecily.

Cecily wished she could disappear. Not only did the conversation make her uncomfortable, but she also felt even more clumsy and untidy next to Lady Margate's petite grace. She was relieved when Severin said he must depart. Lady Margate waited until he disappeared around the corner of the house before speaking.

'He really can be quite charming, but he is also quite ruthless when he wants something. You must not let him turn your head.'

'He was not trying to. You are quite mistaken if you think that.'

'My dear, you must not be so serious! I was only teasing you a little, although I must own I was rather startled to see him touching you in such a way. And on such short acquaintance!' She was smiling, but Cecily sensed she was not completely teasing.

'I had mud on my cheeks and foolishly forgot my handkerchief. He removed the mud for me. I have no doubt he would have done the same for anyone.'

'Well, not quite anyone! Do not worry, he meant nothing by it. If he does anything to distress you, then you must tell me. I have known him for a very long time so I can speak freely with him.'

'Thank you, but I am certain that will not be necessary.'

'You are no doubt right. Goodbye, dear *signora*.'

Cecily slowly walked up the steps to the house. Her cheek still burned from Severin's touch. Since her husband's death, no man had caressed her face as intimately. Not that she thought he meant anything by it, as Lady Margate had pointed out.

All of this was ridiculous. She was ridiculous. A widow of eight and twenty should not be making such a fuss over a mere touch of a hand. Nor should she allow Lady Margate's words to affect her. She needed to think of Mariana.

She realised she had no idea why Lady Margate had even called.

'Severin!' Nico, who had just passed through Signora Renato's gate, halted. Thais Margate was hurrying down the path towards him. She reached his side, her usually pale cheeks becomingly pink with the exertion. 'I was not certain whether I would catch up with you or not!'

'Your visit with Signora Renato was not very long.'

She looked up at him, her rosebud lips parted in a charming smile. 'I merely called to see how she was getting on. I will own I hardly expected to find you there!'

'No?' He felt rather bored. 'Did you walk? Or do you have a carriage lurking about?'

'I walked, of course. And now I expect you to escort me home.' She took his arm. 'Do not seem so surprised. Since coming to Avezza, I have discovered the benefits of exercise. The weather is so much nicer than at home.'

'Why are you in Italy? And why Avezza?' Nico asked as they began walking down the hill that led to the centre of the town.

'Because you are here, of course.' She flashed another smile at him. 'Do not flatter yourself. After dear George died, I realised I needed to go away. So many memories, of course, and then his family was never very kind to me. They accused me of keeping them away from George when he was ill, but I was only following Dr Johnson's orders. I have bought a little pal-

azzo in Venice for not very much. The poor family—
they had lived there for three hundred years, but now
they cannot afford it. But Venice was rather tedious so
I decided to come here—I remember it as such a peaceful place. But I am certain you do not wish to hear about
that! I should really ask—why are you here?'

'For various reasons.'

'You are being elusive as usual! Shall I guess? You
worry that Lord Ballister is becoming too fond of a certain young lady and you wish to put a stop to it, which
of course you must. I cannot imagine what Rafaele
would do if he discovered your cousin wished to marry
his cousin. He is her trustee, you know, although she is
in Signora Renato's care. What an odd coincidence that
your cousin and Rafaele's should meet and fall in love.'
She spoke in a guileless manner that made him wonder
what she was up to.

'Are you not presuming too much?'

She gave an amused little laugh. 'I do not think so.
Everyone can quite see that Lord Ballister and Signorina Renato are rather too fond of one another. Why
else would you call on Signora Renato if not to warn her
not to pin her hopes on attracting a viscount for her
daughter?'

She had always possessed the shrewd ability to sum
up a situation, but her assumption that because of that
she had the right to make it her business both amused
and irked him. As did her certainty that she knew the
motives of the parties involved. He could not help toy-
ing with her a little.

'There are perhaps other reasons I wished to call on Signora Renato,' he said deliberately.

'Really? What might those be?' She looked up at him, still laughing. 'Do not tell me you find her attractive?'

'Then I won't.'

She stopped in front of a house that sat slightly back from the cobbled street and was surrounded by a wrought-iron fence. She looked up at him with her large blue eyes. 'Why, Severin, I believe you actually do! I would not have thought she was at all your style. However, I must warn you that it will not do for you to become too attached.' Her smile was now gone. 'I have heard from several sources—several very reliable sources—that Signora Renato already has an admirer. A man who has been in love with her for an age, although it is not possible for them to marry—at least, not quite yet.' She paused as if waiting for him to ask. 'Rafaele Vianoli. Unless you want history to repeat itself, you must stay away from her.'

'Why were they here?' Barbarina spoke from her chair near the window overlooking the lane, and nearly caused Cecily, who had just entered the salon, to drop her basket.

'Goodness! You frightened me.' Cecily set the flowers on the table and went to Barbarina's side.

'What did he want, the Duke? He does not like it that his cousin wishes to court Mariana, no? Now we have only to wait for Rafaele to come and fight the Duke.'

'I will send Mariana to Vittoria and Serefina as soon

as possible. So no one needs to worry about fights. I have brought you a rose. There was only one blooming.' She realised Barbarina was staring at her with a peculiar expression. 'What is it?'

'You must leave Avezza as well.'

'I will accompany Mariana to Padua, of course. Then I will return.'

'You must stay away from the English Duke. You must not return to Avezza until he is gone.'

Cecily stared at her, a peculiar chill creeping down her spine. 'I assure you I have no desire to be anywhere near the Duke. I do not particularly like him.'

'That does not matter.' She kept her gaze on Cecily. 'For I saw the way he looked at you just now in the garden. You will be in danger as long as he is here.'

'Why would I possibly be in danger from him?'

'Not from him. Because of him.'

'That does not make any sense. What do you mean?'

'He will bring danger to you. Just as he did to Angelina.'

Chapter Four

Cecily received a reply from Vittoria a few days later. Yes, they would be delighted to have Mariana. She should come for a month, perhaps two. Cecily, of course, must stay for as long as she wished as well. Although Caterina's relations, rather than Marco's, they had always been quite kind to Cecily and their warm response made her feel guilty that she did not visit them more often.

Perhaps she should consider staying with them for an extended visit. Since the day in the garden, Barbarina's words hung heavily over her. *He will bring danger to you. Just as he did to Angelina.* Not that Cecily really thought she was in any sort of peril; she was more disturbed by Barbarina's implication that Angelina had been in danger and that Severin was somehow responsible. Did she think that Angelina's death was not an accident, but something more sinister? But Barbarina would not answer Cecily's questions and Cecily could only hope it was another one of her peculiar notions.

She wished she knew what had happened between Severin and Raf, but Barbarina was unlikely to tell her. Perhaps none of it would matter once Mariana was safely away from Avezza. She wondered if Viola would know. She had not spoken to her since the night at Signora Bartolini's. She decided she would call on her today.

Viola lived in one of the narrow streets on the other side of Avezza's small piazza. The day was fine; a dog slept in the sun near the butcher shop and across the square two Austrian soldiers lingered near the café. No one was sorry to see the French leave Venice and its former territories, but whether her new Austrian masters were an improvement was yet to be determined.

She passed the old church, now undergoing repairs, which made her think of Thais Margate and her peculiar idea that Severin might be interested in Cecily. In many ways, she was as odd as Barbarina in regard to Severin.

If only he had never come to Avezza—since his arrival, everyone and everything seemed overset.

Viola leased the top floor of one of the tall narrow houses that lined either side of the street. A maid let Cecily in and Cecily followed her up the steep stairway to the upper floor. Viola greeted Cecily with a hug. Like Cecily, Viola was now a widow, her husband killed at the Battle of Borodino while fighting under Napoleon. Along with many other men in the towns that were once part of the Venetian Republic, he had been conscripted into the French army against his will, which only made his death more tragic.

As soon as they were seated on the small sofa, Viola turned to Cecily. 'So, my dear Cecily, I have heard the handsome Duke was seen leaving your house yesterday. This following the *musicale*, when he insisted on escorting you home.'

'It was not a social call. He wishes to make sure I am not encouraging a match between Lord Ballister and Mariana.'

'Are you certain that is all? A little flirtation with you might soften his heart towards Mariana and her young suitor.'

'Even if I wished to do so, I would never think of flirting with him. At any rate, we are in agreement; neither of us wants a match between them. They are far too young.' She did not want to discuss Mariana and Lord Ballister any further, for she suspected Viola sympathised with the couple's predicament, although she had never exactly said so. 'Not only that, but Barbarina has told me if Raf finds out about any of this he will fight not only Lord Ballister but the Duke as well. She speaks of some sort of quarrel between the Duke and Raf, but will not tell me why. Have you ever heard about any sort of quarrel?'

Viola frowned. 'No, but I do remember that some people were surprised when the Conte announced that Angelina was to marry Lord St Gervase, as he was then, for everyone had always thought she would marry Rafaele Vianoli.'

'Angelina and Raf?' Cecily was truly shocked. 'Why would anyone think that?'

'Because he was the Conte's heir and it seemed only natural that they would marry.'

'Was Raf in love with Angelina?'

'I do not know. No one doubted, however, that Lord St Gervase was in love with Angelina and that she was equally in love with him. Everyone could see how happy they were together, as if fate decreed it to be. I only saw him once after she died and he looked as if his heart had died with her.'

'I did not know that,' Cecily said slowly. So Severin had loved her. 'No one has really said much about Angelina except Barbarina. She seems to be one person Barbarina truly cared about.'

'Angelina was beautiful. She reminded me of the Madonna in one of Bellini's paintings. No one said a word against her because she was always laughing and teasing and had a smile for everyone. I do not think there was anyone she disliked, even the Lady Margate.'

'She knew Lady Margate?' For the second time in the past hour Cecily was stunned.

'She was not Lady Margate, of course, but Miss…' Viola frowned a little, 'Miss Winters, I think. Yes, it was Miss Winters. She also stayed with the Conte's family that summer. Her father was a friend of the Conte's.'

'Lady Margate has said nothing of that, nor has anyone else.'

'I do not think anyone has recognised her. She was only there that one summer and she was the sort of pale, thin girl that no one ever notices. She is quite different now. It is very odd, but I did not recognise her until I saw her with the Duke at the *musicale*. There was a certain way she tilted her head when she looked at him and suddenly I remembered her doing the same all those years ago. As was every other girl that summer, she was a little in love with him. Not that he noticed, for he saw only Angelina.'

'I wonder why she has said nothing.'

'Perhaps she does not want to be remembered as she was.'

'Perhaps not.'

It was all so peculiar. Did Barbarina recognise her? Perhaps that would explain why Barbarina had regarded her with such animosity from the very beginning, but not what she had done to incur it. Why had Barbarina not told her she knew Lady Margate? So many secrets and for what purpose?

'I do not know if any of this explains why Rafaele and the Duke quarrelled unless it was over Angelina,' Viola said.

'That is possible, but if the Conte announced the betrothal it seems *he* must have approved. If he really wished Raf to marry Angelina, he surely would have tried to stop a marriage between the Duke and his daughter.'

'Perhaps you should ask Rafaele. Or the Duke.' A hint of mischief appeared in her eyes.

'Raf is not here and the Duke would send me scurrying away with a cool set-down.'

Viola laughed. 'You are not such a coward. Is Raf still in Verona? He has not been to Avezza for a long time, but should we be expecting him now that the Duke is here?'

'I certainly hope not. Yes, he is still in Verona. We have not seen him for nearly three months. Mariana misses him; we both do.' During Marco's prolonged illness and after his death, he had been like a brother to her; helping her with legal matters, holding Mariana when she cried and then making her laugh, teasing Cecily into smiles when she became too serious.

'At least he will not starve,' Viola said, always practical. 'And he still has the palazzo, no? He has not been forced to sell that?'

'I hope he will never need to. He would be devastated.' It was all that was left of his family's holdings for the French policies had impoverished a good portion of the Venetian nobility, including his family as well as the Guiliani family. After the Conte's death, he had been forced to sell many of the holdings of both families.

'Perhaps he will fall in love with a wealthy woman and then his troubles will be gone.'

'Perhaps, although there does not seem to be an abundance of such women around.' Cecily could not imagine Raf marrying for such reasons, for she suspected that his laughing eyes and cool intelligence hid a romantic heart.

Their talk turned to other matters, such as the fête at the end of the week in the gardens of Signor Palmero's villa. They agreed to share a supper box, then Cecily rose to leave.

She stepped out into the narrow street and started for home, so occupied in thought she barely noticed her surroundings. She had come away from Viola with more questions than before. Questions about Angelina and Raf, Raf and the Duke, and, to add to the confusion, Lady Margate. The only thing she knew for certain was that Severin and Angelina had been in love and were to marry, she had died, and in the thirteen years since her death he had never married.

Cecily had decided she would wait until after the fête before telling Mariana they were to leave for Padua. She knew Mariana looked forward to this affair each year and Cecily hated to spoil it for her. Mariana had been compliant and almost too subdued over the past few days. Except for a visit from Teresa, she had spent most of her time reading or sitting in the garden and Cecily was now troubled by visions of a decline.

On the night of the fête, Mariana appeared to have recovered some of her usual spirits. She wore a muslin gown in a soft rose colour. The gown itself was several years old, but, newly trimmed with ribbon and lace and set off with a new sash in a darker shade of rose, it looked quite presentable. Her black curls were gathered in a knot at the top of her head and fell in a cascade of ringlets to her shoulders and her eyes held some of their old sparkle. To Cecily's eyes, she was beautiful and she could hardly blame Lord Ballister for falling in love with her.

Cecily herself was dressed in pale peach muslin. It

was a trifle outdated—the skirt was not quite as full as the current fashion, but at least it was not very worn. She was stunned, however, when Barbarina suddenly appeared in the salon and announced she planned to attend the fête with them. Cecily was equally taken aback by her appearance. Over her black dress she wore a black mantle, instead of her plain black veil she wore one of black lace, and, if Cecily was not mistaken, she had even applied a touch of rouge.

'How pretty you look!' Cecily exclaimed and then prayed she had not offended Barbarina. Barbarina merely gave a 'hmph' but Cecily thought she looked a little pleased. She did not protest when Mariana fingered her lacy veil and told her she must wear such things more often.

Shades of purple, pink and orange tinted the sky by the time Cecily, Mariana and Barbarina arrived at the Palermos' villa. A long line of carriages already stood in the villa's drive so they were forced to dismount a small distance away. A number of other guests were doing the same. Cecily worried that the distance would be too much for Barbarina, but she managed the walk to the garden entrance without complaint, albeit slowly.

They joined the crowd drifting between the stone pillars to the garden. As they entered the grounds, Cecily wondered if Severin and Lord Ballister would be here, for this was the villa that had once belonged to Angelina's family. Would Severin find it too difficult to visit this place with its surely painful memories?

She had found herself thinking far too much about him and Angelina since her visit to Viola. Tonight, she must make an effort to put them from her thoughts or she feared she would see their ghosts everywhere, which would make for a most melancholy evening.

The gardens were behind the house itself. Signor Palermo been quite taken with a visit to Vauxhall a number of years ago and had attempted to recreate the English pleasure garden. He added a pavilion for musicians and a number of supper boxes. Although lacking a Thames river, the garden could boast of a small artificial lake with a fountain in the middle. He had left the old maze that proved to be one of the most popular attractions.

A footman showed their party to the supper box. Viola and Teresa were already there; Viola arched a brow in astonishment when she saw Barbarina. After Barbarina had been seated near the front of the box so that she could observe the crowd, and Mariana and Teresa were deep in conversation, Viola turned to Cecily. 'How did you persuade Signora Zanetti to come?' she asked in a low voice.

'I did not. She decided on her own.'

'How very strange. Has she ever been here before? At a fête, that is, for I know she stayed here quite often with the Guiliani family.'

'I do not think so. I have no idea why she wanted to come.'

'Mama,' Teresa said, 'Paolo and Frederico wish to take Mariana and me to the maze. May we go?'

Cecily saw that Paolo, Teresa's brother, and their cousin, Frederico, a pleasant-looking, plump youth, were standing just outside their supper box.

Viola glanced at Cecily. 'If Signora Renato does not object.'

Cecily hesitated. What if Lord Ballister were here and joined them? On the other hand, Severin had said they must not make it too obvious they wished to separate them. And Mariana scarcely mentioned Lord Ballister this week.

'Please, Mama,' Mariana said, regarding Cecily with large pleading eyes.

'You may go, but please stay together.'

'Thank you.' Mariana gave her a radiant smile and, after planting a brief kiss on Barbarina's cheek, left with the others. By now the evening shadows had fallen and the servants had begun lighting various lanterns and torches scattered throughout the garden, giving the garden a festive air.

Barbarina seemed disinclined to talk and spoke only to ask for a glass of lemonade from one of the waiters. The strains of a Vivaldi concerto reached them from somewhere in the garden. Viola suddenly touched Cecily's hand. 'He is coming.'

'Who?'

'Your duke. He is very certainly most handsome.'

'He is not my duke!' Cecily half-turned her face to the back of the box and pretended very hard to be studying the painting of cherubs dancing around a fountain. He most likely would walk by.

The skin at the back of her neck prickled and she knew he had come to stand next to them.

'*Buonasera*, Signora Zanetti, Signora Carasco. And Signora Renato.' He switched to English. 'A fascinating work, Signora Renato. What is it that has caught your attention? The cherubs dancing in drunken abandon around a fountain or the cupid peering from beneath the leaves?'

'There is a cupid? Where?' Then she coloured and forced herself to turn around. 'Good evening, your Grace.'

'It must be the cherubs, then, since you did not notice the cupid.'

'I was admiring the use of colour.'

'Can you even tell in this fading light?' He was openly amused, which only served to fluster Cecily more.

Viola was watching with rapt interest. 'You must join us, your Grace.'

'If Signora Zanetti does not object.'

Barbarina was staring at him with something like consternation. 'You must stay away from Signora Renato. She is not safe with you.'

Viola's mouth fell open and Cecily wanted to sink through the floor of the box. She could not look at Severin.

'What precisely do you mean by that?' he asked. His voice was level, but there was a hardness to it.

'She will not be safe with you,' Barbarina repeated.

'Have you visited the maze, your Grace?' Viola asked brightly.

'Not yet.' He glanced down at Cecily. 'Where is Signorina Renato?'

'She has gone to visit the maze. With Signorina Carasco and her brother and cousin.'

His eyes narrowed. 'Has she? An interesting coincidence. My brother has gone there as well.'

She did not like his implication. She spoke in English, hoping Barbarina would not understand very much. 'I hope you are not suggesting what I think you are. If you are so worried about that, then you should keep a tighter rein on him.'

'Just as you should keep a tighter rein on your daughter, madam. I believe I will visit the maze after all. Good evening, ladies.' He walked briskly away.

Cecily was not about to let him confront Mariana without her. She started to rise, only to find Barbarina's hand clasped around her wrist. 'Where are you going?'

'To the maze. To find Mariana.'

'You must not go with him.'

'I am not going with him. I am going by myself.'

'Then I will come with you.'

'No, you must stay here with Viola.' She gently removed Barbarina's hand. 'I will return shortly,' she said to Viola.

'Of course.' Viola looked as if she wanted to laugh.

Cecily hurried after Severin, whose progress had been slowed by a trio of jugglers. He started to move around them when he caught sight of Cecily. He stopped. 'I doubt there will be much benefit in both of us showing up.'

She gave him a tight smile. 'Then you may go elsewhere while I find them. I am going to find my daughter because I do not want her subjected to one of your intimidating stares.'

'I've no intention of intimidating her. You are wasting time by arguing. You may do as you please.'

He stalked off. She followed him, although she grew a trifle breathless as she was forced to trot in order to keep up with his long strides. The crowds had grown and she had a hard time weaving around them. Despite the number of lanterns the gardens were not particularly well lit and some of the paths were dark.

Most of the crowd seemed to be heading towards the grotto where the musicians played. By the time Cecily reached the maze she had lost Severin because of a crowd of people who had got in her way. She felt more than a little trepidation when she entered the first path with its tall, shadowy shrubs. It suddenly seemed very dark and foreboding despite the voices and laugher coming from within. She stopped, uncertain which way to proceed.

'What happened to you? I turned around and you were gone.'

Severin's voice made her jump. He was standing near the entrance.

'I thought that was what you wanted.'

He made an impatient sound. 'I wanted you to stay with Signora Carasco, not get lost in the dark. Despite Signora Zanetti's dire predictions, you are better off with me.'

'I am sorry that she said such stupid things to you. At any rate, I have been here any number of times. I can manage quite well on my own.' Although the maze did look quite different in the dark.

'Not unless you wish to be the object of some man's attentions.' He caught her arm. 'You are wasting time again.'

'Me?' But he was already leading her into the first winding passage between two tall rows of yews.

There were not as many people as she had expected. Once they entered the second passage she knew why. Without the benefit of sunlight or a full moon, it was nearly impossible to see much. She could still hear laughter and voices from somewhere in the maze and she froze when she heard Mariana's breathless laugh and then Simon's deeper voice.

'Oh, dear.'

'Yes.' The grimness of Severin's tone made her shiver.

He glanced down at her face. 'There is no need to look so frightened. I'm not planning to beat either of them. Just lock Simon up until your daughter is safely away from Avezza. You might consider doing the same thing for your daughter.'

'I am beginning to agree.' How could Mariana do this? Did she not know, did neither of them realise, that they were both risking their reputations? Or perhaps that is what they meant to do so they would be forced to marry. The thought made her blood run cold.

They rounded another corner and found themselves

nearly careening into a couple locked in a passionate embrace. For a horrid moment, Cecily feared it was Mariana and Simon, but realised the man was much too stocky. Embarrassed, she backed up and stepped on Severin's foot. 'I beg your pardon.'

The man lifted his head and saw them. 'You will need to find your own corner, *signora*.' His lady made a breathless little protest as her swain pulled her harder against him.

Severin steered her back around the corner. 'We've taken a wrong turn. We will have to retrace our steps.'

She nodded and followed him. By now, the clouds had covered the moon and the maze was even more dark and shadowy. The music and voices seemed far away and Cecily no longer heard anything from inside the maze. It was if they were the only ones here except for the couple they had just left behind.

Severin suddenly stopped. 'We've hit another dead end.' He ran a hand through his hair. 'You said you've been here a number of times. Do you have the faintest idea how we make our way out of here?'

He was asking for her help? Astounded, she stared at him before speaking. 'I have only been here during the day.' He was not going to like what she had to say next. She forced herself to meet his eyes. 'And I have lost my way every single time. Mariana has always had to rescue me.'

She braced herself for the derision in his voice. To her astonishment, he laughed. 'Of course. And you had hoped to find them yourself?'

'I had planned on following you.'

His mouth curved in genuine amusement. 'Next time you should think twice before you decide to follow me.'

'I doubt there will be a next time.' She rubbed her arms as a cool breeze brushed her bare arms. 'If we can find the centre of the maze, there is one path that leads directly to the back entrance near the lake.'

'If I recall, the centre of the maze is to the left.'

'How do you know that?'

He slanted a look at her. 'I have been here as well, although it has grown considerably since I was last here. The paths seemed to have been rearranged, which is why I made the wrong turn.'

'Signor Palermo changes the paths each year. He digs up some of the shrubs and then replants them so the paths are never the same.'

'Very clever. But one should be able to find the old path by observing where the shrubs have been replanted.'

'I suppose,' she said doubtfully.

'Come. We will test my theory.' He took her hand, his hand warm and strong around hers, and began to walk. She glanced at his face and then looked away, her breath catching. She was suddenly aware it was too dark, too quiet, too alone. Too intimate.

A peculiar pit formed in her stomach and she felt almost panicked. Of course they would find their way out. He had been the perfect gentleman. She could not fault him for that at all. She would be safe with him.

'This way, I think.' He tugged her around a corner. She realised she had been paying no attention at all to where they were going. In a moment they were in the centre of the maze. He dropped her hand and looked around. 'I do not recall a statue last time I was here.' He spoke almost to himself.

He had been here with Angelina. She was certain of that. 'Signor Palermo added them only recently.' Her words seemed an intrusion on his memories so she moved away.

It was then she heard the faintest rustling in the bushes surrounding the small garden. She jumped and looked around, but there was nothing. She rubbed her arms, suddenly cold, her light shawl not at all adequate.

She heard the small sound again almost as if someone was in the bushes. Her sense of uneasiness increased and, when Severin appeared behind her, she jumped. 'You have the most damnable habit of disappearing,' he said.

'I did not want to interrupt you.'

'Interrupt me in doing what?'

'Thinking.'

'Thinking?' The edge of his mouth lifted. 'I can do that any time. Shall we go?'

'Yes, we should. In fact, we should leave now.' She realised her teeth were chattering.

'Why didn't you tell me you were cold? I can give you my coat.' He started to shrug out of the garment.

'It is not that. I…I don't like it here. I wish to go back. The way we came.'

'And get lost again?' He looked at her more closely. 'You are frightened. Do not worry, I won't let anything happen to you.' He removed his coat and draped it over her shoulders. 'Come, we'd best leave before you start to imagine ghosts or other such unnatural beings.'

She managed a smile. 'I suppose I have been reading too many of Mariana's novels lately. There always seems to be some sort of spectre or headless monk.' Coupled with Barbarina's odd predictions, it was no wonder she was imagining things.

A smile tugged at his mouth. 'You should find different literature in the future. Come.'

They passed through the arch and entered the straight, dark walk that led to the artificial lake on the other side of the maze. The yews were tall and forbidding and, despite her attempts to reassure herself she had only imagined hearing footsteps earlier, she found she was increasing her pace. Severin glanced down at her once, but said nothing.

She nearly collapsed with relief when the walk opened on to a small grassy lawn with the lake beyond. A number of people strolled near the water and she even saw a few daring souls had taken out the rowboats. The normality of the scene filled her with the same relief she felt after waking up from a disturbing dream.

'You really were frightened. Why?'

She looked up at him and found his gaze fixed on her face. 'I…I had the oddest sense that someone was watching us. I was being ridiculous, of course.'

'Perhaps.' His eyes were still on her.

'I suppose we should go and find Mariana and Simon.'

'We should.' He took a step towards her. 'But first there is something else I want to do.'

'What?'

'This.' He took another step towards her. His hands slipped under his coat and caught her shoulders and slowly drew her towards him. Mesmerised, she made no protest as his lips descended on hers in a surprisingly gentle kiss.

Perhaps her nerves were still on edge, but a faint movement caught her attention just as her eyes started to drift shut. The prickle of danger she'd felt in the maze struck her with renewed force. She pulled away from him and jerked her eyes open in time to see a shadowy figure drifting towards them, the glint of metal in the raised hand exactly like one of Mariana's gothic spectres. The cry broke from her throat just as the hand plunged towards Severin's back.

He half-turned and the stiletto caught his arm. 'What the hell?' he exclaimed. The assailant fled into the shadowy maze.

He stared at Cecily, his hand going to his arm for a moment. He pulled it away and her stomach lurched when she saw the blood on his hand. 'You are hurt,' she said stupidly.

'A mere scratch. Are you all right?' he asked quickly.

'Yes.'

'Stay here. I am going after him.'

She caught his other arm. 'No, you are not. Unless you want to bleed to death in Signor Palermo's maze.'

His eyes glinted down at her. 'That is unlikely.' And then he swayed.

She managed to steady him. 'Sit down. Please.'

He did not argue. He sat down on the grass, still holding his arm. She dropped his coat from her shoulders and knelt beside him. 'Let me see your arm.'

'It is fine.'

'It is not.' She gently removed his hand and suppressed a shiver when she saw the jagged slash. 'I think it will need to be stitched. First we must stop the bleeding.'

'Use my cravat.' His voice was thick.

'Good God! What has happened?'

Cecily looked up and with some astonishment saw two men and a woman standing over them. She had nearly forgotten they were at a fête. 'He has been stabbed. I must stop the bleeding and he needs a doctor.'

'Of course.' One of the men began to shout and the other dropped down beside Cecily. 'Allow me, *signora*. I have seen such wounds when I was with the army. Your sash, if you please, *signora*. I am Signor Canelli.' He produced a handkerchief and Cecily, with trembling fingers, untied the pale green sash encircling her bodice and handed it to Signor Canelli. He formed the handkerchief into a pad and pressed it to the wound, then began winding the sash about the pad.

'Severin!' Lady Margate's voice broke through the crowd that now surrounded them. 'What has happened?' In a moment, she had dropped to her knees next to Cecily. 'Oh, dear God! Who did this to you?'

'A robber of some sort.' He glanced at Cecily as if challenging her to deny it.

'Dear God!' Lady Margate stared at him, her expression horrified.

Signor Canelli finished his task just as Signor Palermo appeared. He took charge; two burly men were assigned to assist Severin to the house; another man was sent for Signor Palermo's physician. In the midst of all this, Cecily caught sight of Simon leaving the maze, followed by Paolo. She ran to them.

'What has happened?' Simon exclaimed when he saw her face.

'Your cousin…he was stabbed, just as we were coming from the maze.' She caught his hand when she saw his face. 'His arm was injured, but nothing vital. The bleeding has been stopped and Signor Palermo has sent for a physician. He is to be taken to the house.'

'And you? You are not hurt?' he asked quickly.

'No, I am fine.'

He nodded and dashed towards the small crowd around his cousin. Paolo looked shaken. 'He was stabbed? Who would do such a thing?'

'We do not know. Mariana, where is she?'

'With Mama and Teresa. Frederico has gone to look for Signora Zanetti. When we returned to the box, not only had you disappeared, but Signora Zanetti as well. Mama said she and Signora Zanetti had gone to view the fountain and became separated.'

Barbarina was missing? She recalled the black-clad figure and a frightening thought crossed her mind. 'How long has Signora Zanetti been gone?'

'I do not know. Only that she was not there and Mama was worried because both you and Signora Zanetti had not returned. She sent Lord Ballister and me to find you.'

'I see.' No, it was not possible, Barbarina would not have attempted to harm anyone. Despite her odd ways she had never shown any signs of violence. The assailant had been much too tall, or had he?

'Signora Renato? Are you unwell?' Paolo asked.

'No, I am quite well.'

'We should perhaps return to the box.'

She glanced towards the others and saw that Severin now stood supported by the two men. Lady Margate hovered nearby and, as Cecily watched, Simon took her arm as if to comfort her. Cecily turned away, a pang darting through her. 'Yes, we should. We can do nothing more here.'

Barbarina had been found by the time she and Paolo returned. The others were horrified by the news. Even Barbarina looked stricken. Cecily tried to tell herself that surely she would not look so if she had committed such a terrible act.

Later, in her bed, she was not so certain. She went over and over the assault in her mind, but somehow the shadowy figure turned into Barbarina, no matter how hard she tried to think otherwise.

When she finally fell into a restless sleep, however, she did not dream of assailants and daggers, but of being kissed by a tall, dark stranger who bore a disturbing resemblance to the Duke of Severin.

Chapter Five

Nico sat on the edge of his bed and waited for his head to clear. He'd slept a good part of the day away if the light peeping through the curtains was any indication. His arm hurt like the devil, but at least he had only a mild headache from the brandy he had drunk last night to dull the pain while the doctor stitched his arm.

As much as he would like to, he could not afford to lie in bed. His first business was to call on Barbarina Zanetti. For a stomach-wrenching moment last night, he thought the assailant would stab Signora Renato as well. The thought continued to trouble him. What if Cecily Renato had indeed been the intended victim? The attack seemed too much of a coincidence after Barbarina's warning.

He had no idea if she actually possessed some sort of ability to predict the future. Her odd black clothes and strange way of looking at one, combined with her dire pronouncements, had prompted Raf to laughingly call her *una strega*, a witch.

Did she know something? Or had she been the assailant? The person had fled and he could not imagine Barbarina moving that quickly. It was possible her shuffling walk was merely an act.

Why would she want to hurt Cecily? It would make more sense if she tried to hurt him, for she had never wanted Angelina to marry him. But if she intended to stab him, why had she said that Cecily would be in danger?

Or was the attack completely unrelated and the assailant had some other purpose in mind, such as robbery? Or had they been mistaken for someone else?

He did not like it at all. After he spoke with Signora Zanetti, he would see Cecily. For until he found out who was behind the assault, he did not want Cecily Renato anywhere near Avezza.

'Why? Why must I go? They are old and fat and I might as well be locked up!' Mariana clutched the sheet covering her with white-knuckled hands and regarded Cecily, who sat on the edge of her bed, with an accusing, angry stare.

Cecily forced herself to remain calm. She had slept very little last night and was in no mood to argue. 'You must not speak of Vittoria and Serefina in such a disrespectful way. They love you very much and quite look forward to your visit. We will leave tomorrow.'

'It is because of Simon that you wish me to go, is it not?'

'I think it best if you are away from Avezza for a while.'

'Because you do not want me to marry Simon,' Mariana said flatly.

Cecily hesitated. 'It is not possible for you to marry Lord Ballister,' she finally said. 'I am truly sorry.' The stricken look on Mariana's face nearly broke her heart, but she could not allow Mariana to nourish any false hopes.

Mariana bowed her head and said nothing. Cecily rose from the bed. 'We must begin packing today. I hope you will collect yourself enough to decide if you wish to take any books or your sketching implements.'

Mariana lifted a tear-stained face. 'If…if my mama were here, my real mama, I know she would understand! She would not make me go away. She would let me marry Simon.'

A knife tore through Cecily's heart. Never in the seven years Cecily had been her stepmother had Mariana ever said such a thing. She silently closed the door behind her and realised her hands were trembling. Of course, Mariana was hurt and angry and wanted to lash out at Cecily any way she could. Still, her words stung.

And then there was Barbarina. When Cecily questioned her this morning, Barbarina had been no more forthcoming about her disappearance than she had been last night. She had become separated from Signora Carasco in the crowd and then lost her way. Finally Cecily had asked her if she knew anything about Severin's attack.

Barbarina stared at her for so long that Cecily wondered if she had gone into a trance. She finally spoke. 'I wanted to find you because you were with him.'

'Do you know who did this?'

Barbarina shook her head. 'I know nothing else.' She suddenly looked very tired.

Cecily was beginning to wonder if Barbarina was possibly mad. She sometimes suspected Barbarina's dire warnings and predictions were a way of making herself important, but never before had anything much come of them. Certainly nothing like this.

She slowly went downstairs. Her housekeeper met her at the bottom. 'The Duke of Severin is here, *signora*. He is in the salon.'

Severin? Whatever was he doing here? She could not imagine that after the wound she saw last night he would wish to leave his bed, let alone pay a call.

'*Signora?* Do you wish to see him?'

'Yes. Yes, I will.'

The first thing she noticed was his arm in a sling, his coat draped across his shoulders. His white shirt was tucked into his breeches and he wore no cravat.

He noticed her gaze. 'I apologise for my attire.'

She crossed the room. 'You should not even be dressed at all. I cannot imagine what you are doing out of bed.'

'I needed to see you.'

'Surely it could have waited. Or you should have sent for me.'

'No.'

His pallor alarmed her. 'You must sit down.'

'After you, *signora*.'

She took the nearest chair. To her relief he took the

chair across from her. He winced a little as his arm brushed the back. The scowl on his face kept her from expressing any sort of sympathy. 'How are you feeling?'

His eyes flickered over her and, for some idiotic reason, she suddenly recalled last night's dream. Heat crept into her cheeks and she hoped he did not notice.

'Well enough.' His gaze was still on her. 'I came to see Signora Zanetti, but your housekeeper informed me she has gone out.'

'She went to the market. Is there something in particular you wished to see her about? Perhaps I can help you?'

He looked at her for a moment. 'Tell me why you knew someone was in the bushes last night,' he said abruptly.

'I heard something…a rustling. At first I thought it was perhaps the breeze or an animal, but I saw nothing. Then I had the most odd feeling that something was not right. That we were being watched. It was so dark and no one seemed to be around and I knew we needed to leave as soon as possible.'

'That was all? Just a premonition of sorts? You did not see anyone?'

'Not until you were…we were occupied.'

'Apparently you were not so well occupied that you failed to notice a person with a dagger behind us,' he said drily.

She flushed. 'I was still very uneasy, so I could not really think of anything else.'

A glint appeared in his eye. 'Next time I will make certain there is nothing to distract you when I decide to kiss you. Not that I am complaining this time—if you had not been distracted, one of us might have been gravely wounded. Do you have any idea of who it was?'

'No, I thought…' She pulled her gaze away from his mouth and tried to concentrate on the matter at hand rather than on the idea he might kiss her again. 'No.'

He looked at her hard. 'But you do suspect someone? Barbarina Zanetti, perhaps?'

'She was missing last night. Paolo told me that when he and Simon came to find us, but by the time we returned to the box Mariana and Viola had found her. I asked her this morning where she had been, but she would only say that she had gone to look for me because I was with you.' She swallowed. 'Do you think it was Barbarina?'

'I think it unlikely. Regardless of who was behind the attacks, you need to leave Avezza. Go to Padua with your daughter.'

'You will leave Avezza as well, will you not?'

'Not right away. I have business here.'

'What sort of business do you have here once Mariana is gone? You cannot stay here after last night. For if you do, then I will as well.'

'For what purpose? To protect me?'

'If I need to.'

Surprise crossed his face. 'My dear, I am touched, but I am in no need of your protection. If you recall, Signora Zanetti said you would not be safe with me. She proved to be correct. If you had any sense, you would stay as far away from me as possible.'

'But you were the one who was injured, not I.'

He rose, although she could see it was an effort. 'Have you considered that perhaps you were the intended victim?'

She stood as well. Frustration and fear washed over her. 'I cannot imagine why anyone would wish to hurt me. But then I do not know why anyone would wish to hurt you either. Why? What has happened? Barbarina will tell me nothing! Only that you and Raf quarrelled, but I do not even know why!' She realised her voice had risen alarmingly and she made an effort to collect herself. 'I should not shout at you. You are not well… and…' To her horror, her voice broke.

He took a step towards her, the cool arrogance gone. '*Cara*, don't.'

'I think you should…should go.'

'*Maldezione,*' he muttered. The next thing she knew he had pulled her against him. 'Don't,' he said roughly. He released her, but only to tilt her chin towards him. His lips came down on hers and her mouth parted under his as reality and dream merged into one.

He finally released her; for a moment, she had no idea where she was. Her eyes shot open and she stared at him, the blood pounding in her head. He looked equally dazed and then his expression closed. 'As you can see, I pose another danger to you as well. For, if you stay, I have every intention of seducing you.'

Nothing came to her mind for a moment. 'I…I do not think I would be that easy to seduce.'

He laughed, but it held no amusement. 'That very fact would present a challenge I could not possibly resist. I've no doubt I would have you in my bed within a fortnight.'

'I think you are impossibly conceited.'

'Perhaps.' He moved towards her, standing so close his body was a hair's breath away. 'Shall we find out? I would start by kissing you again.'

'If it was like your last kiss, then I doubt I would be in any danger at all. I do not like such…such assaults. Besides, I think you only want to frighten me into doing what you want.'

'Oh, it wouldn't be like that at all. It would be like this.' This time his mouth was gentle and firm, his lips moving over hers in a slow burning caress. His body was pressed into hers, his knee gently parting her legs, then he shifted and she could feel his arousal through her thin skirts. She melted into his embrace, her lips parting beneath his.

It wasn't until he finally lifted his head that cold sanity returned. A great pounding wave of shock and embarrassment washed over her.

'Cecily?'

The use of her first name startled her. She jerked her eyes open. 'I suppose you are quite right. I am so stupid that I would allow a man I scarcely know to seduce me.' She did not look at him.

'You are not stupid,' he said quietly. 'Merely a passionate, desirable woman, which is why you had best leave Avezza.'

'Very well. I will travel to Padua with Mariana,' she said.

'Good.' He looked at her and then hesitated. 'Good-bye, then.'

'Please be careful. I…I should not want anything to happen to you.'

A sardonic smile touched his mouth. 'If you continue to say such things, then I will be sorely tempted to take you here and now. I do not think that would be wise for either of us.' He was gone.

Nico stepped into his carriage and sank back against the cushions. Why the devil had he kissed her? Because she had looked so damned distressed that he'd wanted to comfort her. Once she was in his arms, it had been only natural to kiss her.

She was right—he had intended to scare her for, despite her sweet response to his kiss, he had guessed she would be appalled if he told her he planned to seduce her. He hoped that would be enough to drive her away from Avezza. Until he had a chance to determine what was going on.

There was another reason as well. He could not allow his attraction to Cecily Renato to get any further out of hand. Not if there were the slightest chance that Rafaele Vianoli was in love with her.

Chapter Six

Cecily rose early the following morning. She had slept poorly again and, as she had the night before, spent the night in restless dreams. Most disturbing of all was the dream in which she was trying desperately to save Severin's life from a faceless murderer while she attempted to persuade him to leave Avezza.

She had woken suddenly in the night with the realisation that he had never said he would leave Avezza. What he did was none of her affair. Not even if his kisses did make her long for something she could not have.

During one of her lengthy periods of restless tossing she had convinced herself that he had only meant to scare her into leaving Avezza. She was not the sort of woman that would interest a man such as the arrogant Duke of Severin.

Her head was beginning to hurt again from all the questions to which she had no answers. It was no use lying abed any longer. She threw on her dressing gown and went downstairs. Most of their luggage was piled in the hall. Perhaps if she ate she would feel better. She went into the small breakfast room and forced a few pieces of buttered toast and a cup of steaming chocolate down her throat.

She finally stood. She must wake Mariana for their journey.

Her soft rap on the door brought no response. She pushed the door open. The bedcovers were rumpled. 'Mariana?' She approached the bed and her heart stopped when she saw that it was empty.

'Oh, dear lord,' she whispered. Then she saw the note. She unfolded it with trembling fingers.

I cannot bear being parted from Simon. Do not worry, I will be quite safe. Your loving daughter, Mariana.

Not worry? Her daughter had decided to elope and she was not to worry? Where would they even go? And how was she to find them?

She could think of only one person who could help her.

Nico had just poured himself a second cup of strong coffee when he heard rapid footsteps and an agitated feminine voice. He rose just as Signora Renato burst into the dining room.

Her hair, tied back in a loose knot, trailed down her back. Astonished, he realised she wore a night rail underneath her pelisse. 'She is gone!' she said.

'Who is gone?'

'Mariana! She…she has run away with your cousin!'

He set his cup down and took her arm. 'Sit down.'

'No! I…I cannot. Where is Lord Ballister?'

'Sit.' This time she took the chair. 'Now tell me what has happened. Calmly, if you please.'

She took a deep breath and stared up at him. 'We…we are to leave today. I rose early for I could not sleep and went downstairs to eat—I thought I might feel better—but when I went upstairs to wake Mariana, she was not there. She left this…this note.' She held out a crumpled piece of paper.

He took it and perused the contents. 'Why do you think she eloped with my cousin?'

'Because she said she could not bear to be parted from him. Why else would she write such a thing?' She stood, obviously too agitated to sit. 'Please, you must see if Simon is here. If she did not run away with him, perhaps he has some idea where she has gone!'

'Stay here. I'll find my cousin.' He strode out of the room and saw the housekeeper hovering outside the door. Undoubtedly high drama. 'Is Lord Ballister still abed?' he asked.

'I do not know, milord.'

'Can you find out?'

'*Sì*, milord.' She scurried off.

He returned to the dining room where Cecily was pacing. She turned. 'Is he here?'

'I've sent my housekeeper to find out.' He took her arm. Deep circles surrounded her eyes. 'You need to sit. You did not even take the time to dress properly.'

Colour stained her pale cheeks. 'I needed to see you straight away. I did not want to waste time dressing.'

Hell. She looked as if she had just tumbled out of bed. Her pelisse had parted slightly and he could see the nipple of one rounded breast through the thin fabric of her night rail. His body responded with a lust that was completely inappropriate at the moment. He dropped her arm just as Flavia bustled into the room. 'He is gone. His bed has not been slept in. Oh, milord, do you think it is the same person who attacked you at the gardens?'

'No. I am quite certain Lord Ballister has gone of his own accord. Did he leave a note?' Not that he expected Simon to leave a message on his pillow.

'A note?'

'Allow me to see for myself. Send Enrico to the study. I want to speak with him.' He strode out of the room, only to find Cecily on his heels.

'Wait for me in the dining room. There is coffee and I've no doubt Flavia can make you tea if you'd prefer.'

Her face closed. 'Very well, your Grace.'

Flavia was correct: Simon's bed was untouched. He saw no note, but his cousin did indeed seem to have deliberately disappeared. His small valise was gone and, although most of his clothing remained, his favourite pair of boots was missing and several shirts and waistcoats were flung over the chair as if he'd pulled them out and rejected them.

Enrico waited for him in the salon. He answered Nico's questions in his rather vague way. No, Lord Ballister did not return home last night. No, Lord Ballister said nothing about a journey. Nico dismissed him, but just as Enrico reached the door he turned. 'Ah, but the young lord did wish me to give you this.' He pulled a folded paper from his pocket and held it out to Nico. The paper was now grubby with dirt and sweat. He opened it. The ink had smeared but he was able to make out part of the message.

Gone to V... Tell Signora Renato not to worry. Mariana...

'When did he give this to you?'

Enrico shrugged. 'Last night. He said to give it to you today.'

Nico cursed and returned to the breakfast salon. Cecily stood by the window. She whirled around.

'It appears they are together,' he said.

'Oh, dear lord! How do you know?'

'He also left a note. I cannot read all of it, but he does mention your daughter's name and that you are not to worry.'

'Mariana wrote exactly the same. They must be mad if they think we will not worry!' She looked shaken, but to her credit she made an effort to collect herself. 'If they plan to marry, where would they go?'

'There is an English vicar in Vicenza who, for the right fee, is said to be amenable to conducting marriages under rather clandestine circumstances. It is possible they have gone there. He might refuse to marry them if he thought Mariana was not of age, but if they convince him that Mariana is old enough then he might. At any rate, the legality of the marriage would be in question. Not that it makes a whit of difference if this gets out. Go home, I'll find them.'

'You cannot go. Your arm!'

'My arm is fine.'

'I am going with you.'

'You are not. You've no need to ruin your reputation as well by leaving with me. At any rate, I will go by horseback. There is a shortcut I know.'

'That is quite insane. I am going with you.'

'Then you will need to make your own way,' he said carelessly. 'I doubt if you want to leave in your current dishabille, so by the time you dress and are ready to go, I will be far down the road.' He hoped to God that would discourage her.

She stared at him, her expression a mix of worry and anger. 'Very well, your Grace.' She turned without another word and left.

Cecily stood outside the villa gates for a moment. His words rang in her head. *Then you will need to make your own way.*

Very well. She would dash off a note for Vittoria and Serefina with some excuse why Mariana was suddenly unable to make the journey. Her things and Mariana's were packed, so there would be no worries there. There was Barbarina… Perhaps she could tell her that Mariana was too distraught to say goodbye.

And then, she would do exactly as he told her.

Cecily brushed a strand of hair from her forehead and then glanced up at the darkening sky. She should climb back into her carriage, but she had become restless as she sat in its musty interior waiting for the bridge to be cleared. Shortly before she arrived at the bridge, a horse pulling a loaded wagon had shied. A wheel had caught in the groove where the road and bridge met and the wagon had tipped, spilling cabbages everywhere.

Now her carriage was stuck along with a number of other carts and wagons. There had been a great deal of loud talking and shouting while everyone argued about what should be done and how best to move the wagon. The wheel had broken and someone had gone to fetch a blacksmith. She suspected it would be another hour before the bridge would be passable.

She was so close to Vicenza. Only another few miles. She had briefly considered walking except she would still be faced with the problem of crossing the stream. Now it looked as if it were about to rain. She had no idea if she wanted to cry. Or throw something. What were Simon and Mariana doing? Had they already been married? Or were they turned away and forced to go elsewhere? But where would that be? Had Severin discovered anything?

Her mind kept spinning in circles and this idleness had not helped.

She walked down the grassy slope towards the stream, hoping to see progress of some sort. No one seemed to be doing much; several men were standing in a small cluster and talking with much waving of arms. Her coachman, Figaro, was leaning against the carriage, his eyes closed.

A drop of rain fell on the brim of her bonnet and hit her on the nose. 'Drat!'

'Somehow this does not surprise me.'

She whirled around, her heart thudding. Severin sat astride a large bay horse, a sardonic expression on his face.

She lifted her skirts and climbed towards him. 'Did you find them? Were they in Vicenza?'

'No. There was no sign of them.'

Disappointment coursed through her. She stared at him and then looked away, praying she would not cry. 'I see.'

'She will be safe with Simon.' His voice was surprisingly gentle.

She looked back at him. 'I…I suppose. That is, yes, I…I know.'

Another drop of rain hit her on the nose. He frowned. 'It is too late to return to Avezza. I doubt the bridge will be repaired any time in the next few hours. There is an inn, not far from here. Your coachman will need to turn the carriage around, however. Where is your maid? In the carriage? She had best dismount.'

'I did not bring my maid. She becomes exceedingly carriage-sick.' His expression told her what he thought of that. 'I will speak with Figaro now.'

'I will do so,' Severin said. He urged his horse before she could say a thing.

She eyed the narrow road, really not much more than a lane, with some misgiving and wondered how they could possibly turn the huge lumbering coach around without becoming stuck in the soft dirt next to the road.

She walked around the back of the coach and was astonished to see that Severin had dismounted and was involved in an animated discussion with several of her fellow travellers who were pointing at the coach. One of the young boys ran forward to hold Severin's horse. But when Figaro helped him slide his good arm from his coat, her amazement turned to dismay. Surely he did not intend to help.

At first he gave directions, but when one of the heavy wheels temporarily stuck in the mud, she was alarmed to see him set his good shoulder to the coach. She bit her lip to keep from calling out to him—she doubted he would welcome her concern.

Another quarter of an hour passed before her carriage was finally facing the right direction.

Severin returned to her side. A circle of dirt stained his white shirt and a smear of mud was on his cheek. 'It is safe for you to ride inside now.' He eyed the heavy old coach. 'There are lighter vehicles, you know. Ones that do not look as if they are about to lose a wheel at any moment.'

'Since I rarely use a carriage, I cannot see much sense in purchasing a new one. This suits me very well. It has proved to be very reliable.' She certainly did not intend to spend her small portion on such a thing. She frowned at him. 'Whatever possessed you to help move the carriage? What if you have injured your arm again?'

'I haven't,' he said briefly. 'Get into the carriage. I will ride alongside you to the inn.'

She searched his face, suddenly noticing he looked rather tired. 'Are you not going to stay there? I do not think you should travel any further.'

'I am fine,' he said curtly.

She turned and mounted the carriage before he could notice her flushed cheeks. She did not look at him as he closed the door. She stared out of the window at the sky, which was darkening. She hoped it would not rain on him. But, of course, what did it matter to her? He did not want her concern.

They had gone perhaps a mile, before the wind whipped up and rain spattered on the carriage roof. She saw a flash of lightning towards the distant hills. When the thunder came, she jumped, clutching her reticule. Then the storm began in earnest as hail pelted the roof of the carriage. The vehicle ground to a halt and she saw Figaro had stopped under a clump of trees. The pelting of the hail and rain lessened. In a moment, the door opened and Severin appeared. Water dripped from his hat down his face. 'We must halt until the hail stops.'

'You and Figaro must come inside.'

He shook his head. 'We cannot. We must stay with the horses.'

'Is there anything I can do?' She did not like the idea of remaining inside while they were out in the elements.

'Stay here.'

He closed the door. She cringed at the next crash of thunder. What if they were hit by lightning? Her worries turned to Mariana, who had always been afraid of such storms. Would Simon be able to comfort her? What if they, too, were on some road, seeking shelter from the storm instead of somewhere dry and warm?

She could feel the horses' nervousness for, when they

moved, the carriage rocked. She peered out the window and saw Severin standing with his horse under another clump of trees. He was speaking to the animal, stroking its neck as water dripped down their necks. A lump rose to her throat. Not only because they both looked rather forlorn, but because she had not expected him to show such tenderness.

The thunder rumbled again, but this time further away and the rain suddenly let up as quickly as it had come.

Severin gathered the reins of his horse and led him to the carriage. Cecily opened the door. 'Are you all right?'

'Yes. And you?'

'I was not out in the rain. You must ride the rest of the way inside. Could we not tie your horse to the back of the carriage?'

'I could, but he is limping a little and I don't want to risk further injury. We are not far from the inn. I'll lead him the rest of the way.'

'But what if you catch a chill?'

'You are fussing again,' he said, his expression cool. 'Don't.'

Feeling rebuffed, Cecily sat back against the cushions, as the carriage started forward. He had made it clear he did not welcome her concern, so why she persisted was beyond her.

The sudden rain had left great puddles on the road. The carriage lumbered into the inn yard only a little ahead of Severin. By the time she had dismounted, he had arrived. His horse was indeed limping. She caught up to Figaro and spoke to him in a low voice so Severin would not hear. 'Please see to the Duke's horse. Even if he refuses to allow you, you must do so when he is not present.'

Figaro nodded. *'Sì.* I will not allow him to refuse.'

'Grazie.' To her great relief, Severin handed over the reins without argument. She hesitated for a moment and then decided Severin would most likely favour her with one of his sarcastic remarks if she appeared to be waiting for him.

The inn was old and dark and smelled of dampness and onions. From somewhere down a hall drifted the low murmur of conversation punctuated with laughter. No one appeared behind the heavy wooden counter, so she rang the bell. A man came through the door, wiping his hands on the dirty apron covering his large stomach. 'May I help you, *signora*?'

'I wish to procure a room for the night. No, two rooms.'

'Alas, I have only one, which another gentleman has requested. But since he has not yet paid and you are here, I will allow you to have it. But only if you pay now.' He named a sum that nearly sent her reeling.

Only one? Severin would need it. He could not possibly travel any further. She would think of something. Perhaps there was another inn nearby. 'I will take it.' She started to open her reticule.

'I would at least demand to see the room before handing over such a sum.' Severin spoke from behind her. He turned to the proprietor and spoke to him in rapid Italian. 'I require two rooms for the night. With a private salon. At a reasonable price.' His cool manner brooked no argument.

The proprietor, whose name was Signor Bernelli, now appeared apologetic. His prices were always reasonable; perhaps the *signora* had misunderstood. Certainly there was a second room, although it was small and, since it was over the common rooms, noisy as well, but he would charge next to nothing for it. But a private salon…! After much haggling, Severin managed to procure a private parlour for an exorbitant price. He paid no heed to Cecily's protest that it was not necessary. 'I've no doubt I could purchase the inn several times over if I desired,' he said after they were shown to the small, musty room.

'Sit down. I've requested tea to be brought to you and a fire lit.' He started towards the door.

She remained standing. 'Where are you going?'

'To the stables. I need to see to my horse.'

'I asked Figaro to do that. You must sit.'

'I have been sitting all day.'

'Sitting on a horse is hardly the same thing. Perhaps you do not recall that two nights ago you were badly injured.'

His half-smile was sardonic. 'Oh, I recall it all right.'

'Then I forbid you to go out.'

'You are beginning to sound like my sister.'

'I am beginning to think a sister is exactly what you need.'

'I do not quite envision you in that role. Don't fuss. I don't like it.' He left.

Cecily plopped down into the chair. She felt a great deal of pity for his sister. Reasoning with him was impossible, which perhaps came from him being a duke, though she strongly suspected he would be just as intractable if he were a peasant. Not that it was her affair if he chose to injure himself further except that he would be useless in looking for Mariana and Simon. She would look for them herself.

None the less, she found herself on edge until she heard his footsteps. A rather sullen maid had come in and lit the fire so the room had lost some of its chill. He entered, water dripping from the brim of his hat.

She jumped up. 'Now you are soaked as well!'

'Yes.' He removed his hat and shrugged his good arm out of his coat. 'I forbid you to say any more about my condition.' He draped his coat over a chair in front of the fire and set his hat on the seat. He stood there for a moment and then turned just as the maid returned with a tray.

Severin directed her to place it on the table. This time she smiled in quite a flirtatious fashion, and lingered to inquire if milord needed anything further.

Cecily sat back down in her chair and waited as the girl removed the covers. Severin took the chair across from her. The maid left and the room suddenly seemed too quiet despite the sounds coming from elsewhere in the inn. She glanced over at Severin. His face was drawn and his eyes had a peculiar glassiness about them she had come to associate with a fever. She had no doubt that, if she said anything, he would snap at her. His eyes locked with hers for a moment so she looked away and picked up her fork.

The food was remarkably good and she found she was actually hungry. She had eaten a good quarter of her meal when she glanced up and found Severin watching her, his plate untouched. She put down her fork. 'Are you not going to eat?'

'I am not hungry.'

'You should at least eat a few bites.'

'I prefer not to.'

'Then at least drink some of your wine.'

'You are beginning to sound like my old nanny. Or a wife,' he said deliberately.

If he hoped to quiet her, he succeeded. 'I certainly have no desire for those roles either.' She rose, her appetite suddenly gone. 'I am finished as well. In fact, I am extremely fatigued. If you do not object, I believe I will retire.'

He stood. 'Of course.'

'Are you retiring as well?'

'Yes.'

He looked terrible, but she doubted he would listen if she said anything. 'Goodnight then, your Grace.'

'I will escort you to your chamber.'

'I am certain I can find my way.'

'Not tonight.'

She bit back the sharp retort that sprang to her lips. 'If you wish.'

The room was at the end of a long passage. He waited until she stepped inside. *'Buonanotte, signora.'* He leaned heavily against the doorpost, his breathing laboured. It was then that she noticed the bright red stain on his sling.

'Your arm. It is bleeding.'

He glanced down. 'So it appears. I will bid you—'

'I need to look at your arm.'

'I assure you there is no need.' His face had that haughty duke look that made her want to hit him.

'You look as if you are about to swoon as well. You must come in and let me look at your arm. If you do not do it willingly, then I vow I will force you!'

'I rather think I might like that,' he drawled.

'Stop it! Must you say such idiotic things now? You are bleeding; if you dare tell me to stop fussing over you, I will hit you!'

'I wouldn't dream of it.' He pushed away from the doorpost and then swayed. She caught his good arm. 'Please come with me.'

'If you insist.' He followed her into the room and sprawled down on one of the chairs. 'Now what?'

'I must remove your sling.'

'I can do it.'

'Let me do it.'

He did not protest as she knelt next to him and untied the cloth from his shoulder. He wore no waistcoat under his coat, only a loose linen shirt, and her stomach knotted when she saw how much blood had seeped on to his sleeve. His shirt was soaked with sweat and, from the heat radiating from his body, she feared he was feverish as well.

'You are not about to faint, I trust.'

She looked up and found his eyes on her face. 'Of course not. I am going to remove your shirt.' She reached for the first button, only to find his hand on hers.

'I think not.'

'There is no need for modesty. I was married, you know.'

'The only women who undress me are those I plan to make love to.'

She willed herself to meet his eyes, despite the heat in her cheeks. 'Then you must make an exception this time. I am not planning to completely undress you.'

'A pity—I suspect I would quite enjoy that.'

'I am beginning to think you are delirious.'

'Only with your presence.'

Her cheeks must be as flushed as his by now. She shook off his hand. 'I am going to remove your shirt because I must look at your wound. I pray you will cease teasing me.'

'But I am not teasing you. I told you in Avezza that I would very much like to seduce you.'

She finally looked at him. 'I am about to lose my temper regardless of whether you are hurt or not. So I suggest you allow me to continue before I do something you will not like.'

'Then I had best allow you to have your way with me,' he said softly. His hand fell away.

'Yes.' She undid the remaining two buttons, pleased her fingers did not tremble despite her proximity to him and her tingling awareness. She finally rose. 'Can you raise your good arm? I can then slip the shirt over your head on one side and slip it down your injured arm without your having to raise it.'

'Very well.'

She managed to get his shirt off, although he tensed as she gently pried it from around the wound. Some of the blood had dried and, as gentle as she tried to be, she had no doubt it pulled on his skin. 'I am sorry if I hurt you.'

'On the contrary, you seem remarkably skilled at this sort of thing.'

'I often helped my husband when he was ill.' She brought the candle closer and suppressed a shiver. The wound was an angry red and the flesh around it was swollen. Although much of the blood was dried, she could see fresh blood seeping from one side of the jagged wound. 'How long have you been bleeding like this?'

'I've no idea. Hardly enough to concern yourself over.'

'I think some of the stitches have come loose, but I will have to clean the wound before I can tell.' She rose. 'I will ask Signor Bernelli for clean cloths, brandy and water. And to send for a physician. First you need to get into bed.'

'Then you will need to help me into my clothes. I've no intention of walking the halls half-naked.'

'I meant you must get into this bed.'

'Any other time I would be delighted, but I fear I cannot oblige you tonight.'

She gave him an exasperated look. 'Don't be difficult.' She picked up his shirt. 'I will see if these can be washed. By the time I return I expect to find you in bed.' She did not wait to hear his reply.

She suspected he was attempting to fob her off by his improper remarks, but she had no intention of allowing him to do so. She very much feared he had developed an infection and the thought terrified her.

She found Signor Bernelli in the taproom. She hesitated in the doorway of the crowded room but then the man spotted her and bustled forward. He listened to her, a little frown on his brow, and then his face cleared. 'You are more than fortunate tonight for at this very inn a most distinguished physician is staying. Doctor Pascali is doctor to the most prominent of personages many of them your fellow countrymen. I will inform him that his services are needed at once.'

Cecily was rather alarmed to see Signor Bernelli approaching one of the more boisterous tables and speaking to one of the men. The last thing she wanted was a man in his cups examining Severin. To her relief, the tall man with a pair of intelligent eyes in a thin face that followed Signor Bernelli, appeared sober enough. She was even more reassured after he followed her into the hall and inquired what he could do for her in a pleasant, cultivated voice and questioned the symptoms.

'Allow me to fetch my bag and then I will join you in your chamber immediately. I will have Signor Bernelli send up a basin of water and cloths.'

She returned to the room. Severin sprawled halfway on the bed, his eyes closed. She thought he was sleeping until he opened his eyes. 'I've taken your bed. My apologies, but I don't think I can leave it any time soon.'

'I would not allow it.' She resisted the urge to brush

the dark locks away from his forehead. 'A physician will be here shortly.' Someone rapped on the door. 'In fact, he may be here now.'

'You constantly surprise me,' he murmured.

Cecily opened the door and found Dr Pascali, accompanied by one of the innkeeper's pink-cheeked daughters carrying a basin of water and some cloths.

Cecily stayed back while Dr Pascali examined Severin. He finally straightened. 'Your wound has developed a slight infection and the *signora* is quite correct in suspecting that you have torn several of the stitches. We must clean your wound and put in new stitches. And then you are not to move until your fever has gone unless you wish serious consequences.' He turned to the girl. 'Kindly fetch some brandy. You, Signora Renato, will assist me in cleaning and restitching his wound.'

'Of course.'

'I would prefer she leave the room,' Severin said.'

'I will need an assistant and I have no doubt Signora Renato is quite capable.'

Severin made no more protests. He refused the laudanum, but was finally persuaded to take a small glass of brandy. From his clenched fists and gritted teeth, she could tell he was fighting pain as they cleaned and then closed his wound. By the time the doctor finished, his forehead was dripping with sweat and he was breathing heavily. He fell back against the pillow.

Dr Pascali instructed her to bathe his forehead with water to bring down his fever. She could send for him if his condition worsened. Then he departed, leaving Cecily alone with Severin.

She dipped the cloth in the basin of water and wrung as much of the excess from it as possible. She turned to the bed and, as she leaned over him, he opened his eyes. 'My apologies, *cara*.' Then he promptly closed his eyes again.

Cecily finally collapsed into the chair next to the bed. Severin had fallen into a fitful sleep, the strong features of his face unexpectedly vulnerable. She realised with shock that she had not even thought of Mariana and Simon.

Chapter Seven

❧〜✦〜❧

'*Signora, signora.*' The soft, urgent voice jerked Cecily awake. She opened her eyes, disorientated for a moment to find Signora Bernelli, the innkeeper's wife, standing next to her chair. Her mind cleared. She was in the parlour of the inn and she must have fallen asleep while reading.

'*Signora*, the Duke has awakened and asks for you.'

She bolted up. 'Is something wrong?'

'No, no. He wishes to see you.'

'I will be up directly.' She stood and winced. If she continued to sleep in chairs, she would barely be able to move.

She followed Signora Bernelli to Severin's room, the book clutched in her hand. He was sitting up in bed. He wore a loose white shirt, which she suspected belonged to Signor Bernelli since it appeared far too big. A scowl crossed his face when he saw her. 'Where were you?' he demanded.

Any worry she had entertained vanished. 'In the parlour. I suppose you had some reason for summoning me other than ascertaining my whereabouts.'

'I did not know where you were.'

'Did you ask Signora Bernelli?'

His scowl deepened. 'I wanted to see you.'

'Did you need something?'

'What were you doing?'

'Reading, and then I fell asleep. Is there something you wanted?'

His gaze raked over her. 'No. Nothing. I apologise for disturbing you.' Now his voice was stiff.

She bit back a sigh and advanced towards the bed. 'Is your arm giving you much pain?'

'Nothing to signify. Go back to your book.'

Something was obviously amiss. 'What is it you wanted? I thought by going to the parlour I might give you a chance to rest quietly. I did not intend to abandon you.'

'I've no doubt you find sitting with me damnably tedious.'

'Do you wish me to sit with you?' It had never occurred to her he might actually want her company.

'I do not wish to bore you.'

So he did want her company. At least that is what she read into his cryptic conversation. She took the wooden chair next to the bed, vaguely noting that Signora Bernelli had left the room. 'That is quite understandable when one is ill. Marc…my husband complained of the same thing.' Until the end when he was too weak to do much of anything. 'I would read to him or we would play cards or sometimes just converse if he wished to.'

Something flickered in his eyes. 'So I do not suppose you would care to do any of those things with me,' he asked carelessly.

'If you want me to. Which do you wish? I would not recommend having me read to you unless you have a taste for Gothic romances.'

A little smile touched his mouth. 'Ah, yes. I recall you mentioned reading about headless spectres when we were in the maze.'

'It is not my romance, but one left behind by another English traveller. Signora Bernelli loaned the volume to me.'

'But you intend to read it?'

She flushed. 'I did not wish to offend Signora Bernelli by refusing it.'

His eyes held a wicked gleam. 'Of course not. Then you may read it to me. I should not want you to insult the good *signora*.'

She stared at him. 'You wish to hear a romance?'

'I suspect it will be quite entertaining.' He settled more comfortably against the pillows. 'You may begin whenever you wish.'

She eyed him, attempting to determine whether he meant to annoy her or really wished her to read to him. She could tell nothing by his expression. When she did not begin, he raised an expectant brow.

Very well. She would read *The Count of Bleakwood Forest* to him. It would undoubtedly serve him right if he was completely bored by the end of the first chapter. She opened the book.

Ten minutes later she glanced over at him. His eyes were closed, which reminded her of how sleepy she felt herself. Now that he was asleep she could attempt to wake herself by walking down to the parlour and back. She closed the volume.

'What does Amelia do now that her father has gone mad?'

Cecily jumped. 'I thought you were sleeping!'

'How could I when the fair heroine is about to be evicted from her picturesque cottage?' he murmured. His eyes were now open.

'You were actually paying attention?'

'I would not insult you by falling asleep in the middle of such a riveting tale.'

She suspected he was amusing himself. 'I would hardly be insulted. Do you wish me to continue?'

'A few more pages.'

'Very well.' She reopened the book and began to read. She stifled a yawn after the first paragraph and forced herself to go on. Her voice trailed off and she refocused her eyes with an effort.

Cecily's voice had grown so soft Nico could scarcely hear her. Her head was nodding as if she were about to fall asleep at any moment. He was not faring much better. Her sweet, soothing voice had nearly put him into a pleasurable sleep and it was all he could do to keep from fading away himself. He was tired, but she must be equally so. Forcing her to read to him because he was bored was hardly gentlemanly. 'Signora Renato. Cecily.'

When she did not respond, he realised she had indeed read herself to sleep. Her head drooped to one side. He should have realised how tired she was. She had been up with him most of the night. His gaze roved over her flushed cheeks, her lips slightly parted. His groin tightened. He could almost taste her mouth under his; imagine carrying her half-asleep to the bed. She would lie beneath him, her hair tousled around her face, her eyes opening in sleepy invitation as he bent over her. He would…

He jerked his lustful thoughts back to reality. What the devil was he thinking of? No matter how desirable he found Cecily Renato, he could not afford to involve himself with her. He could not make her his mistress even if he knew she would agree, which he very much doubted. She would be too complicated and not only because of Simon and Mariana.

She turned a little and made a small sound. She must be uncomfortable. He scowled and threw back the covers. He sat on the edge of the bed for a moment, pleased his head did not spin quite so much this time. He stood and looked down at her. He doubted she weighed much. If he was careful, he was unlikely to re-injure his arm. He slipped his good arm under her arms and his injured arm under her legs. Making certain his uninjured arm supported most of her weight, he lifted her from the chair. She murmured something, but did not wake as he gently laid her on the bed. He drew the sheet up over her shoulders and then sat on the bed next to her, annoyed to find he was slightly dizzy from the exertion. He gazed down at her for a moment and he found himself wanting to plant a tender, intimate kiss on her forehead.

He rose abruptly, ignoring his spinning head. He could not afford any tender feelings towards this woman.

Cecily awoke with a start to the sound of rain pounding on the window. She had no idea where she was and could not fathom why she was in a bed, fully clothed. She vaguely remembered reading to Severin and she must have fallen asleep. She sat up abruptly and saw she was in Severin's bed. Her gaze fell on the chair next to the bed and she saw he was sprawled in it, eyes closed, his head lolling against the back.

Her confusion increased. Why was he in the chair and she in the bed? And how long had they both been sleeping? She glimpsed the sky through the window and thought it was still early evening despite the dark sky.

She swung her legs over the side of the bed. Severin did not move. He must be terribly uncomfortable. She had been cramped, but he must be doubly so with his long, muscular frame. It was a wonder he had been able to fall asleep. It occurred to her, then, that he must have carried her to the bed, for she could not remember stirring enough to make her way on her own.

Her cheeks heated just thinking about it. At the same time she wondered what had possessed him to do so in the first place. What if he had opened his wound?

Worried, she slid from the bed so that she could look more closely at him. Thank goodness, she saw no tell-tale red staining the rough linen of his shirt. She should wake him and insist he return to the bed. He stirred a little. Her gaze fell to his mouth and her knees felt almost weak as she suddenly remembered how his mouth had felt on hers. What would it be like to kiss him again? But this time she would want to tangle her hands in his thick dark hair and then…

She drew away, horrified at the direction of her thoughts. Whatever was she thinking of? She could not possibly be lusting after the Duke of Severin. Respectable women did not do such things. At least she did not do such things. She had enjoyed the intimacy of the marriage bed, as brief as it had been before Marco became ill, but had not thought about such things at all since his death.

He stirred again and she stiffened. He slowly opened his eyes and she jumped. 'You are awake,' he said.

'So…so are you.' She prayed he would not guess the direction of her thoughts.

'Yes.' He raised his head and winced.

'Your neck must be very stiff. I…I have no idea why you are not in bed.'

A faint smile touched his lips. 'Because you were there. I was not certain you would appreciate my joining you.'

'I should not have been there in the first place. I am not the one who is wounded.'

'You needed to sleep. In a bed. I've no intention of allowing you to collapse because you've worn yourself out by nursing me and sleeping in chairs.'

His kindness touched her. 'You should have wakened me.'

'And deny myself the pleasure of holding you in my arms?'

She flushed and decided to ignore his ridiculous comment. 'You might have reopened your wound.'

'But I did not.' He rose. 'This argument is pointless since the deed has already been done. You will be glad to know, however, that Signor Bernelli has informed me that the room next to this one is available for your use.'

'Yes. That will be nice.'

He watched her with his impenetrable expression. 'You do not seem over-enthused at the prospect.'

'Of course I am. As long as you are certain you will not need anything in the night.'

'Any needs I might have are ones I am certain you would not wish to fulfil.'

She managed to keep her voice calm. 'Then I had best move my possessions next door. Are you well enough to come to down for dinner? Or do you wish a tray in your room?'

'A tray in my room.'

'Very well.' She inched towards the door. 'I will inform Signora Bernelli, your Grace.'

She turned, but not before she saw his swift frown.

By the next day, the rain had let up and the sky was blue and cloudless. Cecily ate breakfast and then made her way out to the stables. She was forced to skirt around several large puddles, one of which seemed to be the size of a small pond. She was relieved to see the horses were in good condition, although the fetlock of Severin's bay was still a little swollen. Figaro did not seem very hopeful about the condition of the road, however, and thought it would be another day before they dried enough to make a journey at all possible.

She picked her way back to the inn, disappointed by the news. Now that Severin did not seem to be in imminent danger, she was anxious to resume the search for Mariana. She would not worry that, if she left him, he would have no one to look after him. Not that he seemed to want her anyway. He had avoided her since she had moved to the adjoining room and they had barely spoken, which was just as well—she had made every attempt to avoid him as well. He would not mind if she went on without him.

At least, she hoped he would not.

She wiped her now muddy half-boots on the old rug in the inn's hall and then wandered into the parlour. Whatever was she to do for the day? Her room, although neat, was small and cramped. She could take a short walk, but she would probably ruin her half-boots. Or she could—

'Good morning.'

She gasped when Severin suddenly rose from a chair on the other side of the room. He was dressed in one of Signor Bernelli's loose white shirts, with his injured arm in a sling, and a pair of borrowed breeches that were both too short and too loose. The ill-fitting clothes did nothing to detract from his dangerous masculine appeal and her heart thudded much too hard. 'What are you doing up?'

'Looking for you. I had almost begun to think you had deserted me.'

'Of course not.' At least not for a while. 'Why ever would you think that?'

'I have not seen you since yesterday when you woke up in my bed.'

He did not need to make it sound so...so provocative. 'It was my bed to begin with, might I remind you.'

'You are correct. Your bed, then. I have not seen you since you woke up in your bed.'

'I rather thought you did not wish to be disturbed.'

'It depends on who is disturbing me.'

'I see.' He was going to be difficult again. When was he not? 'Are you certain you should be up?'

'Quite certain. I need to check on the horses.'

'I have already done so. They are in good health, although the swelling on your bay is not completely gone. Figaro does not seem to think the roads are yet passable.'

He looked faintly surprised. 'You have gone to the stables?'

'I wished to see if it was possible to leave today.'

'I trust you intended to discuss these plans with me.' He finally moved into the room.

'Well, yes. I thought, if you were still not very well, that I could perhaps go on to search for Mariana.'

'Sit down.'

She frowned at him and then realised he still appeared rather pale. He would not sit if she did not. She took the chair near the small table and he seated himself in one across from her. 'I doubt if one more day will make much difference,' he said coolly. 'Simon will see that Mariana is safe. It is possible they are already married. If they are not, they will be. He will not ruin her, if that is what worries you.'

'I never thought he meant to ruin her. But they are so young…what can they possibly know about marriage? I know how much you object to a marriage between them and I would not want her to be unhappy because you…his family does not approve. Nor do I want your family to be unhappy because they do not approve of Mariana. One does not marry just a person; one marries their entire family. I could not bear for Mariana or Simon to be miserable because they have married like this.'

'You do not need to worry about how Mariana will be received. I suspect my mother will be more than delighted to have someone in the family who is from her own country. Her family knew Mariana's uncle's family very well.'

She had forgotten that. 'Dear Lord, what will I tell Raf?'

His expression hardened a trifle. 'I will deal with Vianoli.'

She took a deep breath. 'Is it true that you and Raf have quarrelled?' For a moment, she did not think he would answer.

'Yes,' he finally said.

'Will you tell me why? Barbarina will only talk of duels and fights, but will tell me nothing more. Raf has never said anything. I would not ask if it were not for Mariana and Simon.'

'You know nothing about it?'

'No.'

'Very well, I will tell you.' His eyes did not leave her face. 'We quarrelled, if one can call it that, after Angelina, my fiancée, died. He said that, if he ever discovered I had anything to do with her death, he would kill me. I blackened his eye.' His voice was cold, emotionless.

She stared at him, a sick feeling in her stomach. 'Why? Why would he say such a thing? Marco told me her death was an accident.'

He rose. 'She asked to meet me that day. She was agitated, upset when she left the house. Raf also knew that Angelina and I had argued the day before.' His hand gripped the back of the chair in front of him. 'Her death was ruled an accident, but there were bruises on her arm as if someone had grabbed her. The physician said they were a result of her fall.'

Dear God. Beneath his cool recital she sensed his deep anguish. She had felt a sort of general sorrow that Angelina's young life had ended so tragically, but until now had not really experienced the full impact of her death on those around her. She wanted to go to him, put her arms around him as she would Mariana, but he would reject her. Instead she said, 'It is hardly unnatural that you and Angelina argued, for people do. And unless one knew why Angelina was upset, one cannot assume it had to do with you. It does not make any sense at all for Raf to even think of blaming you.'

'Oh, but it does.' His gaze was fixed on her face, his eyes bleak. 'For Angelina had begun to have doubts about our marriage. I fully expected her to end our betrothal that day. Raf knew about her misgivings. There is one more thing, something I did not believe to be true until I saw his face that day. He was my friend; I should have known. Known that Raf, too, was in love with Angelina.'

She stood then and went to him and placed her hand on the sleeve of his coat. 'I am so sorry,' she whispered.

He stared down at her for a moment. 'Don't be.' He pulled away from her. 'I must make my apologies. I am going to the stables and then for a walk. We will leave for my villa tomorrow. It is possible Mariana and Simon are there. If not, we will continue on to Venice. You will stay with my mother until we discover Mariana and Simon's whereabouts.'

She could not manage any sort of reply. He sketched a brief bow and walked away while a little part of her heart seemed to die within her.

Chapter Eight

Nico finished tucking his shirt into the top of his freshly washed breeches and then leaned back against the dresser for a moment, biting back a curse. He was still weaker than he cared to admit, but he was determined they would leave this place today.

As well as apologise to Cecily for walking out on her in such a boorish fashion. He still saw the stricken look on her face when he pulled away from her.

He'd never told anyone why he and Raf had argued. He had never spoken the words he'd carried in his heart and mind: Raf was in love with Angelina. The compassion in Cecily's eyes only increased his guilt and, in some strange sense, made him angry. He wanted neither her kindness nor her pity—he did not want her concern stirring up the feelings he'd long buried.

Which did not excuse his rudeness. They could not afford to be on poor terms, particularly since they were most likely to soon be related—which would pose a new set of damnable complications.

'*Signora.*' Cecily started out of her reverie and looked over at Severin who sat in the opposite corner of the carriage. He had decided to stable his horse at the inn and ride in the carriage with her. He'd said little as they readied for the journey and she had been in no mood to attempt conversation. Not after yesterday. Not when he made it clear he wanted nothing from her.

'Yes, your Grace?'

'I wish to speak to you for a moment.'

'If you wish.'

'I wish to apologise to you for my rudeness yesterday when I walked away from you.' His voice was cool, but the hint of stiffness in his tone told her that the apology did not come easily.

'You do not need to apologise. I quite understand that you were—'

'I do not want your understanding. I am apologising to you, not asking you to justify my behaviour.'

'Very well. I accept your apology.' She knew her voice was equally icy, but she did not want him to guess how much his coldness hurt. She turned her gaze to the window, telling herself it did not matter. His affairs were none of her concern. He was none of her concern. Once they found Simon and Mariana they would part company and she would never need to lay eyes on him again. Except if Mariana and Simon were married, then they would be related by marriage and she would be forced to see him. She would treat him coolly and quite put aside—

'Hell. Cecily.'

'Yes?' she said, her gaze now on a passing vineyard.

'Will you at least look at me?'

She finally turned to him. 'Why?'

'Because I'd at least like to see your face when I offer you another apology.'

'I have no idea why you would wish to do so.' She was being quite childish. In fact, she was behaving very much like Mariana did when she was hurt.

'For—' He stopped. 'For being so damnably difficult.'

'I do not suppose you can help it.'

He stared at her and then laughed shortly. 'You never fail to surprise me. Do you not wish to take me to task over this?'

'I doubt that would change anything. We would probably quarrel and then the rest of the journey would be exceeding uncomfortable.'

'You are undoubtedly right.' His eyes were still on her. 'Do you think we could possibly declare a truce? I'll promise to be less difficult and you…' he paused '…you will promise to converse with me.'

'How can I tell when you are fulfilling your terms?'

'You mean to say I am always difficult?'

'Yes.'

'You are wrong, I can be very agreeable at times.'

'Most likely when you are getting your own way.'

This time his laugh held genuine amusement. 'Of

course. So, if you converse with me, I can demonstrate how very agreeable I can be.'

Her hurt was fading and she found she was starting to enjoy herself. 'I imagine the topics must be ones of your own choosing as well?'

'Yes, although I might be generous and allow you to choose one.'

'Only one?'

'It depends. Perhaps another if you meet certain terms.'

'What terms?'

'First you must call me Nico.'

'That is hardly proper.'

'But since I have been improper enough to address you by your given name, it is only fair that you do so in return. Say it.'

'Nico.'

His gaze fell to her mouth. 'Very nice,' he said softly.

She felt as if she had stumbled into dangerous waters. 'Which topic should we start with?' Her voice was too bright. Too breathless.

He leaned back against the squabs. 'Tell me how you came to marry Marco Renato.'

For a moment, she was taken aback. 'I met him when he came to London to visit a cousin. We were married shortly after that.'

'That hardly tells me anything.'

'What is it you want to know?'

'Were you in love with him?'

She stared at him and then looked away for a moment. 'Yes, I loved him.' But not at first. No, at first jovial Marco, with his ready laugh and twinkling, intelligent eyes, was only an escape from another marriage she knew would break her heart. She did not know then that her marriage to Marco would break her heart as well.

'And your family? I cannot imagine they were pleased to have you so far away.'

'My parents died when I was fourteen. I had only my grandmother. She was not pleased when I married Marco.' She tried to smile. 'Perhaps we could choose another topic.'

'Why?' he asked quietly. 'Why was your grandmother displeased?'

'Because I was to marry someone else. I…I broke the betrothal and then I met Marco. We were married in Scotland.' She waited for his condemnation, but there was none. 'I fear my past is quite disreputable.'

'Why did you break the betrothal?' His voice was impersonally curious.

'Because the man I was to marry kept a mistress. I know I should not have been shocked and accepted it— it is not at all unusual—but he made no secret of his relationship. Once I saw them together. It was at a ball… I did not mean to see them and they never saw me.' Her cheeks heated and she stared down at her folded hands. 'After that I could not bear the thought of marrying him.' Or having him touch her. She had thought herself in love with Charles Winstead and had treasured the thought that his attentive behaviour and charming manners meant he had begun to care for her. Stumbling upon him locked in an embrace with his mistress shattered her illusions.

'He was a damnable idiot.'

She looked up, taken aback to see the anger in his face. 'He was only doing what most men do, I suppose.' That is what her grandmother had told her.

'You are wrong. Not all men would behave so despicably. Any man who would keep a mistress when betrothed to you is a fool. And wholly undeserving of you.'

She shook her head, not believing his words. 'His mistress was very beautiful and sophisticated. All the things I was not. Sometimes I could scarcely utter a sentence when I was around him. I have no doubt he found me very dull.'

'You are anything but dull. As for the other, you are quite lovely.'

'I really am not. I am very ordinary—'

'Quite lovely, as I have told you before. And very desirable.'

Something in his cool tone told her he was not paying her an idle compliment. She glanced away, feeling oddly vulnerable and a little afraid. Of what, she did not know. He had flirted with her and kissed her and she had not been half as shaken as she was now with him sitting across from her in the close confines of her carriage.

Thank goodness he said nothing more, although conversation would have been difficult for, as they continued on, the road became increasingly uneven and the carriage bumped and jolted along. She hung on to the strap and prayed the carriage would not fall apart.

The carriage suddenly shuddered and jerked to an abrupt, rocking halt.

'What is it?' she asked.

'I don't know. Wait and I'll find out.' He opened the door and stepped out. A moment later he returned. 'The back wheel is loose. We are fortunate Figaro noticed something was amiss and halted before it came completely off.' He held out his hand. 'I will help you down. You should not remain in the carriage much longer.'

'No.' She took his hand and cautiously stepped from the carriage. The road was deserted and nothing but vineyards stretched in either direction. The fresh air was welcome, but the sight of the back wheel was worrisome.

'Can you manage the horses while Figaro and I examine the wheel?' Nico asked.

'Yes.'

He gave her a brief smile. 'Good.'

She went to the horses' heads. They appeared unconcerned about the matter, the bay gelding merely blowing on Cecily's cheek while his companion stretched his neck towards an enticing patch of weeds. She heard Severin and Figaro speaking in rapid Italian, but could not quite make out the words. The late morning sun was warm on her cheeks, the sky a peaceful cerulean blue. She took a deep breath, willing her headache to go away.

Nico returned. 'The wheel is about to come off. The inn is perhaps a mile from here. We can walk while Figaro stays with the carriage or remain here while Figaro goes for help.'

'I would prefer to walk. Will Figaro be safe?'

'I doubt there are any *banditti* about now. I will leave him one of my pistols.' He looked down at her. 'Are you certain you want to walk?'

'I will be fine.' Anything was better than remaining idle along the road.

He did not look completely convinced, but said nothing more.

She waited while he gave Figaro instructions. She was beginning to wonder if they would ever find Mariana and Simon. She could only pray they were safe and trust Nico when he said Simon would not let anything happen to Mariana.

He returned to her side and then set off towards the village. The road ran along a river, which Nico said was the Brenta. A passage-boat passed them, towed by horses and across the river, through the trees, she could see the stucco roof of a villa.

The inn was located just outside the village. A grey cat sunned itself on a bench and opened one lazy eye as they approached. Inside, the stone hall was cool. Sounds of conversation and laughter came from one of the rooms. Nico turned to her. 'Sit down while I find the proprietor. I will procure rooms as I've no idea how long it will take to have the wheel repaired.'

Cecily took one of the benches just as a short, stocky man entered the hall. He came forward. '*Signor, signora.* I am Benvenuto Salvidori. How might I assist you?'

Nico told him, but when he requested two rooms the proprietor frowned. 'Two?' A slight frown crossed the man's face. 'I fear we only have one. There is a party of the English staying here a number of days. Perhaps as husband and wife you would not object to sharing a room. It is quite large and I am certain your lady would be most comfortable.'

Husband and wife? Her startled gaze flew to Nico's face. Wholly expecting him to deny it, she nearly fell off the bench when he said, 'Very well, we will take the room.'

The proprietor beamed. 'Good. Good. The room is prepared, so if the *signor* wishes to discuss the arrangements, my wife will be delighted to show the *signora* to the room.' He turned towards the door. 'Sophia!' he boomed out.

Almost instantly, a well-endowed woman who stood several inches taller than her husband burst through the door. He spoke to her in rapid Italian and she turned to Cecily. 'Of course, you must go immediately to the room and rest while the *signor* sees to the carriage.'

Cecily rose and cast an uncertain glance at Nico, but Signora Salvidori was already walking away. Cecily had no choice but to follow her.

The room was indeed large, much larger than those at the previous inn. Sunlight flooded the room with cheerful warmth. The bed was high and old.

Signora Salvidori was speaking. 'You did not bring your maid? Then I will send my Portia to you. And then you will sleep. You must remove your pelisse and boots and I will find Portia.'

Signora Salvidori bustled away before Cecily could tell her she really did not need to rest. She unbuttoned her pelisse and removed it and then sat on a chair to remove her half-boots. She rose. The bed really did look quite inviting. Perhaps she could lie down for a very short time. A plump girl who must be about Mariana's age entered the room. 'Mama wishes me to assist you,' she announced.

She did not really look much like Mariana, but Cecily felt a tug at her heart and a surge of longing for her daughter. She smiled. '*Grazie*, but I do not intend to rest for very long. I can sleep in my gown.'

The girl's face fell and Cecily relented. 'Very well. Just my gown, then.'

Portia helped her from her muslin gown and her stays with surprising alacrity. Cecily thanked her and, as soon as Portia departed, climbed into the bed. She closed her eyes, images of the carriage and Severin's face swimming before her eyes as he told her she was lovely. And desirable. Soon the images blurred together and then she faded away.

Cecily opened her eyes and for a moment, had no idea where she was and why she was in bed in the middle of the day. Then she remembered; she had gone to bed intending to take only a short nap. It appeared, however, she had been asleep for a very long time.

She sat up abruptly and nearly gasped when she saw Nico's long frame sprawled in a wing chair near the window. His head lolled against the high back and from his deep even breathing she knew he was asleep.

Heat stained her cheeks when she realised her shift had slipped off one shoulder, exposing far too much flesh. No matter that he was hardly in a state to notice, she still felt self-conscious. How was she to dress if he were still in the room?

She spotted her gown draped over the back of a chair. He seemed to be sleeping soundly; she could quietly retrieve her gown and at least put it on over her shift. She could probably manage to tie the tapes of her gown and, after Nico left the room, summon Portia to help her into her stays.

She threw back the covers and slipped from the bed as silently as possible. Fortunately, the gown was on the opposite side of the bed from Severin. She slipped it on but her attempts to tie the tapes proved futile.

She reached around and found she could not quite close the back 'Drat!'

'What are you doing?'

She gasped and her head jerked up. Horrified, she froze and the gown slid from her shoulder. Cecily tugged it up and crossed her arms over her chest to keep it from falling any more. She forced herself to meet his gaze. 'Putting on my gown.'

'The procedure does not seem to be going well. You appear to need help.' To her mortification, he stood and she backed up as he came towards her.

'I assure you I do not.'

He stopped in front of her. 'But I think you do.' He held out his hand. 'Allow me.'

'I couldn't possibly.' She took another step back.

'I only wish to return the favour.' A slight smile touched his mouth. 'I believe you helped me numerous times with my, er…personal needs over the past few days.'

'You were ill, so there was a difference. This would not be at all proper.'

'We seem to be far beyond the proprieties at this point. Turn around. I merely wish to help you into your gown, not out of it.' His voice was rather impatient.

She had no doubt he would persist. Complying now would save further argument. Besides, his voice was too impatient to imagine he had seduction in mind. She turned.

As soon as she felt his fingers at her back, she knew this was a mistake. A shiver ran down her spine and languidness crept over her as he tied the tapes. When he lifted the hair away from her neck, she thought her knees might crumble. She closed her eyes and willed her body to stay still as he did the tape at the neck of her bodice. She prayed he would step away quickly.

He did not. He stood so close behind her she could almost hear his heart beat. She nearly stopped breathing and then his hand again brushed the hair from the nape of her neck. His arm came about her, pulling her back against his chest. His mouth moved across her nape and a little moan escaped her.

His mouth travelled to her ear and to her shoulder where he pushed down the left sleeve of her gown and rained kisses upon the exposed shoulder. When his hand cupped her breast through the layers of shift and gown, she thought she would explode. Her body was on fire, the warm throbbing growing between her legs and, for the first time since Marco, she felt a pure, hot desire that shocked her.

Panicked, she forced her eyes open, her hand going to the hand that covered her breast. He lifted his head almost right away and released her. He waited a moment before speaking. 'I was wrong. I do want to help you from your gown after all. But not against your will.'

'No.' She forced herself to turn although she could not quite make herself look at him. 'Th…thank you for fastening my gown.'

A surprised laugh escaped him. 'Ah, my sweet Cecily, I have just declared my desire to seduce you and you respond by merely thanking me.'

'I cannot think of what else to say. I imagine you merely wish to…to…' Words trailed off. Last time she had suspected that he meant to scare her from following him; this time, she sensed his purpose was far different.

'Make love to you, take you to my bed, be your lover,' he said bluntly. His eyes were on her face.

'I…' Her knees trembled and she thought her cheeks must be on fire. 'I…I fear I have not been offered *carte blanche* very often. I have no idea what one is supposed to say.'

'No, in most cases.'

'And this time?' The words sprang out of their own accord.

His eyes darkened, but his words were deliberate. 'I think you would be wise to say "no" this time as well.'

'Do you?'

'It would complicate matters damnably.'

'I suppose it might.'

'It would. Believe me, sweetheart.' He moved away from her. 'I will leave you to finish dressing.' He stalked to the door. Once there he turned. 'I had hoped to reach my villa tonight, but it appears the wheel will not be fixed in time so we will put up here. You do not need to worry about tonight's sleeping arrangements. I'll sleep in the stables if necessary.'

Cecily sank down on the chair, with the sensation of having been run over by a team of horses. Had the Duke of Severin really just declared he wanted to be her lover? He was undoubtedly mad, but then so was she.

Or else completely wanton…because the idea did not shock her half as much as it should.

Chapter Nine

Cecily watched as Nico's strong lean fingers curled around his wine glass. She forced her gaze to her nearly untouched plate. It was not the first time during dinner she'd found herself covertly watching him instead of eating. What would he do if she were to tell him she wished to accept his offer—well, not quite an offer, for he only said that was what he wished to do before he then proceeded to discourage her. What would he do if she told him she actually wanted to…to lie with him?

She closed her own eyes, an embarrassing stab of desire shooting through her. No doubt dozens of women had thrown themselves at him. She would be only one of many. He probably desired many women and, due to the unfortunate circumstances of finding themselves together, he had developed some sort of strange attraction to her, which would vanish as soon as they returned to society. Thank goodness, they would reach Venice in another day.

'Are you unwell?'

She jerked her head up and found him staring at her with a slight frown. 'I beg your pardon?'

'Are you not well? Your eyes were shut and you've hardly touched your dinner.'

'I am not very hungry. But I am perfectly well. Just rather tired. In fact, I will go to my room as soon as we finish the meal.'

'I am done.'

'Are you? You have not eaten much either.'

'It appears we share a common affliction, then.' He finished off his wine and rose. 'I will escort you to your room.'

She hesitated to ask him where he planned to spend the night. She doubted from his cool, polite manner he would tell her. She had just reached the door when it opened. She jumped back and found herself face to face with a man who stood on the other side. She saw his face and gasped. 'Raf?'

Rafaele Vianoli looked equally startled. 'Cecily? So it is your carriage. I…' He caught sight of Nico. His mouth fell open. 'Domenico?'

'Good evening, Vianoli.'

Raf stared at him and then back at Cecily, his expression incredulous. 'You are with him?'

'Well, yes.'

Raf's gaze returned to Nico and his eyes narrowed. 'I trust you have a reasonable explanation for your presence.'

'I've no idea whether you'll consider it reasonable or not. Nor do I particularly care.' Nico met Raf's eyes, his own hard. 'At this moment, I am taking Signora Renato to her room. She is tired.'

'She is coming with me.'

'She is under my protection. She stays with me.'

'I must contradict you. She is under my protection.'

'The hell she is.' Nico's hand closed over Cecily's arm. 'Step aside, Vianoli.'

'Release her.'

Horrified, Cecily saw Raf point a small pistol at Nico. 'Raf? What are you doing?'

Raf paid no attention. 'Let her go or I will shoot you.'

Nico dropped her arm. 'Go ahead.'

Furious, Cecily placed herself directly in front of the pistol. 'You will have to shoot me before you shoot him. But if you so much as touch him, I will spend the rest of my life making you pay.'

'Cecily, stay out of this,' Nico said.

Raf stared at her and lowered the pistol. He looked back at Nico, his expression cold. 'So you have seduced her. Why? Revenge? Because of Angelina?'

'You bastard,' Nico said softly. 'Put down the pistol. I want an equal chance to kill you for insulting Cecily and suggesting I would dishonour her in such a despicable way. I'll send you to hell before I let you near her.'

Raf dumped the pistol on the table near the door. 'You are accusing me of insulting her?'

'Yes, damn you.'

Raf lunged at Nico. They both went down, crashing into the table, sending it and its contents to the floor.

'Stop! Stop!'

They were oblivious to Cecily's shouts as they tumbled over each other like a pair of deadly, snarling dogs. She was terrified Nico's wound would open and equally terrified they would succeed in killing each other. They rolled into an elegant wing chair, Rafaele hitting his head, and then he had his hands around Nico's throat. Then Nico's hands were around his.

'No!' She snatched the pistol from the floor and pointed it at them. 'Stop! Or I will shoot you!'

They paid her no heed. She looked around and her eyes lit upon a vase filled with flowers. She snatched it up and dumped the contents over the nearest man. Raf reared back in shock as water and flowers poured down his neck.

'Maledizione! What are you doing?'

'Stopping you from killing each other.' With a shaking hand, she pointed the pistol at them. 'If either of you moves, I will shoot you.'

Nico had managed to sit and was now slumped against the wall. Water dripped from his head and he was breathing heavily. None the less, a corner of his mouth twitched. 'Do you even know how to use that thing?' he managed to ask.

'I can swear she does not. She refused to allow my cousin to instruct her.' To her astonishment, Raf looked amused. 'You had best give me the pistol before you do shoot one of us.'

'No, for I think you have both gone mad. How dare you accuse him of seducing me? He was ill most of the time!'

'Cecily, I did not mean…' Raf held out his hand. 'You are upset. At least give me the pistol.'

'No!' She backed up and stepped on something soft and slick. Her foot slid and she was falling. She attempted to regain her balance and then was pitching forward on to the floor. A sharp pain shot through the side of her head and for a moment the world spun around her. She closed her eyes.

Someone knelt next to her. 'Cecily. Damn it! Can you hear me?'

Nico. He touched her cheek.

'Swearing at her less might help.' Now Raf was next to her.

She forced her eyes open and attempted to roll to her side. She could not allow Raf to hurt Nico. 'No. Stop.'

Nico's face hovered over hers, his eyes dark with worry. 'Don't talk, sweetheart.' He slipped one arm under her head and the other under her legs and rose with her in his arms. The movement made her head hurt and she moaned.

'I am taking her to her room. Tell Signor Salvidori to send for a physician. Send Signora Salvidori to her as soon as possible.'

'Yes.' Raf's voice sounded equally grim. 'I will go now.'

'You cannot carry me. Your arm.'

'My arm is fine. Don't argue.' He strode from the room and she could do nothing but close her eyes while he carried her up the stairs and down the passage to the room. Somehow he managed to unlock and open the door and set her gently on the bed. She winced when her head touched the pillow. To her surprise he sat on the bed next to her. 'Where does your head hurt?'

'Only on the right side.'

'Let me see.' Despite his gentle touch, she jumped when his hand brushed over the spot.

'There is a small cut and you will undoubtedly have a nasty lump.' He drew back and she saw the bruise across his cheekbone.

'You are hurt.'

'Not as badly as Vianoli, however.' He took her hand. 'Do not do such a foolish thing again. Give me your word you will never step in front of a pistol again.'

'I did not want him to kill you,' she said softly.

'Cecily,' he said hoarsely. He lifted her hand to his lips.

'Perhaps I should call you out after all.' Raf had entered the room.

Nico jerked back and dropped her hand. 'As you wish.'

Cecily shot up and her head spun for a moment. 'No! I will…will strangle both of you if you even say such a thing again!'

Raf's expression was hard to interpret, perhaps due to his swollen lip. He, too, sported a bruise across one cheekbone. 'I was only teasing, *cara*. I assure you I have no wish to have another vase of flowers thrown at me.'

Nico scowled at him. 'I suggest you do nothing more to distress her. Unless you want a bullet through you.'

'Nico, please.'

He looked back down at her, his expression softening. 'I am sorry. I promise no more fights.' Nico stood just as Signora Salvidori bustled in, carrying a basin of water with several cloths draped over one arm.

She went directly to Cecily. 'Ah, the poor *signora*!

What have you done?' She set the basin on a table and looked at accusingly at Rafaele and Nico. 'Go, I will attend to the *signora*, for she needs a dry gown. Doctor Tartelli will be here soon and after he sees the *signora* I will have him see you.'

Raf glanced at Nico. 'We both need to change and then we will talk.'

'Yes.' Nico's expression had hardened.

'Raf!' Cecily said desperately.

He moved to the side of the bed. 'What is it?'

'Promise me you will not fight him again.'

He observed her for a moment. 'I promise I will not.'

He bent and brushed a kiss across her forehead. When he straightened, she caught a glimpse of Nico's face. His bleak expression made her shiver. He met her eyes and looked away.

Doctor Tartelli came shortly after that. He cleaned and dressed her cut and said it was not very deep, but she must rest for a few days. He closed his bag and announced he would see to the *signori*. He promised Cecily he would examine the Englishman's arm. She could only hope Nico would allow that.

Signora Salvidori had just left the room when she remembered Raf did not know about Mariana and Simon. She sat up, dizziness overtaking her. She would probably faint if she attempted to get out of bed to look for him. She could only pray Raf would not find out until she had a chance to talk to him. For she dreaded to think of what Raf would do when he learned they had run off together.

* * *

Doctor Tartelli finished applying a plaster to the cut on Nico's forehead and straightened. 'There is one more thing. The *signora* asked me to look at a wound on your arm.'

Nico rose from the hard-backed chair. 'It is not necessary.'

'She was quite adamant, *signor*.'

'Then I suggest you allow him to do so,' Raf said. 'Unless you wish to distress Cecily further.'

The slight amusement in Raf's eyes hardly helped Nico's temper. 'There is no need for you to stay.'

'Except to ensure you comply.'

'I will, damn you. Go.'

Raf merely raised a brow. Nico slid his coat off one shoulder and then winced as it brushed against his injury. He nearly cursed when he glanced down and saw the small red stain on the sleeve of his linen shirt.

'We will need to remove your waistcoat and shirt, *signor*.'

The waistcoat came off easily enough, but raising his arm to allow the physician to help ease his shirt over his head made his arm hurt. He sat back down and then scowled when Raf crossed the room to his side and watched in silence while Dr Tartelli examined the wound.

'A stitch has come out, but I do not think it will be necessary to restitch it. The bleeding has stopped and there are no signs of infection. You would do well to restrain yourself from doing battle until the wound is properly healed.' He put his implements away, shut his bag and, after saying he would find someone to help Nico dress, left.

Nico saw Raf staring at his arm, his expression grim. 'When did that happen?'

'At the Villa Guiliani,' Nico said shortly. 'During the local fête. Cecily was with me. The attack occurred just outside the maze. She came very close to taking the knife instead of me.'

Raf's eyes hardened. 'What was she doing with you?'

'We were looking for my cousin and Signorina Renato. We thought they were in the maze together.'

'And were they?'

'Yes.'

'Do you have any idea where they are now?'

Nico eyed him, his eyes narrowing. 'No. Do you?'

'Yes. They are in Venice. At the Ca' Cappelletti.'

'Damn you,' he said shortly. He rose and reached for his shirt. 'Have they wed?'

'Not yet. They will as soon as you and Cecily reach Venice.'

Nico tugged the shirt over his head and winced. 'Contrary to your suspicions, I have not run off with Cecily for nefarious purposes. We hoped to stop them.'

'In Cecily's carriage? I am surprised you made it this far.'

'Her carriage has been the least of our problems.' He eyed Raf. 'What are you doing here?'

'I have just returned from Avezza, looking for you and for Cecily. No one seemed to know where either of you had gone. However, I did not expect to find you together.'

'I have not seduced her.'

'I apologise for that.' Raf hesitated. 'I must apologise to you for other words as well. The ones I spoke thirteen years ago. I know you had nothing to do with Angelina's death.'

Nico looked at the man who had once been his best friend. He had changed; his face was still handsome, despite the bruises, but more chiselled, and there was a hardness that had not been there before. At this moment, Nico had no idea whether he hated him or not.

'Perhaps you will tell me what has led you to this conclusion?' Nico could not keep the bitterness from his voice.

'You loved her.'

'So did you.'

'Yes. I loved her.'

'I did not realise that until after her death. I never intended to take her from you,' Nico said.

'But she was not mine. She loved you. Just as you loved her.' Raf glanced away for a moment. 'I understand if you do not wish to accept my apology. It seems very little in comparison to what we have lost.' He started towards the door, then paused. 'You are much in Cecily's debt. She would not threaten me if she did not believe in you. I promised her I would not hurt you. But if I find out that you have hurt her in any way, I will change my mind.'

'We are in agreement. For I would have no hesitation in calling out any man who even thinks of hurting her. Including you.'

'I believe you would.' Raf left the room, closing the door quietly behind him.

Chapter Ten

Cecily rose from the edge of the bed. She held on to the bedpost for a moment while the room spun and then righted itself. She released it and took a few steps, pleased to find she could walk without swaying.

Through the open shutters she could see the brilliant blue of the sky. Although Signora Salvidori had informed her that the *signori* wished her to remain in bed for the day, Cecily had insisted on dressing. She was not about to stay in bed while there was any possibility that Raf and Nico might kill each other. Particularly after Raf learned of Mariana and Simon.

She left her room and entered the passageway outside her room. The staircase was to her left. She descended it and halted in the hall below. If she recalled, the room where she and Nico had dined was to her right. She skirted around a mound of luggage and started down the short hall. She found the room easily enough and the door was slightly ajar. She peered in and saw

Raf and Nico standing together at the other end of the room. To her great relief, she saw no signs of impending violence.

Nico saw her first. A swift frown crossed his brow. He broke away from Raf and strode towards her. She saw he was wearing a clean shirt and breeches and a coat she did not recognise. He was shaved. 'What the devil are you doing out of bed?' he demanded as he reached her side.

'I needed to speak to Raf.' She looked up into his face, now so familiar that she thought she had memorised every feature. The bruise across his cheekbone was now a dark purple. She resisted the urge to touch his face. 'Are you all right?'

'Yes,' he said shortly.

'You should be in bed as well.'

'Cecily.' His voice held a warning.

'I know. You don't like me to fuss and I remind you of your old nanny.'

A reluctant grin tugged at his lips. 'I apologise for that. You are nothing like my old nanny.' The look in his eyes suddenly made her feel shy.

She looked quickly away, only to find Raf's interested gaze upon them. For some reason, she felt even more flustered. To cover it, she said quickly, 'Raf, I must talk to you. I do not know what Ni…Severin has told you but—'

'What he did not tell me I have guessed. Nico is right, however. You should not be up.'

'But I am, so it is no use telling me I should go back to bed.'

Raf glanced at Nico over her head. 'Then come and sit down. We have things to discuss.'

She took the sofa he indicated and looked up at him. His lip was still swollen and he wore a dressing over the cut across his brow. 'You look horrid,' she said. 'In fact, both of you do.'

His smile was lopsided. 'I hope you will remember that when you hear what we have to tell you.' He glanced at Nico, who now stood next to him.

'What is it?' A knot started to form in her stomach.

Nico spoke. 'Mariana and Simon are in Venice with my mother and sister.'

'Thank God!' Relief washed over her. 'Thank you. Oh, thank you.' Her daughter was safe. Then a thought struck her. She glanced from one to the other. 'Did you know that last night?'

'Yes.' Raf spoke this time. 'I told Nico after you were in your room. I was on my way back from Avezza and saw your carriage in the road, which is how I found you here.'

She stared at him. 'And you said nothing about it last night?'

He spread out his hands. 'I apologise. I fear that seeing you with Nico drove all other thoughts from my mind.'

'If you saw them, you must know that they ran away together! And that I would be frantic with worry! Instead you must fight after hurling the most stupid accusations at him! Could you not have guessed that we were travelling together because of them? I should strangle you! Both of you, actually!' she added when she saw the faint amusement in Nico's face. 'You knew last night as well!'

The amusement fled. 'By the time I knew, you were in bed.'

'You should have wakened me. But it does not matter now.' She took a deep breath, almost dreading the answer to her next question 'Did they…they marry?'

'They started out intending to do so, but changed their minds. By then it was too late to turn back to Avezza,' Raf said. 'They spent the night at an inn and the next day travelled to Venice. Lord Ballister brought her to the Ca' Cappelletti. The Duchess knew I was in Venice and sent for me. Lord Ballister assured us his behaviour towards Mariana was honourable. I have no reason to doubt his word.'

'Is it possible, then, that they may not need to marry?'

'No, it is not possible,' Raf said gently. 'They spent the night at an inn without a proper chaperon. We could not insist they marry until you and Severin gave your consent.'

She looked at Nico, her heart sinking. He met her gaze. 'I have given my consent. We only need yours.'

She stared down at her lap and felt as if her heart was breaking. The reality she had tried to push away broke over her. Mariana would be gone, starting a new life in a faraway place where Cecily would never be welcomed. Her daughter's lovely face swam before her eyes and she already felt the pangs of missing her.

'Cecily?' Raf asked.

She looked up. 'Of course you have my consent.' She rose, her head spinning from the sudden movement. She waited until the world righted itself. 'I must beg your pardon. I believe I will take a walk.' She brushed past them before they could see how devastated she felt.

'Cecily. Wait,' Nico said.

'No.'

'Cecily. At least return to your room.' Raf had followed her across the room.

She shook her head and left them both staring after her.

'Are you going to let her walk away like that?' Nico demanded. 'She's hardly well—she looked as if she was about to swoon a moment ago.'

'I have found that it is impossible to force Cecily to do anything she does not want to do. Or stop her from doing something she has set her mind to. You did not discover that in the time you spent with her?'

Nico scowled. 'I would expect you to exert more control over her. Particularly when it comes to her health.'

Raf's brow raised a fraction. 'What would you suggest? I carry her back to bed and lock her in her room?'

'If necessary, yes.' He wanted to wipe the crooked grin from Raf's face. 'What?'

The grin on Raf's swollen lips only widened. 'I suspect your journey together was most interesting.'

'Hardly,' Nico snapped. 'I was in bed a good part of the time with an infection and she was forced to nurse me.'

'Poor Cecily. I trust you were not too difficult.'

'I was damnably difficult. Are you going to find her or not?'

'I will leave it to you to do so,' Raf said blandly. 'I

do not relish the prospect of informing Cecily I plan to lock her in her room after I carry her into the house.'

'Damn you,' Nico said and stalked out of the room before he broke his promise to Cecily and strangled Raf.

He found her sitting on a bench in the small over-grown garden on one side of the inn. He stopped and watched her for a moment. She sat on a bench in the shade of a tree. In her cream-coloured gown, her head bare and her hands clasped lightly in her lap, she looked like some sort of lovely, vulnerable creature in need of protection. His protection.

She was no longer his concern. Not with Raf here. Only a fool would fail to notice the affection and ten-derness between them, the easy way they spoke to one another. He could imagine that once Mariana was gone, she would turn to Raf for comfort. Raf would—

He jerked his thoughts away, angry with himself for caring about her. Angry that once again he was in dan-ger of wanting a woman already claimed by Raf.

He entered the garden. 'Cecily.'

She looked up at him and sniffed. He wanted to gather her into his arms and kiss away her tears. He frowned at her in an attempt to hide his traitorous thoughts. 'You should not be out here. You are far from well.'

'I am fine.' The little tremble of her lip betrayed her true state. She looked away from him as if she wanted him to leave.

'You are not. You are clearly distressed. Why? Be-cause of Mariana and Simon?'

'I...I will be quite fine. As soon as I have composed

myself I will return to the inn. Please go.' Her face was still averted.

'I meant what I told you before. Mariana will be welcomed into our family. You do not need to worry that she will not be accepted.'

'I…I know.' She half-looked at him now, her lips slightly parted.

'Then what is it? Simon? He will be a good husband and he loves her.' He was finding her soft vulnerable mouth distracting. 'You will miss her,' he finally came up with.

'Y…yes.'

'They will return to Italy probably quite often since Napoleon is gone. You can always come to England. And stay as long as you want.' He would do his best to stay away from her.

He was shocked when her mouth suddenly trembled. 'No, I…I can never return to England.' She stood. 'I…I must go to the house.'

'No.' He stood as well and caught her shoulders. 'Why can you not return to England?'

She held his gaze. 'Because I…I left in disgrace. My grandmother will not speak to me…and….'

'And?'

'There…there was a scandal when I ran away with Marco. I…I cannot let that hurt Mariana or Simon.'

'I will see to it that it will not.'

'You are very kind, but—'

'I am not kind,' he said roughly. 'But I vow I won't let anything or anyone hurt you.'

'You are kind,' she whispered. Her eyes, wide and vulnerable, and her slightly parted lips threatened his control.

'Cecily,' he said hoarsely. He bent his head towards her, but before he could possess her mouth some instinct made him look up. It was as if a fist slammed into his stomach when he saw Raf standing there. He dropped his hands from her shoulders as if he'd been burned. 'I beg your pardon.'

'Why?' Nothing in Raf's demeanour indicated he found anything amiss.

'Because—' He stopped. Confessing he was about to kiss Cecily would only make matters worse. 'We were about to return to the inn.' He sounded like a nodcock.

'Is that it? I hardly think you need beg my pardon for that. Or was it Cecily's pardon you wished to beg?'

'I've no idea.' What the devil was wrong with Raf? He was an idiot if he hadn't noticed anything amiss and damnably casual about Cecily if he had. Last night he'd been ready to kill Nico over Cecily but today he acted as if nothing had happened. 'We need to talk,' he told Raf.

'First you should greet your mother?'

'My mother?'

'The Duchess. She has just now arrived.'

He nearly reeled. 'What is my mother doing here?'

'She was at the Villa Cappelletti. I sent for her.'

'You sent for her?'

'Yes. She is understandably anxious to see you and Cecily.'

'She knows that I am here?' Cecily looked stricken.

Raf's lip twitched. 'I could hardly keep your presence a secret.'

'No, of course you could not.' She managed a wobbly smile, which made Nico want to gather her into his arms and reassure her all would be well.

Raf, damn him, should be doing exactly that. Nico intended to make certain that Raf understand exactly what his responsibilities were regarding Cecily. And that if Raf did not fulfil them, he would answer to Nico.

Chapter Eleven

The petite, dark-haired woman who caught Nico's hands looked nothing like the formidable Duchess of Cecily's imagination. She looked up into her son's face, half-smiling, half-crying. 'I should scold you terribly, only I was so worried when you disappeared and no one knew anything! Then we discovered Signora Renato was also gone, so Rafaele brought me to the villa and I was to wait there until he returned from Avezza. You cannot know how I felt when I received his message telling me that both you and Signora Renato are safe. Except now I see that you and Rafaele have fought and I will scold both of you for that.'

Nico lifted her hand and brushed a kiss over the back. 'We have called a truce, so you do not need to worry. I must apologise as well for not sending a message to you, but I expected to reach Venice long before this.'

'Next time you will do so.' She stepped back and her gaze fell on Cecily, who stood a little behind Nico and next to Raf. 'You are Signora Renato? But no one told me that you are so very young!' She went to Cecily and took her hands. 'Before I say anything, I must reassure you that Mariana is quite well for I know you must be anxious about her.'

'Thank you.' For she had not expected the Duchess to greet her with such generous warmth. 'I do not know how to thank you for caring for her, particularly under the circumstances. You are more than kind.'

'You do not need to thank me. I am only grateful that Simon thought to bring her to Venice and to us.' Her large dark eyes searched Cecily's face. 'Are you well, my dear? Your face is quite pale.'

'I am fine, only a little tired.'

'She is hardly fine,' Nico said. 'She fell and hit her head last night.'

'Then why have you allowed her out of bed?' The Duchess shot a reproving look at her son. She took Cecily's hand. 'You must sit down and after that Domenico and Rafaele will explain to me why they permitted you to hurt yourself in such a way.' Her hand on Cecily's arm, she guided her to the sofa. After Cecily sat, she turned a cool eye on the two men.

Nico glanced at Raf before he spoke. 'Cecily threw the contents of a pitcher over us. She slipped in the puddle.'

The Duchess started. 'And why did you do that, my dear?' she asked Cecily.

'They were fighting and I wanted to stop them. I feared they would kill each other.'

'I have heard it is very effective in stopping a dog-fight. Did they come to their senses after that?'

'Only after Cecily threatened us with a pistol,' Raf interjected. 'She slipped when I attempted to take it from her because she thought I intended to shoot Nico. I consider myself responsible for her fall.'

The Duchess stared at them. 'I consider both of you at fault for behaving in such an ungentlemanly and unseemly manner.' She pressed Cecily's hand. 'I think, my dear, that you have had too many things to worry you in the past few days. For now you must go to your room and rest and after that I will take you back to Ca' Cappelletti so that I can properly look after you for a few days. We will leave for Venice after that. I am certain both Domenico and Rafaele will agree.'

'Of course,' Nico said politely. He did not quite look at her, nor was his manner any more warm when she left with the Duchess to go up to her room.

Cecily sat on the bed after the Duchess left her inn room, too restless to sleep. It was as if Nico had with-drawn from her ever since Raf had come upon them in the garden. For an instant she thought he intended to kiss her, but when Raf appeared he looked stricken as if he'd been caught committing a crime. Perhaps he thought Raf would call him out, but Raf had not seemed to no-tice anything amiss.

She sensed it was more than that—that it had some-thing to do with her. It was possible that he regretted his earlier words when he had said he would not let anything or anyone hurt her, that he really did not want anything to do with her. Which was for the best, for she feared that he might have the power to hurt her most of all.

They had arrived at the Villa Cappelletti in the late afternoon. The house, situated on the Brenta River, in the midst of a large park, was built in the classical style with wide shallow steps leading to the entrance with its row of columns. The Duchess had insisted that Cecily be shown straight to her room and that for tonight, she would have her dinner on a tray. Cecily had just sent the tray away when the Duchess entered her room. 'I came to see if you would object to a visitor.'

'No, of course not.' She looked up and then fought down a stab of disappointment when she saw Raf. The Duchess quietly left them as he came to her side. He pulled a chair to the bed and sat down. 'We have not had a chance to talk. How are you feeling?'

'Better. And you? Your face still looks horrible.'

He flashed her a crooked grin. 'Thank you.' He took her hand. 'But it is you that I worry about.'

'I am fine.' She hesitated. 'I am sorry about Mariana. I should have guessed that matters were more serious between them. I never thought that she…that they would run away together. I would hardly fault you if you were very angry with me.'

'I am not. Mariana and Lord Ballister both assured me that you did everything you could to stop them. In fact, Mariana seemed to worry I would hold you to blame. However, it is not Mariana's affairs I wish to discuss, but yours.'

'Mine? I have none worth discussing.'

'Not even Nico?'

'Nico? He is not one of my affairs!' She flushed. 'Not that I have any affairs…that is, not those sort of affairs.' Under Raf's interested gaze, her words seemed even more tangled.

'You mean affairs of the heart? But why not? You are still young. Now that Mariana is to be married it is time that you consider your own heart. Marco never intended that you spend the rest of your life alone and without love.'

'I am not without love,' she said, stung. 'I have Mariana and you, and Vittoria and Serefina are very fond of me. I will have Barbarina, so I will hardly be alone.'

'Barbarina is not quite what Marco intended. Or what I meant. I am speaking of a husband or perhaps a lover.'

She flushed. 'I do not want to remarry and I have always thought that a lover would be most inconvenient!'

'Even Nico?'

'Why would you say such a thing?'

'I have seen the way he looks at you,' he said gently. 'If I had not come upon you today, he would have kissed you. Nor would you have objected, I think.'

'We were together on the journey and I…I suppose it was not unnatural for some sort of bond to develop. There is nothing more.'

'Are you certain?'

'Yes, of course.' Even as she spoke, the day at the inn flashed through her mind when Nico had told her he wanted her. Heat flooded her cheeks. 'Please, Raf, I pray you will say no more about this.'

'As you wish.'

'I do wish! Can we not speak of something else?'

'Then we will. I do not wish to distress you, but there is one more thing I must ask. Nico told me you were with him the night he was stabbed. He said the man wore a cloak and mask. Can you tell me anything more?'

'Only that I felt someone was watching us when we were in the maze.'

'But you saw no one?'

'No, no one. I thought perhaps I heard something in the bushes, but I was not certain. It was so dark and quiet.' She hesitated and decided she must tell Raf the whole of it. 'Barbarina had been saying such odd things that I wondered if I was being fanciful.'

'What sort of odd things?'

'Earlier that night, when we were in the supper booth, she told Ni…the Duke that he must stay away from me because I would not be safe with him. But he was the one who was hurt.' The sudden change in his expression alarmed her. 'Raf? What is it? Do you know why she would say such peculiar things?'

The dark look disappeared. 'No, I can think of no reason. I can only think she is becoming increasingly eccentric. I am only sorry she has frightened you.'

'You think, then, that Nico's attack had nothing to do with…with Barbarina?'

He took her hand. 'What I think is that you must not worry.' He released her and stood. 'I will leave you for now. I wish to tell you, however, that I am leaving to-morrow for Vicenza. I will return to Venice in time for Mariana's wedding.'

'Must you go?'

'Yes. It is possible I will have another commission. Do not look so worried. Everything will turn out as it should.' He bent and kissed her cheek. 'Be kind to Nico.' He left.

Be kind to Nico. The words echoed in her head. How could Raf suggest that she consider Nico for a lover? But then, two days ago she had been tempted to tell Nico that was exactly what she wanted.

This was madness. She meant to keep a safe distance between herself and Nico. She could not allow herself to think of him as anything other than Simon's guardian. In time, they would undoubtedly come to regard each other in the polite manner of those distantly related by marriage. Their journey together would fade away like a half-remembered dream.

Nico glanced at the clock. What the devil was Raf doing with Cecily? He'd gone into her bedchamber over a half an hour ago. Visions of Raf leaning forward to kiss her soft, desirable mouth, her sweet shy response, assailed him. Would she be surprised? Did she suspect Raf cared about her?

Did Raf suspect how much he desired her?

'Nico.'

He whirled around. Raf stood behind him. 'How is Cecily?' he asked.

'Better. It is good she will be under your care here.'

'She is under my mother's care.'

'But of course,' Raf said in the bland way that filled Nico with the all-too-familiar desire to mow him down. He did not seem to notice, however. 'I need to talk to you.' All traces of amusement left his face.

'What about?' Nico tensed, half-expecting Raf to tell him that he and Cecily were now betrothed.

'You did not tell me that before you were attacked that night, Barbarina told you that Cecily would not be safe with you.'

'I beg your pardon?'

'Shortly before you were attacked, Cecily said that Barbarina told you Cecily would not be safe with you.'

'She did. As it turned out, she was right.'

'Barbarina said much the same thing to me before Angelina died.'

Nico stared at him, a chill creeping up his spine. 'What exactly did she say?'

'She said that because of you Angelina was in danger.'

'When did she say that?'

'Perhaps a week before Angelina died.'

'Why did you not tell me?'

'Barbarina had always assumed that I would wed Angelina, which was one reason she did not approve of you. I thought she hoped that, if she could convince me that you were a danger to Angelina, I would stop the marriage. Afterwards, I thought that…'

'That perhaps you had been right,' Nico said grimly.

'Yes. But I was wrong.'

'You were wrong about me, but Angelina is still dead. It is possible Cecily was the intended victim, not me. If so, then it seems too much of a coincidence.'

'You are suggesting that Barbarina is responsible?'

'I did not think so at first, but now…' Nico looked away for a moment, and then back at Raf. 'Yes, I am beginning to think it is possible. But why?'

'She has always been rather mad,' Raf said slowly. 'But I have never thought her capable of violence. Until we know, we must consider the possibility that Cecily is in danger. I told Cecily that I am leaving tomorrow for Vicenza. I wished to ask you to watch over Cecily while I am away.'

'I would hope that under the circumstances you would remain here.'

'What circumstances?'

'Cecily is here. She has been injured; she is worried about Mariana, and now this. After yesterday, I would think you would realise that I am the last person you should ask to watch over Cecily.'

'After yesterday, I am convinced you are exactly the right person to keep her safe.'

'Perhaps you failed to notice that I nearly kissed her.'

'It was quite obvious.'

'I came damnably close to seducing her when we were together.'

'I suspected that as well.'

'I would expect that, instead of standing there with that devilish calm expression, you would be threatening to put a bullet through me.'

'And risk Cecily's wrath for the rest of my life? I think not.'

Nico resisted the urge to throttle him. 'Are you or are you not in love with Cecily?' he demanded. 'Because if you are, I've half a mind to put a bullet through you for allowing another man to touch her.'

Raf blinked. 'In love with Cecily?' He looked truly astounded. 'Where did you get that idea?'

'From Thais Margate.'

'Thais Margate? I had heard she was in Venice, but I did not know she had met Cecily.'

'She leased a house in Avezza.'

'Has she? Then perhaps she still hopes to become a duchess, so she would naturally try to dissuade you away from Cecily. She did the same with Angelina, did she not?'

'Last time she was right. Do you love Cecily?'

'I love Cecily, but I regard her as my sister just as she regards me as her brother. So you thought I was in love with her. That explains much.'

Nico's relief only made him surlier. 'Then as her brother I would hope you would tell me to stay away from her. If you recall, I just told you I wanted to seduce her.'

'But you did not.' He regarded Nico thoughtfully. 'I think it is perhaps best that Cecily visits England until we are assured she is safe. You will watch out for her in my place. Although she is at an age where she can decide whether she wishes to remarry or take a lover, I would be most grateful if you would see to it that any man who interests her is acceptable.'

The nonchalant tone of this pronouncement made Nico curl his fists. 'I suppose you will next ask me to interview suitable candidates,' he said through gritted teeth.

Raf's expression was bland. 'If you wish.'

'You know damn well I don't wish,' Nico snapped. 'If you continue on in this vein, I might decide to call you out after all.'

Raf eyed Nico's face, a smile tugging at his lips. 'Precisely why I know Cecily will be quite safe with you. I will retire now, for I wish to leave early tomorrow. I will see you in Venice in a week at Mariana and Simon's wedding. I have no objections if you are tempted to kiss Cecily again.' He was gone before Nico could gather his wits together to form a reply.

Why the devil had he worried about coming between Raf and Cecily when it turned out Raf had done everything but thrust Cecily into his arms?

He would laugh at the irony, only the matter was too serious. Now he no longer had Raf to use as an excuse to prevent him from giving in to his desire for Cecily. To make matters worse, he knew she was not indifferent to him. He could not ask her to become his mistress—she would be too complicated and not only because of Simon and Mariana.

Hell. He was known for his cool control. There was no reason he could not keep his head around Cecily. None at all.

Chapter Twelve

The following evening Cecily stood in front of the looking glass and smoothed down the skirt of her peach gown with nervous fingers. The Duchess had invited a cousin and her family to dinner and in a few minutes Cecily would go downstairs to join them. She had been to many a dinner party so she had no reason to feel so apprehensive. Perhaps it was that ever since she had left her house that fateful morning she'd had the sense of living in a different existence. A dinner party seemed so normal that she feared she would hardly know how to go on. Which was ridiculous, of course, she still remembered the conventions of polite society.

The knock at her door startled her. She opened it. Nico stood on the other side. Her pulse quickened at his appearance. Dressed in a bottle-green coat, and snowy starched cravat, his dark hair trimmed and fashionably arranged, he looked every bit the cool, arrogant English peer. The sort of man she would never dare approach in a London drawing room.

Her cheeks coloured when she saw he was staring at her with similar appraisal. 'I am to escort you to the salon,' he finally said. 'If you are ready.'

'Yes. Yes, I am.' She started to step from the room when she realised she had forgotten her fan. 'I must get my fan first.'

She turned and went to her dressing table and found her fan. She took a deep breath. He was still the polite distant host. Raf had been quite mistaken—it was apparent Nico wanted to keep their relationship on a strictly impersonal basis. She would do the same.

He said nothing as they walked down the stairs to the next floor, the *piano nobile*, and entered the salon. The other guests were already there, a pretty, plump woman in a purple gown, a man with greying hair and a young man and woman.

The Duchess spotted them and broke away from the others. She took Cecily's hand. 'How charming you look! Do you not think, Domenico?'

'Signora Renato always looks charming,' he said.

The Duchess's eyes twinkled. 'But of course.' She took Cecily's arm. 'Come and meet Signor and Signora Parvatti and their younger daughter. Domenico once attempted to frighten Octavia away with a large toad, for she used to follow him and Rafaele about like a small puppy.'

'How gentlemanly,' was all Cecily could come up with. She glanced at Nico.

His mouth twitched. 'I was eleven and thought most females excessively annoying.'

She smiled at him and for a moment they were in perfect accord. The accord vanished as soon as she met Signor and Signora Parvatti and their daughter. Octavia was no longer an annoying young girl but an alluring young woman with great dark eyes and a curvaceous figure and, from the way Nico returned her smile, Cecily suspected he would no longer mind so much if she trailed him around.

Their son, Bernardo, was a handsome young man who proclaimed himself most delighted to make her acquaintance. He then attached himself to her until dinner was announced.

Cecily, seated between Signor Parvatti and Bernardo, was determined she would not glance in Nico's direction. Signor Parvatti was a quiet, polite man whom Cecily liked very much. Bernardo, who must be at least five years her junior, persisted in flirting with her. Despite those distractions, she could not completely ignore that Octavia was flirting with Nico almost as persistently as Bernardo was with her. A few covert glances in his direction revealed he did not seem to object at all.

Well, that should not matter to her. She turned to Bernardo and smiled at his latest ridiculous compliment.

She was glad, however, that the guests did not linger too long into the evening. Her head had begun to hurt and she felt fatigued from the effort to make conversation. As soon as the Parvattis departed, she rose. 'If you do not mind, I should like to retire.'

'But of course. I can see that the evening has tired you.' The Duchess smiled kindly at her. 'We will see you in the morning.'

Cecily turned to Nico, who had stood as well. She forced a smile to her lips. 'Goodnight, your Grace.'

'Goodnight, Signora Renato,' he said coolly.

She looked away before he saw the stab of hurt that shot through her. She walked from the room. Even with the door closed safely behind her, she refused to allow more than a tear or two to fall.

Nico unwound his cravat and tossed it on a chair in his dressing room. Instead of summoning Hobbes, he threw himself down in a chair and stretched his legs out before him. He needed to think.

He had scarcely seen Cecily at all today. He had been busy, that was true, but he had been careful to avoid being alone with her. At dinner he attempted to treat her with the polite civility he would show any guest of his mother's.

Not that she showed any particular inclination to seek his company. In fact, he suspected she wished to avoid him as well. He had told himself a cool relationship with her was for the best. Until tonight, when pure hot jealousy seared him as he watched her respond to Bernardo's blatant flirtation. Not even Octavia's smouldering glances and *double entendres* distracted him.

He realised, as he watched Cecily smile at something Bernardo said, that he did not want to let her go. He did not want Bernardo or any other man flirting with her, much less touching her. In the short time he'd spent with her, he had come to think of her as his.

He could marry her.

He needed a wife. He'd made up his mind that he would choose a wife once he returned to England. None of the possible candidates held any strong appeal. He had not expected love; merely a mutual understanding of the duties of marriage and some measure of affection.

With Cecily he would have much more.

He did not know if he loved her. He had loved Angelina with all of his being and he doubted he would ever care for a woman in that way again. But until Cecily, he had not expected to find a woman he would consider marriage to more than a mere duty.

His attraction to her was far more complex than mere lust, although her very presence made him think of nothing but taking her to his bed. He liked her, even the little things such as the way she walked, the way she tilted her head a little when she was listening, the quick flush that sprang to her cheeks when she was flustered. He needed her in some way he could not quite define.

She was not indifferent to him. He did not know if she was in love with him, but he thought she might be.

He would not allow her to refuse him.

The Duchess added more sugar to her coffee before looking across the table at Cecily. They were at breakfast the following day.

'I am glad we have had this time together before we leave for Venice, for I feel I would not have had a chance to know you so well if we had first met there. I hope that after the wedding you will consider staying with us. I know you and Eleanora will have much in common.'

'I look forward to meeting Lady Eleanora.' She was not quite so certain about staying with them, especially if it meant she would see Nico very often.

'I would also like you to consider returning to England with us. You have not been back for a number of years, I think.'

Cecily nearly dropped the cup of coffee she held. She set it down, spilling a few drops on the white table linen. 'I cannot return to England.'

'Of course you can. You need not worry about how Lady Telford will receive you, for I believe she very much wishes to see you again.'

'You know my grandmother?'

'A little. She and my husband's mother went to school together, so she knows of our connection to Avezza. When she learned we were to travel to Venice, she asked me to inquire after you. She is worried about you and I can see the breach between you distresses her.'

'I refused her invitation last year. I told her I would never return to England. It was not a very kind letter. She never accepted my marriage to Marco, nor Mariana as my stepdaughter, and although she invited me to come to England and to bring Mariana, I was still angry.' She felt ashamed thinking about it. 'I was sorry almost as soon as I sent it off.'

'Perhaps it is time for you to forgive your grandmother,' the Duchess said gently. 'Although she does not suffer from any serious malady, her health is not quite what it should be. One does not want to wait too long to forgive.' Sadness crossed her face. 'I did and it is one of the sorrows I still carry.' She glanced away and then looked back at Cecily. 'So you must promise you will consider returning with us, not only for Mariana, but for yourself and your grandmother.'

Cecily stared down at her coffee cup. She had been away so long, England had taken on an almost dream-like quality. 'I will consider it,' she finally said, looking up at the Duchess.

'I am glad.' The Duchess smiled and then her expression sobered. 'There is one more thing I wish to speak of now. I have not yet thanked you for taking such good care of my son. I have no doubt he would be much more seriously ill if you had not looked after him so well. Not only that, you saved him and Rafaele from much foolishness. He told me that it was because of you that he and Rafaele finally reached a truce.'

The sincere gratitude in her eyes made Cecily uncomfortable. 'I did nothing more than anyone else would do.'

'But there is a difference—I think you care for my son, do you not?'

Cecily's startled gaze met that of the Duchess. Hot colour rose to her cheeks. 'I...I cannot imagine why anyone...any woman would not.'

'Not all women see past his title and his appearance. Or into his soul.'

Cecily felt as if her own soul had been stripped

naked. She could only stare at the Duchess, who regarded her with kindly understanding. 'I do not wish to distress you, but I felt I must speak of this. For the first time since Angelina's death, he has lost a little of the hardness. He has a tenderness and a protectiveness towards you that I have not seen for a very long time.' She smiled a little. 'I can see he has tried to hide it, particularly in the past few days, for he has been too polite with you, which has made me wish to scold him. He is always like this, even as a young boy, when he does not wish to reveal his feelings. I hope you will not allow that to send you away from him.'

'I…I fear you are mistaken. We are friends, but there is nothing else between us. We have never…I do not want…' She stopped, stricken.

The Duchess reached across the table and took Cecily's hand. 'He needs you. As I suspect you need him. I only ask that you do not run away from him too quickly.'

'No.' Cecily rose. 'I…I should see to my packing. You are much too kind.' She fled the room, cheeks burning. She went to her bedchamber, where the maid had already started folding her clothes in neat piles. The walls seemed to close in on her and she knew she needed to move, walk, do anything to calm her churning emotions. She grabbed a bonnet from the bed and left the room.

Cecily tugged another weed from the stubborn ground. She had walked down a wooded path before coming upon a small building in the shape of a small temple hidden in the trees. Behind it she could see the roses and lavender and rosemary and her hands had almost itched with the need to clear the weeds around them, freeing them from the vines that entwined them like a sorcerer's spell.

First Raf, and now the Duchess. Why did they both think that she and Nico had some sort of special regard for each other? More puzzling, why were they both encouraging it? They seemed to think that Nico actually needed her, which was ridiculous. If ever a man did not need another person, it was the stubborn, self-sufficient, Duke of Severin. He certainly did not need her if his behaviour for the past two days was any indication. He had confessed to wanting her, but she could only think that had been because of the odd circumstances that had forced them together. In the ordinary world, he never would have noticed her. She would have found him impossibly arrogant.

Cecily pulled out another weed.

'We do have a gardener.'

She gasped and looked up. Nico stood on the path behind her, his expression quizzical.

'Good day, your Grace.' She rose.

'Your Grace? I thought we agreed that you would call me by my given name.'

'Under the circumstances, I do not think that would be wise.'

'What circumstances are those?'

'We are now in society, so it would be most improper for us to address each other with such familiarity. It is best if we keep a certain distance between us.'

He took a step towards her. 'I do not agree. I would prefer that there is no distance between us at all.'

The arrogant Duke had fallen away, but the intense expression in his eyes made her feel vulnerable. 'I had best return to the house. My gloves are quite dirty and I must see to my packing since we are leaving tomorrow.'

He took another step towards her. 'Don't run away.'

His mother had said almost the same thing. She looked up at him and the uncertainty in his face made her pause. 'Why shouldn't I?'

'Because I want you. Need you.'

'Nico?'

He caught her to him. His dark face hovered over hers for an instant before he lowered his head and possessed her mouth in a fierce, seeking kiss. Her knees trembled and she clung to him, returning his kisses, meeting his growing need with her own need.

But when his lips left her mouth and trailed down her neck to the top of her breast, her desire to give dissolved into an even greater need for completion. She arched into him, feeling his hardness through her skirts. She hardly noticed when they sank down on the ground and he was above her, his weight pressing her into the grass and herbs. He lifted his head, his eyes glazed with passion. 'Cecily, *cara…*'

'Don't talk. Please not now.' She threw her arms around his neck, pulling his head towards her. With a groan, his mouth sought hers in brief possession before moving down her neck in a series of fiery, mind-numbing kisses. With one hand he pushed down her bodice and shift and she felt his fingers fumble with the draw-string of her stays. He shoved the confining garment away and briefly caressed her breast before he took the erect nipple into his mouth, licking and teasing the swollen bud. Liquid heat spilled through her and when his hand stroked the silky soft flesh of her thighs, her legs parted of their own accord.

When he finally touched her intimately, she bit her lip to keep from whimpering with need. She pressed down on his hand as he stroked and caressed and when he suddenly withdrew, a little moan of protest escaped her.

'In a moment, *cara*.' He dropped a hard kiss on her lips and rose to his knees, his legs braced on either side of her. She waited, eyes closed, afraid that if she moved the spell would break. The scent of lavender and rose-mary enveloped her while she waited. She finally felt his welcome weight on her and then he cupped either side of her face. 'Look at me,' he commanded.

She opened her eyes and found his face hovered over hers. The hint of gentleness mixed in with passion amazed her. 'Do you want this?' he asked roughly. 'Because if you do not…'

'I want this. I want you.' She touched his cheek.

He stiffened and then his eyes darkened. He pushed her skirts up around her knees, his gaze never leaving her face and then his weight pressed into her. He parted her thighs and lowered himself between her legs. Her body arched in response but he paused, his gaze holding hers. Then he kissed her, a kiss that was surprisingly gentle. She moaned, her body aching and swollen with desire, and when she thought she could bear no more, he entered her.

She closed her eyes and clung to him, biting her lip at the slight discomfort and then he was moving inside her and her own body was finding a rhythm to match, her need for release relentlessly growing with every stroke. When it came, she cried out as wave after wave of throbbing pleasure washed over her and an instant later Nico spilled his seed into her, and then collapsed on top of her.

They lay in silence, his heartbeat melding with hers. After a little while, he brushed the hair from her face. '*Cara*, sweetheart,' he murmured.

She opened her eyes. His face hovered over hers, his eyes still heavy with passion, but with something else as well. 'Marry me,' he said.

Her heart nearly stopped. 'Please, please do not say anything more. It is not necessary to offer me marriage because of this. I am not a young girl but a…a widow and I am—'

'I am not giving you a choice. You will marry me.'

'I will not. I…I cannot.'

He rolled off her and sat. 'I suggest we both make ourselves presentable and then we will talk.' He reached over and gently pulled down her tangled skirts. She sat up and averted her eyes as he pulled up his breeches and then fastened them.

'There is a bench we can sit on.'

He now stood and held out his hand to help her up. He led her to a stone bench near the wall. 'Sit,' he said.

'Only if you will.' She did not intend to have him hover over her while he demanded that she marry him.

He complied and pulled her down next to him. 'Why can't you marry me?' His eyes narrowed. 'Is there someone else?'

'That is ridiculous! Of course there is not!'

'Then why? From your response just now, I hardly think you are indifferent to me. Unless I forced you.'

'No! No, you did not force me. I...I am not indifferent to you but I...I do not wish to be married.' She knotted her hands together to keep them from trembling. 'I would not make you a suitable wife.'

'Why not?'

'I would make a deplorable duchess. I am not very organised and have been away from English society for so long that I would have no idea how to go on.'

'You will have my mother to guide you.' His gaze raked her face. 'I am not asking you only because of what happened today. I need a wife. I want to marry you. I made up my mind last night to ask you.'

'But why me?' she blurted out. 'You must have dozens of women falling over themselves to marry you.'

He almost smiled. 'Not quite. However, I am flattered by your perception.' He held her gaze. 'After this, you can have no doubt that I find you desirable—very desirable. But over the time we have spent together, I have come to hold you in higher esteem than any of the dozens of women you seemed to think wish to marry me. Not since Angelina have I been able to envision another woman as my wife. I can envision you.'

'I see.' Coldness crept over her—Marco had said much the same thing. *Since the death of my beloved Caterina, I had not thought I would marry again until I met you.* She forced herself to look at him. 'I am sorry, but I cannot accept your offer.'

'So, despite your passionate acceptance of my love-making, you cannot bring yourself to marry me. Precisely why did you give yourself to me? Out of pity? Another one of the many services you have performed for me?'

The slight sneer in his voice filled her with cold fury and propelled her to her feet. 'You do not need to insult me. Or yourself. If you think that, then you are beyond despicable. I would never lie with a man I did not care about!'

'You are saying you care about me?' He sounded almost stunned.

'Yes, if you must know!'

'Despite that, you do not want to marry me,' he said flatly.

'No, I…I cannot. I do not want to marry again.' She made an awkward gesture. 'I am sorry,' she repeated when he said nothing.

She was taken aback by the fleeting bleakness in his face. 'There is no need to be. You have made it clear enough that you find the thought of marriage to me repugnant.'

'Not repugnant. I…I do not wish to be married. To anyone.'

'I see. However, there is one thing I wish to make

clear. If you find yourself with child because of today, you will marry me. If necessary, I will force you to the altar. Do you understand?'

'A child is most unlikely. I was married to Marco for two years and there…there was no child.'

'You told me he became ill shortly after you married. How often did you lie together as husband and wife after that?'

'That is none of your concern!'

'Just because you did not conceive with Marco does not mean you are immune from such a possibility now.'

She looked away so he would not see he had guessed the truth. After the first few months of marriage, Marco had rarely come to her bed and eventually he did not come at all.

'If you are with child, you will tell me. Do you understand?'

'Quite.' She forced herself to meet his eyes.

'We should return to the house.' He retrieved her straw bonnet and held it out to her.

She took the bonnet and set it on her head, her hands trembling as she tied the ribbons. When she finished and looked up again, he had his coat draped over his arm. 'Ready?' he asked.

'Yes.'

She hardly remembered the walk back to the villa. They walked without touching, neither of them speaking, until they reached the edge of the garden and Nico halted. He looked down at her. 'I am taking you through the side entrance. There is a small staircase you can use to reach your bedchamber without detection.'

'Thank you.' She could imagine nothing more mortifying than to meet the Duchess in her current state.

He led her through the side garden and to a side door. He halted. 'The staircase is just inside,' he said.

'Yes.' She made herself look at him. His face was cool and set. Any words she might say died on her lips. She brushed past him into the hall.

She reached her bedchamber unseen, slipped inside and closed the door. She pulled off her bonnet and sank down in one of the chairs near the window. What had she done? No, she knew exactly what she had done. She had given herself to the Duke of Severin because he said he'd wanted her, needed her and, if she was honest with herself, she had wanted and needed him just as much.

But not so much she would marry him. How could she explain to him that she could not bear another marriage where the ghost of another love hovered between them? Nico might want her, even need her, but he still loved Angelina, just as Marco had loved Caterina. Why, why was it that she was the sort of woman men wished to marry, but did not love? Charles, Marco and now Nico. She feared that Nico, even more than the others, would tear her heart open. She could not, would not, risk that hurt again.

Chapter Thirteen

'**S**omething is troubling you, I think.'

His mother's voice broke into Nico's thoughts. Dinner was over and they were in the salon. Minutes earlier, Cecily had gone up to bed. It had taken all his willpower to keep from running after Cecily and pulling her into his arms, demanding to know why she would not marry him, especially after their love-making. But her cool, strained manner at dinner had made it clear she would not welcome anything he had to say. He'd be damned before he forced his presence upon her again. Once they were in Venice, he would stay as far away from her as possible.

Exhaustion washed over him, a physical and mental tiredness he could not recall experiencing in an age. 'I must beg your pardon as well,' he said to his mother.

She regarded him with her clear intelligent gaze. 'But first, I must talk to you. Please, come and sit with me.' She indicated the place on the sofa that Cecily had vacated.

'If you would not object, I would rather any conversation between us take place tomorrow.' He doubted he could think clearly enough to hold a rational discussion.

'I do not wish to wait until tomorrow, for there will not be enough time before we depart for Venice.'

'Which is something I did wish to tell you before you retire for the night. I have decided to wait a few more days before travelling to Venice.'

'Because of Signora Renato?' Her worried gaze searched his face.

He hesitated, not knowing how to answer her. She placed her hand on his and continued to speak. 'I had hoped that perhaps there was an affection between you, that you would find the happiness with her that I have wished for you for so long. But I can see something is not right between you. Did you say something to distress her?'

He pulled her hand away from hers and rose. 'Apparently. I asked her to marry me. She refused.'

The shocked dismay that crossed her face made him wince. 'Why did she refuse?'

He shrugged. 'She does not wish to remarry.'

'But I am certain she cares about you. And you care about her, do you not? I have seen it in your face when you look at her. Did you tell her that?'

He could not remember for a moment, then recalled that he had told her that he held her in higher esteem than any woman he knew. And that he wanted her. 'She knows.'

Her eyes were still on him. 'Do you love her?'

'I...' He stopped. 'I have no idea. I like her more than any woman of my acquaintance. I admire and respect her. I wish to take care of her, protect her. I find her lovely. But I cannot say that I love her. Whatever that might mean.'

'I see.' She was silent for a moment. 'Perhaps it is for the best that she did not agree to marry you after all.'

He held out his hands, frustrated. 'Why? Why does it matter if I say that I love her? I have not found any other woman since Angelina that I've the least interest in marrying. I have offered to her everything that I have.'

'Not everything.' She rose. 'Angelina still holds your heart. You do not have that to give. Because of that, you have the power to greatly hurt any woman who might care for you. Including Cecily.'

When he said nothing, she pressed a kiss to his hand. 'Goodnight, my love. Think a little about what I have said.'

'Yes,' he said and watched her go.

Cecily tried to tell herself she was relieved that Nico had decided to delay his journey to Venice and, although he said something about estate business, she had no doubt it was because of her. The Duchess said nothing, however, on their carriage journey to Mestre.

Once in Mestre they left the carriage and stepped into the covered gondola, which would take them across the lagoon to Venice. Although the city was but two days' journey from Avezza, Cecily had never visited Venice. She would never forget her first glimpse of the city, with its turrets and domes shining in the sun that appeared to float on the water as if enchanted.

Her awe did not dissipate as they reached the city and entered the Grand Canal. She had seen paintings depicting various scenes, but none of them prepared her for the sheer wonder of gliding through the water past palazzo after palazzo with their exotic arches, graceful columns and elaborate balconies. Or the domed churches whose steps seem to rise up from the water.

The Duchess touched her arm. 'See, there is the Palazzo Cappelletti although we say Ca' Cappelletti for we consider the Doges Palace the only true palace in Venice.' The Duchess had explained as well that both her family's villa as well as their Venetian palazzo bore the family name of Cappelletti.

Cecily did not realise how nervous she was about meeting Mariana and Simon until she saw the façade of the Ca' Cappelletti. Three floors high, it was an imposing building with its row of arched windows separated by columns of white stone. Balconies of the same stone ran the length of the first and second floors above the canal level.

A servant appeared as soon as the gondola reached the stone steps in front of the water gate. He helped the Duchess and then Cecily from the craft. Cecily followed the footman and the Duchess across the patterned stone floor of the long *androne* to a staircase leading to the *piano nobile*. At the end of the *androne*, just before they started up the steps, Cecily caught a glimpse of an open courtyard.

They were shown to a spacious salon, which Cecily barely had time to notice before Mariana flew up from a sofa at one end of the room.

'Mama!' Mariana flung her arms around Cecily's neck. Cecily pulled her close, revelling in the feel of her slender, warm body.

Mariana finally pulled away. 'Oh! You do not know how worried I was about you! When no one knew where you were, only that you had left very suddenly and you were not to be found, I was so terribly frightened!'

'Just as I was frightened when you went away.' She touched Mariana's cheek, wanting to take the sting from her words.

'I am so very sorry. I did not think,' Mariana whispered.

Cecily glanced up and saw Simon had come to stand behind them. His expression was wary as he moved protectively towards Mariana. Cecily drew away from Mariana and held out her hand. They would marry and no purpose would be served by scolding him. She would not forget how her grandmother had looked at Marco with such cold disdain before informing them that they were never to see her again. She would not do the same thing to Mariana. 'Thank you for keeping Mariana safe.'

He took her hand after a moment. 'I would do anything for her,' he said quietly. 'I am only sorry that…'

She met his gaze. 'You do not need to say more. I will welcome you as my son-in-law.'

His eyes met hers. 'Thank you.'

He dropped her hand just as a young woman entered the room. 'Mama? You are here at last?' She was dark and pretty and Cecily had no doubt she was Nico's sister. She eyed Cecily with an almost haughty gaze that quickly turned to astonishment. 'You are Mariana's mama? Why, you cannot be much older than me! I quite expected you to be—' She stopped. 'I beg your pardon. You must think I am insufferably rude.'

'Eleanora!' the Duchess said with a reproving glance at her daughter.

'I do apologise. It was only that I expected you to be quite different.' Her appraising gaze travelled over Cecily and then she smiled and held out her hand. 'Welcome to Venice.'

'Thank you.' Cecily returned her smile. 'And thank you as well for looking after Mariana.'

'We are already quite fond of her.' She released Cecily's hand. 'But where is Nico? Was he not to travel with you?' she asked the Duchess.

'He has decided to stay at the villa for another day or two.' Nothing in the Duchess's voice indicated she found that odd. 'I have no doubt Signora Renato is quite fatigued. She must go to her room and rest.'

'I have given her the room next to Mariana's.' Eleanora smiled quickly at Cecily. 'I thought you would wish to be next to her.'

'Yes, thank you.' Cecily was touched by Eleanora's thoughtfulness.

Eleanora said she would show Cecily to her room and Mariana insisted on accompanying them. The bedchamber was located on the floor above the *piano nobile* and, like the floor below, consisted of a large main saloon flanked by a series of smaller rooms on either side. Cecily was shown to one of these, a pleasant room with an old-fashioned bed in a small alcove. 'I will send my maid in to help you unpack and change,' Eleanora said. 'I will allow you to be private with Mariana. I am certain you have much to discuss.' She left the room.

Cecily found Mariana watching her, her dark eyes filled with concern. 'Is something wrong, Mama?'

'No, nothing is wrong.' She squeezed Mariana's hand. 'How can it be, now that I can see for myself that you are safe?'

'But you looked so sad.'

'It is only that I am rather tired.' She smiled at her daughter. 'I did not sleep well last night. I never do the night before I am to leave on a journey.' She sat down on the bed and patted the spot next to her. 'Come and sit. You must tell me what you have done this week while you have been in Venice.'

Mariana obligingly sat down and after a question or two, chatted quite eagerly about the many interesting things she had seen. As Cecily listened to her, she vowed to put Nico from her mind. Now that she was in Venice and reunited with Mariana she must keep her thoughts on the upcoming wedding. She could not allow her own affairs to interfere with Mariana's happiness.

Two nights later, Mariana entered Cecily's bedchamber and then stopped, her eyes widening when she saw Cecily. 'Mama! I have never seen you in such a gown before! I did not know you could look so…so beautiful!'

Cecily smiled, flushing a little at her daughter's mixed compliment. 'I have not worn such a gown before. And you!' Her heart caught a little at her daughter's appearance. 'Oh, Mariana, you look so pretty. And so grownup.' For, in her blue silk shot with gold, she no longer looked like a child at all but a young lady.

'It is a wonderful gown, is it not?' Mariana twirled in front of the looking glass. 'I am so glad you permitted me to wear a real colour. I do not think I will ever want to wear pale blue or that horrid shade of pink again!'

Cecily could not disagree, for the pastels deemed appropriate for young English ladies, which so well complimented many of their soft delicate complexions, only dulled Mariana's lovely olive skin.

'What necklace will you wear?' Mariana peered into Cecily's jewellery box. 'This one, I think.' She held up a garnet. 'The colours will looked splendid with the colour of your gown.'

She was right, of course. Mariana's instinct for such things was flawless. She helped Cecily fasten the necklace and then led her to the looking glass. 'See how perfect it is! And how beautiful you are!'

Cecily peered at herself. The gown and the necklace might have been made for each other. But as for the other, she hardly recognised herself. Eleanora had insisted on loaning her a gown for tonight—they had been invited to a *conversazione*. It was to be Mariana and Simon's first formal appearance as a betrothed couple. The gown was indeed lovely and certainly cast even her best gown in the shade.

Now that she was about to appear in company, she was beginning to wish she had insisted on wearing one of her own gowns after all. The bodice seemed to reveal too much of her arms and back and far too much soft rounded breast. Her hair was braided in a circle behind her head, a style Eleanora assured her was all the thing. She had no idea if she was as beautiful as Mariana said, for she looked so unlike herself she could not make a judgement at all.

She turned away. 'I certainly look different,' she said doubtfully.

'Beautiful,' Mariana corrected. 'If the Duke was to see you I am certain he would say the same thing,' she added with a teasing smile.

Cecily nearly dropped her fan. 'The Duke? Why would you speak of him?'

'I rather thought he liked you. Even Simon said so.'

'Indeed.' She prayed Mariana would not notice her suddenly flushed cheeks. 'We had best go downstairs. I dare say they are waiting for us.'

By the time they had been in Signora Fiori's elegant crowded salon for three-quarters of an hour, Cecily was certain she and Mariana had met at least half of Venice. Despite her absence of thirteen years, the Duchess seemed to be acquainted with everyone. They even met Mrs Hoppner, the English consul's wife, who greeted both her and Mariana very kindly.

Now Mariana stood with one of Eleanora's cousins, a pretty girl who was Mariana's age. Eleanora had just suggested that they take a turn around the room when someone said Cecily's name. Thais stood there in a pale yellow gown, smiling. 'I could not believe my eyes when I saw you! I thought you were in Padua. And Lady Eleanora! I had no idea that you and Cecily were acquainted.'

'Cecily is staying with us in Venice,' Eleanora said politely. She did not look particularly pleased to see Thais.

Thais looked momentarily surprised. Then she gave a little laugh. 'Indeed. How did that come about? I was quite certain you would be with Mariana in Padua.'

'Mariana is also here,' Cecily said.

'Mariana? Is she also staying with you?' Thais asked Eleanora.

'Yes. Perhaps you have not yet heard, but Signorina Renato and my cousin are betrothed.'

An odd expression crossed Thais' face. 'How delightful!' she finally said. 'Although I am certain it will be difficult for Cecily to have Mariana so far away.'

'We hope Cecily will return to England with us for a visit,' Eleanora said. 'Signora Abruzzi has arrived. You have not yet made her acquaintance, have you, Cecily? Then you must excuse us, Lady Margate.'

'I had hoped to speak to Cecily for a little while before you take her away. You do not mind, do you?'

Eleanora glanced at Cecily. 'No, but you cannot have her for too long.' She gave Thais a little smile before walking off.

Thais watched her for a moment. 'She is pretty enough, but has such odd manners. But I do not wish to speak of Lady Eleanora, but of you. Let us go into one of the smaller rooms. And Mariana, of course. However did you managed to persuade Severin to allow the match? And Rafaele Vianoli? I presume he must have given his approval?'

'Of course. Both families are quite delighted.' Cecily bit back her annoyance at Thais' offhand dismissal of Eleanora.

'I am so pleased, as I am certain you must be.' Thais appeared genuinely pleased. 'So you will return to England? It would be very odd to return after so long, I would think.'

'I have not made up my mind.'

'I quite understand.' She looked over Cecily's shoulder, then placed a hand on her arm. 'Whatever you do, do not smile at the man who is approaching us. He has the most shocking reputation.'

Before Cecily could say anything, a man appeared next to them. He was heavyset and expensively dressed. 'Good evening, Lady Margate. You have decided to end your rustication and once again grace Venice with your charming presence?' He spoke English with an accent Cecily recognised as Austrian.

'For a little while. I will own I did not expect to find you here either. I have heard rumours that you bought a villa on the Brenta.'

'I did. It has been badly neglected, but the restoration is nearly complete and I will soon hold a little party in celebration.' He turned his clear, almost colourless gaze upon Cecily. 'But we are most inconsiderate to talk of these things when I have not yet been introduced to your lovely companion.'

'Then, Signora Renato, you must allow me to present the Baron Eberhart,' Thais said.

Eberhart took Cecily's hand. 'Enchanted, *signora*.' He raised her hand slowly to his lips, his eyes never leaving her face in a way Cecily found disconcerting. 'But you are not Italian?'

'I am English, sir.'

He finally released her hand. 'An English rose,' he murmured.

Thais tapped his arm with her fan. 'I have already warned her of your reputation, so you must not try to flirt with her. She is, as well, related to Rafaele Vianoli by marriage.'

'Indeed.' The Baron looked at Cecily even more closely. 'He is very talented. I had hoped he would be available to oversee the repairs to my villa, but alas he was not.'

'He has been very busy.' His praise of Raf softened her a little towards him. 'I must find my companions so I beg your pardon.'

'You are not with Lady Margate?' the Baron asked. 'For I had hoped to persuade you to stay to talk with me a little longer.'

'I am sorry, but I cannot.' She started to move away, only to find the Baron's hand on her arm.

'I am quite harmless, no matter what Lady Margate has told you,' he said.

She gave him a polite smile. 'I really must go.'

'But I must insist you stay.'

'And I must insist you release Signora Renato.'

Thais gasped and Cecily froze. Nico? The Baron dropped his hand away from her. 'Good evening, Severin. I assure you, I intended only conversation with the *signora.*'

'Against her will?' Nico regarded the Baron with cold eyes.

'I am beginning to think that perhaps I should be insulted.'

'Really, Severin!' Thais said.

Cecily forced herself to smile at Nico. 'I am quite certain the Baron did not intend to detain me, so there is no harm done. Perhaps you would not object to escorting me back to the salon. I wish to find Mariana. Have you yet spoken to her or Lord Ballister?'

'Not yet. My sister sent me to find you almost as soon as I stepped into the salon.'

'Then we most certainly need to go.'

'Yes.' His gaze fell on the other two. '*Buonanotte*, Eberhart. Lady Margate.' He held out his arm to Cecily. 'Signora Renato?'

His brusque cold tone made her heart sink. 'Yes, your Grace.' She placed her hand on his coat sleeve. 'Goodnight, Thais. Goodnight, Baron Eberhart.'

Nico barely gave them time to respond before whisking her from the room to the salon. He did not pause until they were near a table with a large vase of flowers. He stopped, and she pulled her hand from his arm. 'I would like to find Mariana, if you please.'

He scowled down at her. 'Stay away from Eberhart. He's dangerous.'

'Really? He seemed quite congenial.' She did not particularly care for the Baron, but she was even more irritated at Nico.

'He's a rake of the worst sort.'

'Are there better sorts of rakes than others?'

His mouth tightened. 'Yes. Where did you get that gown?'

'I suppose, your Grace, you intend to tell me you dislike it?' She met his gaze, her own defiant.

'I like it too much. Don't wear it in public again.'

'You've no right to dictate what I can or cannot wear.' She wanted to throw something at him. Or cry. Or both. 'If I wish to wear nothing, then I will do that as well!'

'Not unless you are with me, my sweet.'

She stared at him. 'That will never happen,' she said coldly and walked away from him.

Nico stared after her. What the hell had come over him? He'd planned to treat her with cool indifference, not quarrel with her in the middle of a *conversazione*. He'd arrived in Venice a short time ago, and, after changing from his travel clothes, had left for the Fiori palazzo. The first person he found was Eleanora, who wasted no time in informing him that Cecily needed to be rescued from Baron Eberhart.

As soon as he saw her in the damnable dress, beautiful and desirable and obviously not pining away for him, he'd lost all rational thought. Nor did it help that he saw his own feelings reflected in the Baron's gaze. He'd made a fool of himself over the dress because what he really wanted to do was pull her into his arms and kiss her into submission. Until she knew she had no choice but to marry him.

He thought of his mother's words after he said he did not know if he loved Cecily. *Then perhaps it is for the best that she did not agree to marry you after all.* Her words made no sense, for he could not see why it mattered whether he loved her or not. Cecily had not spoken of love at all—surely if she were in love with him, she would have accepted his offer. Perhaps that was why she refused his offer. She did not love him.

Which should make no difference at all to him.

But it did.

Chapter Fourteen

Mariana and Simon were married a week after Nico returned to Venice. The ceremony itself was quiet, with only family present, but the banquet held afterwards at the Ca' Cappelletti was a much more elaborate affair. After the lavish meal, a trio of musicians entertained the guests in the *piano nobile*.

To her surprise, Raf had managed to persuade Barbarina to attend. He had brought her from Avezza two days ago to stay with her cousin, Signora Gamba, although she insisted that Raf was to take her back to Avezza the day after the wedding. Now she was sitting alone on a sofa in an alcove of the salon in her customary black, an odd little figure among the colourful gowns of the other guests. As soon as she could politely do so, Cecily excused herself from the Contessa Alberti, the older sister of the Duchess, and made her way to Barbarina's side. She sat down next to her. 'I wanted to tell you how grateful I am that you are here. And that you have accepted Mariana's marriage to Lord Ballister.' She had been fearful that Barbarina would make some sort of fuss, but she had not.

Barbarina turned and fixed Cecily with her small dark eyes. 'It is done, so what could I do? At least he is not a poor man, so she will not suffer in that way.'

'He loves her and she loves him. Is that not important as well?'

'Only if both love equally, otherwise it is worse than no love at all. You learned that, as I did.'

'Mariana and Simon will be happy.' She would not allow Barbarina to tell her otherwise. 'Would you like something? A lemonade? Or wine?'

'When will you return to Avezza?'

'I do not know. The Duchess has invited me to stay until Simon and Mariana return from their wedding journey. They are going to Lake Garda.' She had not made up her mind to do so. As much as she wanted to be here when Mariana and Simon returned, she did not think she could bear to stay under the same roof as Nico once they were gone. With the preparations for the wedding and the dinners given in honour of the forthcoming nuptials, she and Nico had managed to avoid each other. But with Mariana gone and the strain between them, she could not imagine staying on any longer.

'You have quarrelled with the Duke, no? So why do you wish to remain in Venice? It is foolish to hope he will love you as he did Angelina. It will be just as it was with Marco. You will love him and he will not love you.'

Cecily rose before she said something to Barbarina she would regret. 'Would you like something to drink?'

'A small glass of wine.'

Across the room in the corner she saw Thais with Nico. She managed to find a waiter and procured the wine and started towards Barbarina, careful to avoid Thais and Nico. Thais, however, met her before she could reach Barbarina. 'I have not yet had a chance to speak with you, Cecily. How beautiful and happy Mariana looks! You must be so pleased, but perhaps a little sad as well.'

'Yes, a little.' If she thought of Mariana's going away too much, she would probably burst into tears.

'Then I have the most splendid idea. You must come and stay with me after Mariana and Lord Ballister leave on their wedding journey. You do not need to give me an answer now, but please consider it.'

'You are very kind,' Cecily said, taken aback by the invitation.

'But I am not. I sometimes become quite lonely in my little palazzo, so I would quite enjoy your company. So you would be doing me a great favour.'

'I will consider it, then.' Cecily saw that Barbarina was now staring at them. What if she suddenly decided to join them and say some peculiar thing to Thais? 'I must take this wine to Barbarina now.'

'Most certainly. Poor creature, but she is so fortunate to have you to look after her.'

'What did she want?' Barbarina asked as soon as Cecily returned.

'Nothing in particular. I hope you will like this.' She handed Barbarina the glass.

'She is wicked beneath her smiles and rich clothes. You must not forget that.'

Oh, dear. She hated to think what Barbarina would say if she discovered Thais had invited Cecily to stay with her. Or worse, what she would say if Cecily accepted.

Nico glanced across the salon to where Cecily now stood with Bernardo. It was apparent from the way Bernardo Parvatti hung on to every word that he was besotted. No matter that she was five years his senior. He found himself crossing the room.

'Good evening, Signora Renato. Bernardo.'

The smile faded from Cecily's face. 'Good evening, your Grace.' She spoke as if they were complete strangers, as if they had never been together as lovers. She turned to Bernardo with a charmingly sweet smile. 'I will leave you so that you and your cousin may converse. I hope we will have the opportunity to meet again.'

Bernardo looked as if he'd been offered a fortune. 'I…I would like that, *signora*.'

Nico reined in his temper. 'Actually, I want to talk to Signora Renato.'

'Ah, yes. I beg your pardon.' Bernardo executed a slight bow and then backed away, almost running into an elderly lady behind him.

Nico looked down at her. 'Are you certain it is sporting to give him false hopes?'

'What sort of false hopes would that be, your Grace? If you have come here to scold me about that, then you are wasting your breath, for I intend to walk away from you.' She spoke in a low angry voice and it occurred to him that she possibly hated him.

He felt completely out of control. Then he saw the distress in her eyes. Hell. 'We can go to the library. I promise I will behave as a gentleman. My mother and my sister will have my head if they think I've overset you. Especially today.'

The almost-smile that touched her lips made his heart thud. He wanted to kiss her. 'Will you come with me?'

'Very well.' She made a few polite comments as they left the salon, undoubtedly for the benefit of anyone who might be watching.

The library was shrouded in shadows; the only light provided by the full moon, spilling through the tall arched windows and across the marble floor. 'What is it?' she asked.

What did he want to say to her? His mind was blank; he could only think of how the moonlight shone across her hair and how much he wanted to take her into his arms.

'Your Grace?'

'I wanted to tell you that I plan to accompany Simon and Mariana as far as Mestre. To ensure that their carriage is ready and they are properly prepared for their journey.'

'Thank you. You are most kind. Shall we return to the salon?'

'I wish to apologise for my ungentlemanly behaviour after the *conversazione*.'

'We were both angry.'

'Yes.' He drew in a breath. 'Damn it, Cecily, why did you refuse my offer?'

She looked up at him, her face pale in the moonlight. 'Because you still love Angelina, just as Marco still loved Caterina. Her ghost would always be hovering between us. I have lived with one ghost; I cannot live with another.'

He did not know if he understood. 'I cannot help loving her.'

'I would not expect you to stop. But I would always be in her shadow. You would look at me and I would see that you regret that I am not Angelina. No woman ever will be, you know.' She sounded almost wistful.

'I hardly would expect you to be. For one thing, you look nothing alike.' The words did not come out as light as he had intended.

Her face clouded for a moment. 'No, I do not suppose we do. Everyone said she was beautiful.'

He had insulted her. 'But so are you. In a different way, of course. Is that it? You think I would compare your beauty to Angelina's?'

She moved a little away from him. 'No. Marco did not compare me to Caterina, at least not like that. But he had loved her since childhood. He adored her, worshipped her, and to him she was the embodiment of all that a woman should be.' She turned her clear gaze on him. 'But I was not.'

'He told you that?'

'No, he was too kind. But I could sense it. I could not

be all that Caterina was. I cannot be all that Angelina was either.'

No response sprang to his lips. For the truth of what she said hit him with blinding force—he held all other women up against Angelina and found them wanting. Even Cecily.

She watched him for a moment. 'We had best return to the others,' she finally said.

'There is one more thing.' He did not move. 'Is there any chance you are with child?'

She shook her head. 'No. I...I knew that a few days after our...our encounter.'

'We were fortunate, then.' Instead of relief, he felt a sense of loss.

'Yes, we were.' She did not quite look at him. 'I must return to the salon. We must before someone notices we are gone.'

'Cecily...' he began and then stopped. Nothing he said would be of much use now.

Cecily waited until after Simon, Mariana and Nico left before telling the Duchess she planned to accept Thais' invitation to stay with her. 'Please do not think that I have been unhappy here, for that is not it at all. I—'

'You do not need to say anything more—I quite understand. My son told me that he asked you to marry him, but you did not accept his offer. You worry that it will be awkward for both of you if you stay.' She took Cecily's hand. 'He told me the night before we left for Venice and only because I asked him,' she said gently.

'I am sorry. It is not because—'

'You do not need to explain. I only wished to assure you that you will always be welcome under our roof whether we are in Italy or England.'

'You are much too generous.'

'No, I am only sorry that I will not have you for a daughter-in-law, but you are still part of our family, no?'

She looked at the Duchess's lovely, familiar face. 'I will miss you and Lady Eleanora very much. You have been so kind.'

'And we will miss you.' She leaned forward and kissed Cecily's cheek. 'If you decide that Lady Margate does not suit you, then you will come back to us. You must promise me that.'

'I will.' Cecily was quite certain she would not set foot in this house again.

A week later Cecily sat next to Thais in a carriage that was taking them to Baron Eberhart's villa. The Baron had invited Thais and her as well as a number of others to his newly renovated villa for a few days. Despite the clear blue skies and pleasing scenery, Cecily felt more than a little trepidation about actually staying under the Baron's roof.

During the week she had been with Thais, the Baron seemed always underfoot, escorting them one night to his box at Le Fenice, accompanying them to a dinner given by the Austrian governor another. He had even gone on a shopping trip with them and afterwards had insisted on taking Cecily and Thais to a small café for a light repast. He had always been courteous to Cecily, but she found the speculative way he sometimes looked at her unnerving.

'Georg looks forward to showing you the improvements he has made,' Thais suddenly said. 'You will be most impressed.'

'I am certain it is lovely,' Cecily said politely.

'Dear Cecily, you must guess that Georg is quite taken with you. I hope you like him a little?'

'I hardly know him well enough to form an opinion.' Cecily could think of no polite way to tell Thais she did not really like the Baron despite his impeccable manners and amusing conversation. She certainly did not like the way he persisted in referring to her as a 'delicate English rose' even after she had told him she did not like roses.

'Now you have a perfect opportunity to know him better,' Thais said. 'My dear, he is not so much a rogue that he will force you into anything. A little flirtation will do you good. You are still young and very pretty and, now that Mariana is married, you cannot hide yourself away with Signora Zanetti in that dull little town. Georg may be exactly what you need to take your thoughts from Severin.'

'I have no idea what you mean.'

'It is quite apparent that you have developed a *tendre* for him.' Her large blue eyes rested on Cecily's face.

'You are quite mistaken.'

'I do not think so, for I know the signs.' Her smile was not unsympathetic. 'It is quite natural for you to do so, particularly when he has not exactly been indifferent to you. You are quite the opposite of many of the women he meets, so it is not surprising he finds you rather intriguing.'

'He…he looks upon me as a relation. Which is exactly what I consider him. Nothing more.' Cecily spoke firmly and prayed the colour in her cheeks would not give her away.

'I hope not. He does feel quite protective towards you now that you are related by marriage, for he told me so. It would be easy for one to mistake his protective instincts for a warmer, more personal regard.'

'I quite suppose it would.' Cecily bit back a stab of hurt that he would discuss her with Thais. She glanced out of the window. Through the trees she caught a glimpse of a large square house with a classical portico. 'Is that Barbarigo?' she asked brightly.

'Yes.' Thais touched Cecily's hand. 'I did not mean to overset you, but I do not want you to be hurt as I was.' Her smile had vanished and she looked at Cecily with wide unhappy eyes. 'You see, I too was in love with Severin. I had hoped that we would marry, but he was to marry Angelina instead.'

Nico looked down at the letter the groom had just handed him. 'My lord, the Lady Eleanora says I must tell you that it is a matter most urgent,' the man added with an anxious look, as if he feared Nico intended to lay it aside. 'I am to tell you also that the Duchess is in the best of health.'

'I am relieved to hear that.' He glanced at the man, who still waited. 'I will open it while you go to the stables and see to your horse.'

'Thank you, my lord.' He bowed and backed out of the study.

Nico frowned for a moment, wondering what the devil was of such urgency that Eleanora must send a groom all the way to the Villa Cappelletti. Particularly when he was to return to Venice in the next few days. He broke the seal, quickly perused the contents and then swore.

If Eleanora was correct, then Cecily and Thais were, at this very moment, guests under Eberhart's roof. More disturbing, Eleanora reported that ever since Cecily had gone to stay with Thais, the Baron had been seen everywhere with them and it was rumoured a bet had been placed on how long it would take Eberhart to seduce Cecily.

He could not imagine Cecily a willing participant in any such scheme, but then why the hell had she agreed to attend this house party? And when he told her to stay away from Eberhart, she had replied that she found him 'congenial'. Cecily might not want him, but he'd abduct Cecily before he'd allow Eberhart to touch her.

If he left within the next hour, he would reach Eberhart's villa in time for dinner.

Chapter Fifteen

Cecily picked up her fan and wondered if Eberhart would suspect she was avoiding him if she pleaded a headache tonight and stayed in her room instead of going down to dinner. She had no real desire to see Thais either—the conversation in the carriage had disturbed her greatly.

Thais had been in love with Nico and expected to marry him? Had there actually been some sort of formal promise between them? Or had Thais only hoped there would be? She must have been in love with Nico that summer, but had anyone noticed? Perhaps not—Viola had described Thais as the sort of pale girl no one seemed to see. Despite living under Thais' roof for a week, Cecily did not feel she knew Thais much better than she had in Avezza, almost as if the pale unremarkable girl still lurked beneath her charming smiles and blonde loveliness.

Even the few confidences she had shared with Cecily did not, in retrospect, reveal much about her. She knew that Thais had been widowed twice, but Cecily had no idea if Thais had regarded either of her husbands with any sort of affection. She had numerous acquaintances, but none of them seemed to be a friend, at least not in the sense that Cecily considered Viola and, if circumstances were different, Lady Eleanora.

Certainly Thais had been hospitable and the week had passed in a whirlwind of social affairs, visitors and shopping, which had left Cecily in a sort of daze. She had scarcely a moment to herself except when she tumbled into bed at night and she was so tired she fell asleep with hardly a thought for Mariana and Simon. Or Nico. She felt as if she had left the Ca' Cappelletti a year instead of a week ago, for although they were in the same city, the only time she had glimpsed Eleanora and the Duchess was when the Baron had escorted them to the theatre. Thais had pointed out their box and Cecily had been taken aback by the jolt of longing that pierced her when she saw their familiar figures.

She was puzzled and a little hurt that neither the Duchess nor Eleanora had made any effort to visit her as they had promised they would. She thought that perhaps she had insulted them after all by leaving in the way she had.

Nothing seemed right. She walked to the window. Below were the formal gardens. Everything looked serene under the clear blue sky of an Italian afternoon. None the less, she felt on edge, as if she expected something unpleasant to happen. She would avoid Eberhart as much as possible but surely Thais was right and he would not do anything she did not want. She had worn one of her less becoming gowns tonight, a pale lavender silk, hoping he would consider her less of an English rose and more of an English thistle.

Someone rapped lightly at her door. She crossed the room, opened it and found Thais on the other side. She was dressed in a gown of delicate pink silk that emphasised her porcelain skin. Around her neck was a stunning necklace of diamonds. 'Dear Cecily, it is time to go down…' She stopped. 'Why are you not wearing the cerulean gown we had decided upon?'

'I found it had a stain.' The lie sprang quite easily to her lips.

'But this gown is so…so dull. Everyone will think you are someone's companion! And that necklace! It is so ordinary!' She pressed her lips together, dismay written all over her face. 'It is too late to do anything now. Perhaps if the bodice was arranged a little lower.'

'No! That is, I was feeling a trifle cold. I should hate to catch a chill.'

'It is too late for you to change, for we must go down. Tomorrow I will insist on supervising your dress.'

Cecily refused to feel guilty over deceiving Thais. She would have worn sackcloth and ashes if she thought that would help her escape Eberhart's attention.

Cecily followed Thais into the richly decorated salon where the guests gathered before dinner. Her hopes for an unobtrusive entry were dashed when the Baron's cousin and hostess, the Countess von Essen, spotted them and crossed the marble floor to their sides. Her cool grey eyes swept over them. 'A most charming gown, Lady Margate.' She turned to Cecily, a hint of surprise crossing her thin features. 'You are in mourning?'

'No, Countess.'

She looked a trifle puzzled. 'Come, my cousin most particularly wishes to greet you and Lady Margate.'

Cecily did not dare look at Thais as they followed the Countess across the room. She had the unpleasant sensation that several of the guests stared and whispered as they passed.

Eberhart stood with a heavyset man Cecily did not recognise. In fact, she realised she recognised none of the fashionably dressed guests she glimpsed as they crossed the room. The Countess excused herself, leaving Thais and Cecily with the men.

'Thais, my dear,' Eberhart said as he took her hand. 'As usual, you are the pinnacle of health and beauty. Another new gown, perhaps?'

'Will you scold me if it is?'

'Only if it did not become you.' He dropped her hand and turned to Cecily.

'Signora Renato,' he murmured. He possessed himself of her hand and brushed a brief kiss across the back of it. He impaled her with his strange colourless eyes. 'Welcome to my villa. I have anticipated your arrival since I learned you were coming.'

She forced her lips into a diffident smile and wondered how long he intended to go on holding her hand. 'Thank you.'

He finally dropped her hand as they were presented to his companion, Herr Schuler, who proclaimed himself in a heavy German accent delighted to meet such beautiful ladies. He too held Cecily's hand a trifle too long, his gaze a trifle too bold, before turning to Eberhart and speaking in rapid German. The Baron smiled and Cecily had the uneasy sense the Baron's comment concerned her.

The Baron started to speak just as a footman appeared at his side. He spoke to Eberhart in a low voice and the Baron frowned. 'You must excuse me, my dear ladies. An unexpected guest has arrived.' He left them with Schuler.

Schuler cleared his throat. 'I am most pleased to once again find myself in your splendid city.' His Italian was laboured as if he read from a schoolroom book.

Thais started to speak and then her attention riveted to something over Cecily's shoulder. 'Good heavens!' Pure dismay crossed her fact. She turned to Cecily and spoke in English. 'Dear Cecily, I fear I must warn you that Severin has just arrived.'

Nico? Cecily nearly dropped her fan. She slowly turned. Nico stood in the doorway. He seemed not to notice his approaching host as his gaze swept the room. Then his eyes fell on her with an intensity that was almost physical and she knew he was here because of her. She turned away and realised she was shaking.

She had no idea whether it was from anticipation, fear or relief. Or something else altogether.

* * *

Nico glanced down the table at Cecily. She was seated between Schuler and an elderly gentleman he did not recognise. Her profile was turned away from him as she listened to her dinner partner, her soft brown hair gleaming with bits of gold from the candlelight. Among the fashionable dress and glittering jewels of the others she looked like a poor relation in her drab gown, but that only rendered her more vulnerable.

His gaze shifted to the Baron, who laughed at a joke before gulping his wine. Although Eberhart was attentive to the lady seated at his side, his gaze frequently fell on Cecily with a speculative interest that raised Nico's hackles. He could not tell whether Cecily was aware of his interest, for she steadily avoided looking at the Baron. As she had steadily avoided looking at him since they had sat down to dinner.

'Are you certain it wise to stare at Cecily so often? Some might decide you are here because of her.'

He forced his attention back to Thais. She wore a little smile, but there was an edge to her voice he did not often hear.

'They would not be wrong.' He was in no mood to dissemble.

Slight colour stained her cheek. She stared at him and gave a little laugh. 'Whatever for? Really, I would think you must know by now that she finds you rather…well, intimidating. If you persist in this sort of thing, you will quite scare her.'

'I had not noticed that she finds me particularly intimidating.'

'Of course you do not! Men always assume that a woman who blushes and looks away from them is merely shy, but it is most often because they find the man too overwhelming. Contrary to what most men wish to believe, women do not in general like men who overwhelm them.'

He felt irked. 'You are speaking of women in general, or of Cecily?'

Her smile held a touch of pity. 'Have you not realised that Cecily wants nothing to do with you? Why else did she leave your house and come to stay with me?'

In that moment, he realised how much he disliked Thais. 'Perhaps, but what interests me is why you were so conveniently at hand to invite her to stay with you? More than that, my dear, I am quite curious as to why you brought her here, a place where most of the guests are no more respectable than their host?'

Her blue eyes widened. 'Dear Severin, I have no idea what you mean.'

'I think you do.' He held her gaze, his own hard. 'What game are you playing?'

Cold anger flickered across her face and then she gave a little laugh. 'Games? Why, none!' She looked away and picked up her wine glass.

What the hell was she up to? She knew exactly what she was doing when she brought Cecily here. He had no idea whether she deliberately intended to hurt Cecily or if Cecily was merely a pawn for some other nefarious purpose.

It did not matter—he intended to remove Cecily from this place as soon as possible.

* * *

The dinner was followed by a tedious tour of the Baron's collection of antiquities, which included two nude male statues. Eberhart chortled. 'I did not wish to offend the sensibilities of the ladies. Or make them dissatisfied with their current pleasures. Rather magnificent, are they not?'

A few crude comments followed, which only served to increase Nico's impatience.

Nico dallied, intending to allow the others to go ahead so he might fall behind and steal away to the salon. Eberhart usurped his plans by suddenly announcing they must join the ladies. He fell into step beside Nico.

'I am quite curious to know exactly why you decided to join my little party.' He glanced at Nico. 'Shall I guess? A certain lady, perhaps?'

'Yes.'

'I would hope you are referring to the delightful Lady Margate.'

'I am referring to Signora Renato.'

There was silence. Then Eberhart turned to look at him. 'I must ask you to turn your attention elsewhere. Perhaps you do not realise that I have an interest in the lady myself.'

'I have heard rumours to that effect. However, I have a prior claim.'

'Then I must ask you to relinquish it.'

'I am going to wed Signora Renato.'

Eberhart momentarily lost his bland expression. 'How very interesting, particularly since I had the impression from Lady Margate that the lovely *signora* had all but run from you.' He stopped in front of a painting. 'What do you think of my most recent acquisition? A present from an unfortunate Frenchman just before he was compelled to leave Italy.'

Nico looked up at the painting. 'Very nice. Which noble family did the Frenchman rob?'

'You are far too cynical, my dear Severin. If you insist on continuing in this vein, I might suspect you of harbouring radical sympathies.'

'My only interest is in Cecily Renato.'

The Baron began to walk again. 'Of course. I am curious if you have yet informed your intended bride she is to wed you.' He cast Nico a sly look. 'Because if you have not, then I still consider the lady fair game.'

'I suggest you rid yourself of that notion. Unless you want a bullet through you.'

'I would take offence, but since you are caught up in the throes of passion I will overlook your lack of gratitude for my hospitality. You would be wise to keep in mind, however, you are here only because I have allowed it.' They had reached the salon. Eberhart paused. 'We will make a little wager. I will give you until noon tomorrow to convince the *signora* to marry you. If she does not agree, then I will continue my pursuit of her without your interference. However, there is one more condition.'

'And that is?'

'If she agrees, we will announce it to the rest of the guests. To ensure that your intentions are honourable.'

'As yours are, no doubt.'

Eberhart smiled. 'Perhaps I am also in need of a wife.'

'You had best look elsewhere.'

'She is lovely, is she not, with an air of innocence despite her widowhood. One wonders if she has ever been brought to the height of passion. I have no doubt that, if properly tutored, she will be a most pleasurable bedmate. I am not certain if I wish to relinquish that task to you after all.'

Nico nearly lost his tight control then. 'The choice belongs to the lady,' he said coolly.

'Naturally. You will understand if I do not wish you success in your pursuit.'

'I do not intend to lose.' He stepped into the room.

Cecily was nowhere in sight.

Cecily had been glad to escape from the salon to the quiet of the bedchamber. But after the maid finished helping her into her nightclothes and left, an unexpected surge of homesickness washed over Cecily. Not for her house in Avezza, but for England. This room, with its silent marble floors and dark bed coverings, seemed huge and strange and she suddenly longed for the cheerful simplicity of her childhood room. For the first time in an age, she missed her grandmother. Lady Telford had been stiff and demanding and not very physically demonstrative, but when Cecily had been truly overset her grandmother would sit with her.

'You may cry for a while, but then you must dry your eyes and decide what you must do next,' Lady Telford told her many times.

After that she would gather Cecily into her arms, rather stiffly, and Cecily had known she was loved. Now, she felt an aching need for someone to hold her.

'Cecily.'

Her heart leapt to her throat. Nico?

'Cecily. It is Nico. Open the door.' His voice held a note of impatience. 'Now.' She did not think he would go away if she ignored him. She padded to the door.

She turned the key and opened the door a crack. 'I was about to go to bed.'

'Let me in before any of the guests find me shouting through the door.'

'Oh.' She stepped back. He brushed past her, closed the door behind him and turned the key.

She stared at the key and then at him. 'Whatever are you doing?' Her voice was a trifle too high.

'Locking the door. So our host doesn't disturb us.'

'Us?' Her voice squeaked.

'Yes. Us. We need to talk.'

'Could we not do it some other time?'

'No.' He folded his arms and leaned against the door, his eyes on her face. 'I told Eberhart I plan to marry you,' he said coolly.

Her heart thudded. 'Why did you do that?'

'So he would cease his pursuit of you.'

'You know of that?' How utterly humiliating.

'Yes, as do a good many others.'

'I see. You are most kind, but it was not necessary to tell him that—'

He stopped her. 'It was. I promised Raf I'd look after

you. I'm not about to let you end up as Eberhart's mistress,' he said roughly. 'Or have your reputation ruined.'

'I am certain Raf did not expect you to go around telling people untruths in order to protect me,' she said coldly. So that was why he was here—to keep some sort of stupid promise to Raf.

'It is not an untruth. We are about to become betrothed.' His expression was grim. 'Eberhart will not touch you if you are under my protection. Furthermore, our betrothal will quell any rumours linking your name with Eberhart. There is one more thing. If Raf returns and discovers you have been compromised in any way, he will come after Eberhart. I doubt you would like to see Raf imprisoned or worse for killing an Austrian baron.'

'No, of course not, although I would hope he would be more reasonable.'

'Not where his family is concerned.' He moved away from the door. 'So you see, by agreeing to a betrothal, you will possibly spare Raf's life.'

'Surely things are not quite that dire!'

'They are.' He had come to stand in front of her and she resisted the urge to back up. 'Why did you leave my house in the first place? Was it because of me?'

'Only because I thought it would be awkward under the circumstances if I stayed.'

'Not because you are afraid of me?' He seemed to really want to know.

She gave a strangled laugh at this sudden change in topic. 'No, although when you stare at me in the grim way you are doing now I quite fear you are about to scold me or attempt to ride roughshod over me. But, no, I am not afraid of you.'

'I am glad.' Some of the harshness faded from his expression.

The air suddenly crackled with tension. She clutched her dressing gown more tightly about her. 'I think you should go. It is late…and…'

'I am spending the night with you.'

She took a step back, her pulse beating wildly. 'Spending the night with me? Whatever for?'

'To protect you from Eberhart. He has an unfortunate habit of roaming during the night. I should not want him to wander into your bedchamber and find you unprotected.' His voice was cool and matter of fact.

'But the door has a lock!'

'I doubt that will stop him. If he thinks we are spending the night engaged in passionate lovemaking, he is unlikely to stray into your room. Or question the veracity of our betrothal. He would like, I think, to discover I am only bluffing.'

'Oh.' She took another step back, crossing her hands over her breasts.

'I am not planning a seduction, if that worries you. I intend to sleep here.' He had crossed the room to one of the chairs near the mantelpiece.

'Th…there is a cot in the dressing room. It might be more comfortable.'

'I would prefer to be in the same room with you. In case, our host decides to investigate.' He had started to shrug out of his coat.

'Surely he would not do that! And if he did, he would think it equally odd if you are in the chair.'

He finished removing his coat. His hands stilled on his waistcoat. 'You are right, my dear. Then perhaps I should share the bed with you.'

She swallowed. Her eyes met his and even in the dim light of the room, she could not mistake the blatant desire in his eyes. The knowledge he still wanted her sparked the aching need for him she had tried to ignore. The strangeness of the day…everything whirled around her, everything but him.

Her gaze did not waver from his face. 'I think, yes, that would be the best thing to do.'

He stared at her. 'I beg your pardon.'

'I think we should share the bed.'

He looked incredulous and then gave a short laugh. 'My sweet Cecily, I was hardly serious. Sharing a bed with you would be disastrous.' He fumbled with the button of his waistcoat.

He was right. Even if his bluntness hurt. She sat on the edge of the bed and wondered how she was ever to sleep. Worse, the lost feeling had returned in full force. Having him in the room only intensified it. She sniffed, praying she would not start to cry like some missish creature.

'Cecily.'

Her head jerked up. He stood in front of her dressed only in his loose shirt and breeches. 'What is wrong?'

'Nothing is wrong.' She looked away. 'We…we should go to bed.'

He did not move. 'Do you really want me to share your bed?'

'N-not really. It…it would be st-stupid.' To her chagrin, her voice shook.

'Stupid. Dangerous. Disastrous. All of those.' He took her hands and drew her to her feet. 'Do you know why? Because I would want to make love to you. Over and over. All night.'

'Would you?' she whispered. She hardly seemed to be breathing.

'Yes.' He moved closer to her, imprisoning her between the bed and his body. She could feel the hard planes of his body against hers, feel the beat of his heart. His mouth was inches from hers and she could almost taste him. She reached up and tangled her hands in his hair and pulled his head towards her. Her mouth found his. He did not move while she explored his mouth. Her hands moved down from his head to his shoulders to the hard muscles of his back. He still stood motionless. She finally lifted her head. 'You do not like this?'

'Not like it?' His voice was ragged. 'My sweet, I can think of nothing more pleasurable than having you touch me. And if you continue, I will lose every vestige of control I possess.'

'What if I want you to?' She touched his cheek.

'Are you attempting to seduce me?'

'I…I think so.' She pressed closer to him.

He stilled. 'Are you certain you want this?'

'Yes. Will you kiss me?' She was beyond caring whether she made a fool of herself or not.

An odd light sprang to his eyes. 'Anything to oblige you.' And then his arms were around her, his mouth crushing hers in a kiss that sent her senses spinning. She clung to him; when he finally lifted his head, her legs nearly buckled.

'What else will please you, my lady?' His voice was husky with desire.

She managed to speak. 'Your shirt. I want it off.' Impatient, she fumbled with the buttons and then started to lift it over his head.

'Allow me.' He finished the task and stood before her. She had seen him partially unclothed before, but not like this, standing before her as a lover. She took him in, the broad shoulders and chest, the muscles, the dark hair on his chest, his narrow hips. He waited under her perusal, his eyes on her face. 'What else, sweetheart?' he asked softly.

She wanted to touch him everywhere. She swallowed and ran her tongue over her dry lips. 'I don't know.'

'It is my turn to make a request. Your shift must go.'

She thought she would explode when he undid the ribbon and then helped her from the garment. Then she stood naked before him. The heat in his gaze rendered her self-conscious for the first time and she crossed her hands over her breasts.

'Don't,' he said softly. He gently removed her hands and held them to her sides. His gaze seemed to burn through her as his eyes took in her breasts, her hips, the juncture of her thighs and her legs. He did not need to tell her he found her desirable; his sudden intake of breath was enough. 'Turn around,' he said hoarsely.

She did and then his arms circled her waist, pulling her back against him. He caressed the back of her neck with his mouth. He cupped her breast with his free hand and then moved down to her stomach, stroking the soft roundness in lazy circles. A whimper of pleasure and need escaped her and when his hand moved to the mound between her thighs, she shuddered.

He removed his hand. 'Come, we will continue this in the chair,' he said thickly.

'The chair?'

He took her hand and led her to the wing chair. He sat and pulled her down on his lap so she was facing him. He looked up at her, his eyes dark and sensuous. 'Kiss me, Cecily.'

She leaned forward, her hands bracing against his shoulders, and found his mouth. She kissed him, tentatively exploring his mouth, tasting him. He responded, his own kiss unhurried. The feel of the bare flesh of her thighs against the rough cloth of his breeches was unexpectedly sensuous and she found herself leaning forward and pressing into him. Her breasts fell forward and he cupped them. When he drew one nipple into his mouth, she thought she would die. She leaned into his caress, wanting more and then his hard length pressed into the sensitive nub between her legs. She shuddered with pure, hot desire.

He pulled his mouth away from hers. 'What next, my lady?' he whispered.

'I…' She was too far gone to think of propriety. 'Your breeches.'

He laughed softly. 'Of course. But we will need to stand for a moment.'

He rose, his arm around her. Her legs nearly buckled when she stood. In fascination, she watched as he undid the fastening of his breeches and then stepped out of them. But when he started to remove his small clothes, she averted her eyes. Whatever was she doing?

But he was drawing her to him. 'No need to be shy, *cara*.' He tilted her chin and kissed her mouth. 'Come and sit back down. This time properly. Or most improperly, as you wish.' He sat again, slightly sprawled, and she could not look anywhere but at his face.

A slight smile touched his mouth. 'Come and kiss me again. Just like before.' He held out his hand.

She took it and again was on his lap. She leaned forward to kiss him and this time he met her mouth with a hard, possessive opened-mouth kiss. Her head spun as his hand cupped her buttocks, lifting her slightly and then he was parting her thighs. She gasped as he slipped two fingers in her swollen opening. She clung to him as he explored, stroking and caressing the most sensitive places in her body until she was completely at his mercy. Her breath came in shallow gasps and when he finally withdrew, she thought she would explode. She opened her eyes. 'Please…' she begged.

'Lift your hips.'

She complied and then drew in a sharp breath when

his hard length filled her. 'Lean forward and ride me,' he whispered.

She nodded and braced her hands on his shoulders and began to rock. Her body seemed to know what to do, moving and adjusting to seek the most pleasure possible. Her body was swollen and full, the movements only increasing her desire for release. He moved under her, matching her rhythm. She climaxed, wave after wave of sensuous pleasure crashing over her. His own climax followed and she collapsed against him, as her breathing slowed.

And sanity returned. She was sitting on the Duke of Severin's most private part after begging him to take her to bed. Except they hadn't even made it to the bed.

His hand brushed her cheek. 'Regrets already, my sweet?'

She opened her eyes. He watched her with a lazy, sensuous expression, but she felt as if he could read her soul. 'No. I...I don't know. I have never been like this.'

'Like what?'

'So...so...brazen.'

Slight amusement lifted his mouth. 'I feel more than complimented.'

'I suppose women often throw themselves at you.'

'But rarely with so much passion.'

She had no doubt this sort of lovemaking was nothing out of the ordinary for him. If his cool, slightly amused manner was anything to go by, he had not felt the same loss of control she had. 'Thank you for...indulging me.' She started to move backwards, only to find his arm trapping her against him.

'But I have not finished indulging you.'

'I really do not expect you to do any more.'

'Don't you? Then perhaps you will indulge me.'

'What do you mean?'

His smile held a hint of wickedness. 'This time I will tell you what I want.'

Her body was already tensing in anticipation. 'What sort of things do you…want?'

'This to start with.' He rose with her and pulled her to him for another raw kiss. He was already hard, his erection pressing against her flesh. He lifted his head. 'I think now we can go to bed.' He took her hand.

The pleasurable warmth of the body cradled against his slowly penetrated his sleep-fogged consciousness. She lay under his arm, her back to him, the soft roundness of her buttocks pressed against his stomach, one leg under his. He kissed the back of her neck and then pulled away. For the first time in an age, he was reluctant to leave a woman's bed. If he did not, however, they would be here for the rest of the day.

He half-turned, easing out from under her and bit back a groan as he moved his stiff arm. He managed to sit on the edge of the bed. His gaze was drawn to Cecily, to the curve of her cheek. One slender arm was flung over the covers. She looked vulnerable and soft, and innocent. Unexpected protectiveness surged through him—something he had not expected after a night of such wild passion.

As much as he'd wanted her, he had not expected to

lose himself in her so completely that he no longer knew where he ended and she began. The pleasure had been nearly unbearable and, for the first time since his youth, he had lost control.

He'd never had such satisfying sex in his life.

He rose and found his shirt on the floor. He slipped it over his head, wincing a little. His breeches were flung over the chair where they had first coupled. The sudden hardness in his groin made him curse. He pulled up his breeches. When he looked up he saw Cecily was sitting, holding the bedcover up around her chest. Soft colour tinted her cheeks when she met his eyes and she looked away.

He walked over to her. Her hair was tousled about her bare shoulders and her mouth was soft. He wanted nothing more than to pull her back into his arms and entangle his hands in her hair, pulling the cover to reveal her breasts and make love until he lost himself in her. 'Once again, *cara*, we must talk.' He forced his voice to remain calm.

'I would like my shift first,' she said quietly. She did not meet his eyes.

'Of course.' He retrieved the garment from the floor and handed it to her. Then he walked to the window although the curtains were still drawn in order to give her privacy.

He waited until he heard her soft footsteps on the floor before he turned to face her. She stood at the foot of the bed, properly covered in the voluminous white gown, which did not render her any less desirable. But he was no longer a youth who could not control his desires. No matter what had happened last night.

'Sit down. Please,' he said.

She took a chair, not the one they'd made in love in. He had no idea whether she intended to avoid it or not. 'I hope you are not planning to beg my forgiveness for seducing me,' she said. 'In fact, I should beg your pardon for seducing you.' Her voice was calm, but the way she twisted her hands together told him she was not.

'Why? Because you regret it or you think I do?'

'I do not know.' She finally looked at him. 'You were here to do me a kindness and instead I…I took advantage of you.'

'My sweet girl, if I had not wanted to be taken advantage of, then there is nothing you could have done to, er…persuade me.' The conversation was not the one he had anticipated. He had never had a woman apologise for having her way with him. 'Will it ease your conscience if I tell you I have never been so enjoyably ravished in my life?'

She flushed. 'Oh.'

'Once we are married, we can repeat the experience any time you desire,' he said carelessly.

'Married? I thought…'

'You thought what?'

'That we were only to be betrothed. You said nothing about marriage.'

'I believe, my sweet, that in general marriage follows a betrothal. After last night, you do not have much choice. I've no doubt Eberhart knows we spent the night together and it is likely the others will suspect as well. Particularly after we announce our engagement today.'

'Today? Must we do it so soon?'

'Yes.' He scowled at her. 'Damn it, Cecily, marriage to me won't be that bad. I won't beat you.'

'I know,' she said quietly.

'Then why do you look as if you've just been sentenced to death?' He demanded.

'I…' She looked at him rather helplessly.

A cold fist slammed through him. She did not want to marry him despite the passion they had shared. It was possible Thais had been right after all, that for some reason Cecily feared him.

'Then we will consider the betrothal temporary. After a suitable length of time you may jilt me. For now, I had best leave your room and allow you to dress.'

'Yes.'

He tucked his shirt into his breeches and picked up his coat, then realised he'd forgotten to put on his stockings and shoes. He collected his shoes and stockings and sat down.

He finished and looked up. She stood near the window and he sensed it mattered not at all that the curtains were drawn, for her eyes seemed to be focused on something far away. Her shoulders drooped as if her thoughts gave her no pleasure. He rose and moved to stand behind her. 'Cecily.'

She turned, her expression rather confused as if she'd almost forgotten his presence. The forlorn look in her eyes tugged at his heart and he reached out to touch her cheek. She flinched and he dropped his hand. 'I am leaving now,' he said.

'Leaving?'

He supposed he should be gratified at the dismay in her face. 'Just the room. Not this villa. I would not leave you here.'

'No, of course not.'

'We will make the announcement before noon. After that we will leave.'

'Together?'

'Together, my sweet. Furthermore, you will return to my house. I will not allow you to go to Lady Margate so do not waste your breath in futile argument.' He did not wait for an answer. He turned and left the room before he could see her undoubtedly horrified expression.

Chapter Sixteen

Cecily rose from the bench. She could not spend the entire day in the villa's lush garden, as tempting as it was. She must return to the house and face the rest of the party. And Nico.

She had been beyond foolish to allow Thais to convince her to come here. The thought had never entered her mind that Nico would find out, much less come after her. Or that he felt such a…a stupid sense of honour that he would offer marriage to protect her.

Before they had made such passionate love.

Her whole body heated even thinking about it. Last night had been far different from the first time. Then, he had needed her and she had responded, but his love-making had held a certain desperation.

Last night had been something entirely different. He had made love to her, not out of need but out of desire. He had wanted her and she had wanted him back with a physical desire that had shocked her. Always slightly embarrassed by her unclothed body, she had stood naked before him, revelling in the knowledge he found her nude body beautiful.

She had run her hands over his body with an abandon she had never shown with Marco, fascinated with the strong male hardness of his muscles, enjoying the feminine power she felt as he lay still beneath her hands, his breath coming harder and harder until she finished her exploration. And then...

No. She must put last night aside before she did something rash such as seduce him again. She must be completely depraved. Women, at least well-bred women, were not supposed to be thinking about such things. As much as she had enjoyed Marco's considerate lovemaking, it had never occurred to her to indicate she desired him.

She started up the path towards the house. She must face the others, including Thais. She only hoped Nico was wrong and no one would know they had been together last night.

She had nearly reached the lawn directly behind the house when she saw Nico coming around the side of the house. He paused for a moment and then he saw her. He strode towards her and there was no mistaking his black expression.

He halted in front of her. 'Where were you?' he demanded. 'No one could find you.'

'I was in the garden,' she said coolly. It was quite apparent he was not thinking about last night.

'Alone? What if Eberhart was to come upon you?'

'Well, he did not.' She must have truly lost her mind to think she would ever want to seduce this arrogant man. 'I am going back to the house. Are you coming, your Grace? Or were you about to visit the gardens yourself?'

To her great satisfaction, he looked as if he were about to explode. He did not. 'We are going back to the house where we will announce our betrothal,' he said through gritted teeth.

'Very well, your Grace.' She started to walk away, only to have him catch her arm.

She stopped and looked up at him. 'Is there something else you wished to say to me?'

'Yes.' He dropped her arm. His eyes still held an angry glint, but there was another emotion as well. 'This.'

He grasped her shoulders and pulled her into his arms. She was too startled to protest as his mouth covered hers. Her feeble attempts at resistance were swept away by his leisurely, seductive kiss and she melted into him, her mouth soft and pliable beneath his.

He lifted his head. 'We can go in now that you look well kissed. We would not want Eberhart to suspect we were quarrelling.' A little smile played about his mouth.

'And you do not appear to have been affected at all,' she said tartly, hoping to cover up her confusion. If he could look so calm and collected after ravaging her senses, then she would pretend the same.

A sardonic light leapt to his eye. 'In that, my sweet Cecily, you are quite wrong.'

* * *

Thais was the first person they met when they entered the house. 'Severin! Thank goodness you found her!' She grasped Cecily's hands. 'I was so worried you were not in your room and then no one knew where you had gone to!'

'I only wished to walk in the garden. I did not think anyone would worry.' Nothing in Thais' face indicated she guessed Cecily had been in Nico's arms a short time ago.

'You should have asked me to come with you. I adore walking in gardens. We can walk together tomorrow.' She smiled at Nico. 'I am certain you will not object if I steal Cecily away?'

'Actually, I do object.'

Thais stared at him, then gave a little laugh. 'Well, really! Then I will ask Cecily instead. I hope you will not go against her wishes!'

'Ah, so Signora Renato has not run away after all.' Eberhart had come up silently behind them.

'Of course she would not,' Thais said. 'But Severin refuses to let her out of his sight. I hope you will convince him he is being quite selfish!'

Eberhart's gaze raked over Cecily in a way that made her think that he guessed exactly how she'd spent her night. Her face heated, which brought a knowing smile to the Baron's full lips. 'You have pleasing news, I see.'

She glanced at Nico. His eyes were on Eberhart. 'You may congratulate us.'

'Most certainly.' Eberhart turned to Cecily. 'My dear,

I must wish you all happiness.' He took her hand and brought it to his lips, his mouth lingering an instant too long, before releasing it. Nico's expression did not change, but he shifted closer to Cecily.

Eberhart turned to Thais. 'Lady Margate, do you not intend to congratulate the Duke and Signora Renato on their upcoming nuptials?' he asked blandly.

Thais had gone very still. For a moment, Cecily did not think she would answer. Then a strained smile crossed her face. 'Of course. I was just rather surprised, but I should have suspected something when Severin appeared last night.' She took Cecily's hand and kissed her cheek. 'I hope you will be happy, but it was very sly of you not to say a thing. In fact, I rather thought you did not care much for Severin at all.' She spoke in her light, teasing way.

'Thank you.' Why did Thais now say she thought Cecily did not care for Nico when yesterday she had accused Cecily of being in love with him?

'There is only a quarter of an hour left until noon, so I suggest we make the announcement without delay. Unless, Severin, you wish to postpone it,' Eberhart said.

'I would prefer—' Cecily began. Everything was happening too fast.

Nico's hand closed around hers. 'We will make the announcement now.'

Eberhart smiled. 'Then let us proceed to the salon.'

Thais insisted on accompanying Cecily to her bed-chamber so she could help Cecily pack. 'Although I think it is very bad of Severin to insist that you must stay with his family instead of me—I would have liked to have held a little party for you,' Thais said as they entered the room. Once inside, however, she closed the door and faced Cecily, the smile gone from her face.

'Perhaps I should not say anything, but as your friend I cannot remain silent.' She hesitated. 'Dear Cecily, are you certain you wish to marry Severin? I only ask because you do not seem happy. I worry that he has somehow forced you into accepting him.'

'Of course he has not.'

'Are you certain? He can be very overwhelming when he wants something. Particularly if he wants a woman. And it has been quite apparent from the very first that he has wanted you.' Her large eyes were filled with concern. 'Just as he wanted Angelina. Poor thing—he pursued her even though she found him quite intimidating. Everyone knew that she and Rafaele were to marry some day, but Severin did not care for that. He only wanted Angelina and would not allow her to refuse him. Sometimes I have wondered if her death was no accident, that perhaps she deliberately threw herself from the path rather than marry him.'

'That is a horrible thing to say.'

'Not if it is the truth.' Thais walked to the door. 'Do not make the same mistake Angelina did.'

Five days later, Raf was shown into the salon of the Ca' Cappelletti where Cecily and Eleanora were seated in front of the long windows facing the Grand Canal.

Cecily looked up from the book she had been attempting to read, her pleasure at seeing him tinged with apprehension. 'Raf! What brings you to Venice? I thought you were in Vicenza!'

He smiled. 'You, of course.' He looked over at Eleanora, who had thrust the sketch she was working on under a paper. The smile left his face. *'Buongiorno,* Lady Eleanora.'

'Buongiorno, Signor Vianoli,' Eleanora said curtly. She stood, clutching the sketchpad to her chest. 'I am certain you wish to speak to Cecily in private, so I will leave you.' She brushed past him.

Cecily glanced at Raf, who regarded Eleanora's retreating back with a slight frown. She had no idea why Eleanora did not seem to like Raf.

Raf said nothing about her when he turned to Cecily. 'A few days ago I met an acquaintance who informed me that a certain Austrian baron has been pursuing you. He also mentioned you were staying with Thais Margate. When I called there today, I was told you were no longer with Lady Margate but were now here.' He regarded her, his face serious. 'Is any of this true?'

'As you can see, I am here.' She had hardly expected such news to reach him.

'I was referring to the rest,' Raf said.

She hesitated for a moment. No purpose would be served by dissembling. He would learn the truth soon enough.

'Cecily?'

'Yes. I went to stay with Lady Margate. I did not wish

to stay here after Simon and Mariana left. It was too
awkward.'

'Because of Nico?'

She flushed a little.' Yes. I met Lady Margate a few
days before they departed and she suggested that I stay
with her. I accepted.'

'Nico allowed you to go?'

'He did not know. He accompanied Simon and Mariana as far as Mestre and then went on to the Villa
Cappelletti.'

'I see. What of Eberhart? Is this true as well?'

'Yes. He…he had an interest in me.'

He swore softly and she put her hand on his arm. 'But
no longer. He invited Lady Margate and me as guests
at a house party at his villa. Just before dinner Nico arrived.' She took a steadying breath. 'He told the Baron
that we are to be married. But only to protect me,' she
quickly added.

A peculiar gleam shone in his eye and then his lips
curved. 'Of course. I should have known that Nico would
not allow such a thing.' He took her hand. 'May I offer
you my felicitations for your future happiness. I must call
on him, however, since he did not ask my permission,
although he can be forgiven under the circumstances.'

She gathered her wits together. 'We are not really to
be married. The betrothal is only temporary.'

'Has it been made public?'

'I suppose, yes. The Baron announced it at the house
party.'

'And did Nico object?'

'No, he quite wished the Baron to do so.'

'He means to marry you. He will not publicly humiliate you by breaking off the betrothal.'

'But he does not mean to marry me!'

'Then he is only trifling with your affections?'

'Raf!' She realised he was only teasing her, but she was uncomfortable none the less. 'No, of course not. I do not want to marry him, either.'

'So you intend to humiliate him?'

'No!' She took a deep breath before she lost her temper. 'I would never do such a thing. We mutually agreed that, after a suitable period of time, we would break off the betrothal. There will be no marriage.'

His mouth curved in a most wicked grin. 'But I have decided otherwise.' He brushed a brief kiss across the back of her hand 'It is time that I speak with your *fidanzato*.'

'Raf!'

But he was gone. She suspected he meant to tease her but she was not completely certain. Not that she was certain about anything to do with Nico. Since their return to Venice she had seen him twice. Both times in company and both times he had treated her with all the solicitousness of a devoted fiancé. Nothing in his manner indicated they had spent a night in each other's arms. She prayed nothing in her manner indicated how his impersonal touch sent her pulse racing and made her knees tremble. She would die if he guessed how much she wanted to throw herself in his arms again.

She feared she was very much in danger of falling in love with him.

Nico looked up from the letter he was attempting to write. He started when he saw Raf. 'What the devil are you doing here?'

Raf strode into the study. 'I heard rumours that Eberhart had been pursuing Cecily. She informed me that you had already dealt with the situation in a most admirable fashion.'

'Her words, I imagine,' he said drily.

Raf grinned. 'Of course. You have my blessing.'

'She does not want to marry me.'

'Do you wish to marry her?'

He stood. 'I have asked her twice. She has turned me down the same number of times.'

'Has she? I wonder why. She cares for you.'

He shrugged. 'Not enough to marry me.' He could not quite keep the bitterness out of his voice. She had given no indication since they had returned to Venice that she had been affected by their night together. When all he could think about was having her beneath him, while he made love to her again and again.

'Do you want to marry her? Or are you only doing what is honourable?'

'I need a wife.'

Raf merely looked at him. Nico folded his arms. 'Well?'

'You are in love with her, are you not?'

Nico stared at him. 'Why the hell would you say that?'

'I cannot fathom why you would put yourself to so much trouble if you were not. But it is more than that. Your face softens when you speak of her. You look at her the way a man looks at a woman he loves. You frown now and swear because you wish to cover your hurt that she has refused you.'

He wanted to shout and call Raf a fool, but the words died on his lips. 'I loved Angelina.'

'As did I. But she has been dead for over thirteen years. You cannot bury yourself with her.'

'I've hardly done that.'

'No?'

'No, damn you.' He eyed Raf coolly. 'I could fling the same accusation at you. For I do not see any indication you have fallen in love again.'

'Perhaps I have not met the right woman.'

Nico said nothing.

'Cecily is not Angelina. But then you are not the same youth who fell so wildly in love with her. I wonder—if you were to meet her now for the first time, would you still want her? Or if you would discover it was Cecily you wanted after all?'

He turned and left Nico.

Nico did not move. He should have cursed Raf. Mowed him down. Finished the mill they started at the inn that night.

For what? Suggesting he might not want Angelina at

all? That he would choose Cecily instead? He should have thrown Raf's words after him, but he had not.

He had no idea why.

The letter arrived the next day. It was written in a thin, uneven hand that Nico did not recognise.

Cecily Renato will come to great harm if you do not end your betrothal. You must stay away from her.

He stared at it, his initial anger followed by a prick of fear. Barbarina. Of that he had no doubt, for the wording of the note bore too much resemblance to Barbarina's other dire warnings. How the devil had she found out about their engagement? The notice of their betrothal had been published only yesterday and few people had known beforehand. Except the guests who were present. Of those, only Thais knew Barbarina.

He frowned. He could think of no reason why Thais would take it upon herself to inform Barbarina. It made no sense.

He dismissed Thais; his greater concern was Barbarina. He had not thought much about Barbarina or the fête until now. Or the discussion with Raf and the possibility Barbarina had tried to harm Cecily.

Hell. Why had it slipped his mind? He stared down at the note, his expression grim. He had promised to look after Cecily and he'd failed when she had gone to stay with Thais. He would not make the same mistake again.

Chapter Seventeen

Eleanora turned to Cecily. 'Would you mind very much if we stop at one more shop? It is not very far from here. If you are not too fatigued, that is. I fear I can go on wandering for ever and never tire while my companions have nearly collapsed. I promise we will not get lost again.' They stood outside a small milliner's shop in one of the many narrow, fascinating streets winding through Venice.

Cecily smiled. 'Even if we did, I would not mind because it is such an interesting place in which to lose oneself.'

Eleanora smiled back at her. 'Oh, Cecily! I am so glad we are to be sisters! Have you tired of hearing that yet?'

'No, for I feel exactly the same.' She would not think about Eleanora's disappointment when she learned Cecily would not be her sister after all. For since her return to Venice nearly a week ago, she was more and more convinced marriage to Nico would lead to nothing but unhappiness for both of them. She shook off her uneasy thoughts—she did not want to worry Eleanora. 'Let us find your shop.'

Eleanora tucked her arm through Cecily's as they started off, Giacomo, the footman, trailing after them. The small streets between the tall narrow buildings fascinated Cecily. As did coming upon the quiet canals where one must cross a bridge in order to reach the next *calle*.

The small shop was located in a tiny *campo*. Several women were gathered around the cistern in its centre to procure buckets of water. A few children and a dog chased after a hoop. They crossed the square towards one of the little shops. The sign proclaimed one could procure papers, paints and brushes.

Cecily turned to Eleanora. 'You are interested in art, then?'

'A little,' Eleanora said carelessly. 'I sometimes like to sketch or attempt a watercolour. We do not need to go in if you would rather not.'

She was not certain why Eleanora suddenly seemed so hesitant. 'I will look for a present for Mariana as she also enjoys drawing.' She stepped into the shop and after a moment Eleanora followed.

No one was in the shop. Eleanora looked around and then went to the display of paints. Cecily looked about her. 'It is exactly the sort of place Raf would like.'

'Raf?' Eleanora started. 'Of course. He is an artist, is he not?'

'Yes, although he does not paint much any more.'

'Oh.' She turned back. After a few moments, she

chose a box of watercolours. 'This is all I want. Have you found something for Mariana?'

'Perhaps some paper and a new set of pencils. What would you recommend?'

Eleanora was soon engrossed in helping Cecily; by the time she stepped up to the counter to pay for the purchases, she was convinced Eleanora was more than an amateur artist, for she sounded exactly like Raf when Cecily had accompanied him to such a shop. Why then did Eleanora seem so reluctant to admit it? She held back her questions, not wanting to pry into Eleanora's affairs.

By the time they left the shop, Eleanora had reverted to her usual cheerful self. 'We can go over the Rialto,' Eleanora said as they crossed the *campo*. 'There is a little place where we can have an ice. It is not as grand as Florian's, but I must admit I like their ices better.'

Cecily was amazed how well Eleanora managed to find her way through the narrow maze of streets. Soon they were on the bridge that spanned the Grand Canal.

They slowly made their way up the shallow steps of the bridge through the crowds, stopping here and there to peer into one of the shops that lined the bridge. As they started down the other side of the bridge Eleanora's attention was caught by a display of books. 'I promise I will look at nothing else after this,' she told Cecily with a sheepish smile.

Cecily laughed. 'Should you promise that? There are certain to be more shops before we are home.'

'Yes, well.' Eleanora crossed to the display and

picked up one of the books. 'Come and look, Cecily. Is this not an odd illustration?'

Cecily was about to move to Eleanora's side when she heard a shout. She looked up and froze in horror, for a small cart was careening down the steps towards her. Just in time she jumped away. Her foot caught on the edge of the step and then she was falling.

'Cecily!' Eleanora cried. She dropped beside Cecily. 'Thank God! I thought the cart was going to hit you.'

Cecily attempted to sit up and her head spun for a moment. She saw the cart lying on its side a few steps below her.

'*Signora!*' Giacomo suddenly appeared. Soon a crowd of fascinated, horrified onlookers surrounded them.

Giacomo helped her to her feet and to the inside of the nearest shop where someone procured a chair and insisted she sit. Her entire body hurt, she had torn her glove on one hand and, to her chagrin, she felt tears prick her eyelids.

Eleanora knelt next to her, her face worried. 'I have sent Giacomo for Nico. You cannot possibly walk home.'

Oh, dear. 'I am fine, really. Just rather shaken. It is not very far. I am certain I will be able to walk.'

'Well, I am not about to let you. Nico would strangle me.' Eleanora rose as a burly man, who appeared to be the proprietor, approached them. With him was a man wearing the uniform of an Austrian officer.

The officer introduced himself as Captain Guttman. He had seen the disturbance and had come to make certain the *signora* had not been badly hurt and to offer his assistance. After Cecily reassured him she had sustained no serious injuries, he offered to see them home.

'It is kind of you to offer, but I have sent for my brother, the Duke of Severin,' Eleanora told him.

'I will wait with you until he arrives,' Guttman said. He had a pleasant face and manner and Cecily had recovered enough to notice the admiration in his eyes when he looked at Eleanora.

Shortly after that, the proprietor announced the *signora*'s cousin had arrived. Expecting to see Nico, Cecily was stunned to see Raf instead.

She half-rose and then winced. 'Raf? Why are you here?'

He strode to her side. 'I was just leaving the Ca' Cappelletti when Giacomo arrived and said you were hurt. Nico was not home, so I came. Are you all right?'

'Yes, of course. Just a little bruised.'

Raf looked at Eleanora. 'What happened?'

'She was almost knocked down by a cart. She fell down the steps when she tried to get away.'

Raf's mouth tightened. 'Whose cart was it?'

'I do not know,' Eleanora said.

Guttman spoke. 'I would like to speak to you for a moment, *signor*.'

Raf turned to him. 'Captain Guttman offered to stay with us until Nico…or you arrived,' Eleanora said quickly. 'Signor Vianoli is a relation of Signora Renato,' she told Guttman. 'Oh, dear, I should have made a more formal introduction.'

'Under the circumstances this will suffice,' Raf said. 'You had something you wanted to tell me, Captain?'

'Yes. If you will step outside with me.'

Raf followed him out and they returned a few minutes later. Raf's mouth was set in a hard line, although his expression relaxed a little when he informed Eleanora and Cecily he would take them home now.

Guttman took his leave, bowing over Eleanora's hand a trifle too long.

It did not escape Raf's notice. 'You have an admirer,' he said.

'Hardly,' Eleanora snapped. She picked up her reticule and then Cecily's. 'Did you bring a gondola?'

'It is waiting near the bridge.' Raf looked down at Cecily. 'I will carry you.'

'I can walk perfectly well.' She rose, albeit rather stiffly. 'Shall we go?'

Raf did not argue, although she suspected he wanted to. The thought crossed her mind that Nico would have swept her up into his arms no matter what she said. Which was one reason she should be glad he was not here.

However, he was on the small dock outside the palazzo with its black-and-white striped poles. He helped Eleanora step from the gondola to the landing and then held his hand out for Cecily. Raf helped her to her feet and she grasped Nico's hand. She stumbled a little, her balance shaky, and then she was on solid ground, his arm supporting her.

'Thank you.' She drew away from him and managed a step before she swayed again.

He was at her side. 'I am carrying you to your room.'

She looked up into his cool, arrogant face. 'I suppose if I said I was perfectly capable of walking, you would completely override my wishes.'

'You are correct in your supposition.'

A strangled giggle escaped her. 'Then I will not argue.'

'Good.' He swept her up, his arms strong and safe around her. He looked down at her, and she saw the worry in his eyes. He was overbearing, but it was because he wanted to take care of her.

She closed her eyes before he could read the truth in her face.

She had fallen in love with him.

Raf whirled around when Nico entered the salon. 'How is Cecily?'

'She is bruised, but nothing more serious, thank God.' Nico met Raf's eyes. 'Thank you for bringing her home.' He'd arrived at the palazzo minutes after Raf had left. Only his mother's calm reassurance that Eleanora was with Cecily and Raf would see her safely home kept him from going after her.

'I am only glad that I was still here when Giacomo arrived,' Raf said. 'It was not an accident.'

'How do you know?'

'An Austrian captain was waiting with Eleanora and Cecily when I arrived at the shop. He took me outside and told me that several witnesses claimed someone deliberately pushed the cart towards Cecily. A person in a black cloak and possibly wearing a mask.'

Nico's blood ran cold. 'I received a letter today. An anonymous letter. The writer said that if I did not end my betrothal to Cecily she would come to harm.'

'Do you still have the letter?'

'It is in my room.'

'I would like to see it.'

'Then come with me.'

Raf followed him to his room. He retrieved the letter from his writing desk and handed it to Raf. Raf read it and looked up his expression, grim.

'Do you recognise the handwriting?' Nico asked.

'I cannot say for certain.'

'Is it possible that Barbarina has returned to Venice?'

'I will call on Signora Gamba and see if Barbarina has returned to her. If she is not there, then I will leave for Avezza tomorrow—we need to know for certain if she has left Avezza and when.'

'And if she has not?'

'Then we will consider other possibilities. For now we must keep Cecily safe.'

'I will not allow her to leave the house unless I am with her. Or Giacomo. Once he understands what we want, he will guard her well.'

'How much do you want to tell your mother and sister? Or Cecily?'

'Not much until we discover Barbarina's whereabouts. I do not want to alarm them or Cecily unduly.'

'Very well. I will call on Signora Gamba now and let you know as soon as possible what I have discovered.

I will show myself out.' Raf looked at Nico. 'I know you will keep her safe.'

'Yes.' He would. He had failed Angelina, he would not fail Cecily.

'You still have not decided what you wish to wear? Perhaps go as Brighella? A shepherdess? Or,' Eleanora said with a teasing smile, 'should we ask Nico?'

'Nico?' Cecily jerked her thoughts back to the topic at hand. 'Ask him what?'

'What you should wear to the masquerade. I do not suppose he has mentioned to you what he plans to wear.'

'No, he hasn't said a thing. I am certain I can think of something. For myself, that is, not Nico. I can always wear a domino and a mask.' She could only imagine what he would say if she attempted to choose a costume for him.

Eleanora made a face. 'You are as bad as he is! That is exactly what he always wears to a masquerade. I had hoped you might persuade him to actually wear a costume. I have a splendid idea. We can go out today and find masks. There is a little shop near San Marco that has the most interesting ones that I have seen. We can find one for Nico as well.'

'Find what for me?' Nico asked.

Cecily started and looked up, her heart pounding much more than it should. He stood in the doorway of the small salon.

'A mask. Cecily and I are planning to visit a shop today to find masks for the masquerade. I suggested we find one for you since you seem too busy to go yourself.'

'Are you certain Cecily is well enough for such an excursion?' He did not look at all pleased by the idea.

'Of course I am,' Cecily said, annoyed that he did not directly address her.

'I will go with you,' he said abruptly. 'When do you wish to leave?'

Eleanora and Cecily both stared at him. 'Well?' he asked impatiently.

Eleanora recovered first. 'As soon as Cecily and I are ready. Before you change your mind.'

Chapter Eighteen

It was not Nico who changed his mind, however, but Eleanora. An hour and a half later, Cecily entered the salon and found Nico there with the Duchess. 'Eleanora is not well, but wants you and Nico to go without her. She would like both of you to choose a mask for her,' the Duchess said.

Cecily glanced at Nico, whose polite expression conveyed no enthusiasm for the idea. 'I do not mind waiting until Eleanora is better. I am certain the Duke has other business to attend to.'

A gleam appeared in his eye. 'On the contrary, I am at your service.'

The Duchess smiled. 'Good. He can take you to Florian's for an ice for you have not yet been there. In fact, Cecily has not even seen San Marco, although it is not at all the same since Napoleon. He was a criminal, no better than the *banditti*.' She spoke with an angry passion that Cecily had not witnessed before. She quickly collected herself. 'But it is still beautiful, he could not destroy that. So Domenico will take you and you will enjoy yourselves and not think of these things today.'

By the time they reached the Piazza San Marco, Cecily wondered why he had agreed to accompany her— he had said very little on the journey through the canals. Once or twice, when they had accidentally touched, he had jerked away as if burned. Not that she had fared much better, for her pulse jumped every time he came close to brushing against her. She wished she had thought of developing a headache.

The shop was located in a narrow L-shaped *calle* several streets behind the Piazza San Marco. Nico pushed opened the door and Cecily stepped inside. It was a tiny shop and masks of every description covered the shelves and counters. A white-haired man emerged from a room behind the counter. Through the curtain Cecily could see half-finished masks spread across a worktable. 'May I be of assistance?'

'We are interested in your masks,' Nico said.

'For the lady or yourself or both?'

'For both of us,' Cecily said before Nico could answer. Eleanora had wanted him to get a mask so she would make certain he did.

'Very good, *signora*.' He came around the side of the counter. 'Do you wish to find a mask for the *signor* first?'

'For the *signora* first,' Nico said.

'Allow me to show you what I have.'

In a few minutes he had set out a bewildering assortment of masks. Some were plain white ovals; others were lavishly decorated with feathers or sequins. There were full masks and half-masks and Cecily hardly knew where to start. She finally picked up a purple one, all too aware of Nico hovering near her shoulder. 'We must choose one for Eleanora first.' She set down the mask and forced herself to concentrate on them instead of Nico. She finally found a silk half-mask in blue and gold. 'What do you think?' she asked Nico.

'I have no doubt she will like it.'

He certainly was no help. 'I will take this,' she told the proprietor. She turned back to the selection, finding she had very little enthusiasm for choosing one for herself. She picked up one of the plain white masks. 'This will do.'

'No.' Nico removed the mask from her hand. 'This one.' He picked up a mask. It was of green silk and exquisitely decorated with small jewels. He stepped back. 'I want to see it on you.'

She stared at it. 'It is very beautiful, but…'

'Turn around. I will tie the ribbons.'

She obeyed and he stepped close to her, his body almost touching hers. His hands brushed her hair as he tied the strings. He moved his hands to her shoulders and she had the sudden desire to lean back into his arms as she had that night at the Villa Barbarigo. Oh, lord, what was wrong with her?

'Let me see you.' His hands fell from her shoulders.

She slowly turned around and faced him, grateful the mask would hide her embarrassing desire. His gaze travelled over her in a way that brought heat to her face. 'I will buy this.' His voice was husky.

'The *signora* is beautiful, no? It is a very fine mask, made by my son.'

Cecily untied the strings. 'I cannot accept this,' she told him in English. 'It is not proper.'

'You are my fiancée, so it is quite proper. Don't argue. I am buying it for you and you will wear it.'

'Indeed. Then it is only fair that I choose one for you that you will wear.'

'I have a mask.'

'But I did not choose it,' she said with a tight smile.

An odd glint appeared in his eye. 'Very well, my dear. Find something for me.'

She turned to the shopkeeper. 'I wish to look at masks for the *signor*.'

'Of course.' He pulled several from a shelf and spread them out before her. While she examined them, he brought out more.

She finally found what she was looking for. 'This one,' she told him. 'I want you to try it on.'

'Only if you will tie the strings for me,' he said softly. He suddenly looked quite dangerous and she wished she had not made the offer. But it was too late and she refused to back down.

'Turn around. You will need to bend a little.'

As soon as her hands touched his thick, dark hair she knew she had made a mistake. Not only by her own pounding heart and trembling fingers, but by the way he suddenly stilled under her hands. She finished tying the strings and stepped back, her mouth dry.

'It suits the *signor*.'

The shopkeeper's voice startled her out of her trance. She glanced at Nico. 'Yes. Yes, it does. He will take it.' She hardly knew what she was saying. To her relief, Nico removed the mask himself. She pretended interest in a display of masks while the shopkeeper wrapped their purchases, every nerve in her body on edge.

Nico finally turned. 'Shall we go?'

She jumped. 'Yes.'

She followed him out the door, careful to avoid touching him. Outside the shop, she paused. 'Perhaps we should return to the Ca' Cappelletti. I am certain your sister is eager to see our purchases.' She started to walk away.

He caught her arm. 'You are going the wrong way.'

'Oh.' She looked up at him and her heart pounded at the expression in his eyes. 'Then I had best turn around.'

'Damn it, Cecily, this is impossible.'

'What is?' She could barely form the words.

'This,' he murmured. He stepped towards her and then his mouth was on hers. Her eyes fluttered shut and she gave herself over to his kiss, hardly noticing when the package slid to the ground. He pressed her to him and her arms circled his neck, her hands finally tangling in his silky hair. His mouth was hard and demanding and she met him kiss for kiss.

A sense that someone watched them broke into her consciousness. She pulled away and he lifted his head, his eyes heavy with desire. He saw her face. 'What is it?'

She looked around. The street was deserted. 'I thought someone was here…watching us. I am being fanciful again.' She shivered. The high walls of the buildings seemed to close in on them.

'You were not fanciful last time. Come, we need to leave this place.' He retrieved the fallen package and then took her hand.

The grim set to his jaw alarmed her as he led her through the narrow street, around the corner and through the short passage to the streets that would take them back to San Marco. The crowded street was reassuring and when they finally entered the piazza, her uneasiness dissipated.

He dropped her hand. 'We can stop at Florian's before we return home.'

'Yes.' He led her across the piazza to the colonnaded row of shops. They sat down and she looked across at him. His face still looked grim. 'What is wrong?' she asked. 'Do you really think there was someone there?'

He looked over at her. 'I do not know…'

'Why such sober faces? I hope you are not quarrelling already!'

They both looked up. Thais stood next to them, a quizzical expression in her blue eyes. She was very prettily dressed in a canary yellow pelisse and matching bonnet.

Nico rose. 'Good day, Lady Margate.'

'Lady Margate? When have you become so formal?' She turned a smile on Cecily. 'How are you, dear Cecily? It has been quite dull without you. You cannot imagine how I have missed our little chats.'

'Perhaps you would join us,' Cecily said.

'If Severin would not object to sharing you. I suspect him of wanting to keep you solely for himself.' She cast a droll look in his direction.

'I do,' he said coolly.

'He is only teasing,' Cecily said hastily. 'Please sit down.'

'Thank you.' Thais took the chair opposite Cecily. After a moment, Nico sat down next to her. 'You have been shopping,' Thais said. 'What have you purchased?'

'Masks,' Nico said briefly. It was quite apparent he did not welcome Thais' company.

'Masks? For the Weston masquerade? How delightful! Where did you go?'

'In a little shop nearby which Lady Eleanora recommended.'

'I shall have to visit it myself for I have not yet purchased anything!' She looked up at the waiter who had returned to take her order and asked him for a coffee. After he left she smiled at Nico. 'I cannot help but think of Angelina whenever I visit the piazza. She so loved St Mark's. Do you remember how devastated she was when Napoleon removed the horses?'

Nico's face tightened. 'Yes.'

'I can only imagine the pleasure she would have felt upon their return!' She turned to Cecily. 'She was such a sweet girl, rather like your own Mariana. When I first saw your daughter I was quite reminded of Angelina. It is a pity you did not meet her, for I am certain you would have adored her, do you not think, Severin?'

A sick feeling rose in Cecily's throat at his bleak expression. She turned to Thais. 'I know I would have liked her very much.' She looked up and saw the waiter carrying a tray towards them. 'Our refreshments are here, thank goodness. I am starving.' She prayed Thais would be distracted by the cakes and coffee.

The waiter put the tray down on an adjoining table and set the plates and cups in front of them. After the waiter left, Thais took a sip of her coffee before speaking. 'Angelina always had a lemon ice when we were here. I quite forgot until now. Does this not remind you of the time the three of us came here? Except you are now betrothed to Cecily instead of Angelina.' She picked up her fork and calmly took a bite of her cake.

The thought darted through Cecily's mind that Thais meant to hurt Nico. She must stop her from saying anything more about Angelina. 'Have you yet decided on a costume for the masquerade? We have talked of nothing else.' She began to chatter about the various ideas Eleanora had suggested and when she had exhausted that topic began describing the plot of a novel she had just read in minute detail. Thais had no chance to do more than say a word before Cecily prattled over her. She was quite aware that Nico stared at her as if she had gone mad, but at least he had lost that horrible stricken look.

As soon as the bill had been paid, she rose. 'How nice to see you, Thais. But we really must return home.'

'I quite understand.' Her smile was guileless. She turned to Nico. 'I hope we will have the chance to speak of Angelina again. I miss her just as I know you do.' She walked off before he could reply.

Cecily touched his arm. 'We must go.'

He looked down at her as if he'd forgotten she was there. 'Yes. We must.'

He said little on the tedious journey home and Cecily had no idea if he even noticed her presence.

At the top of the staircase, outside the doors to the salon, he stopped. 'I will see you at dinner.'

'Yes. Thank you, your Grace.' She turned and left him. He had shut her out and she knew there was nothing she could say to help him.

Chapter Nineteen

Nico looked up just as Cecily appeared in the doorway of the small salon. He caught his breath. Ready for the masquerade, she was dressed as a lady from the preceding century. Her gown of embroidered cream-and-green silk emphasised her small waist and the soft curves of her breast. She wore a white wig, which was unexpectedly erotic, and he felt his groin tighten in response. For a moment she stared at him and he thought he glimpsed a similar awareness until her face closed. 'Good evening, your Grace. You wished to see me, I believe.'

He did not like the impersonal politeness in her voice. The same politeness that had been there since the day at San Marco. He had no idea how to bridge the gulf between them. He kept his own voice cool. 'I do. I have something to give you.'

'To give me?' She entered the room and stood a few feet from him.

He forced his eyes away from her lovely mouth and

pulled the small packet from his waistcoat pocket. 'A ring.' He unwrapped it. 'Hold out your hand.'

She looked at the ring and then quickly up at him, dismay clearly written all over her face. 'But that is the ring the duchess wears.'

'It is traditionally presented by the Dukes of Severin to their intended brides upon their betrothal. My mother wished you to have it now.'

'It is lovely, but I cannot wear it,' she said quietly.

'Why?' He felt angry and frustrated. 'We are betrothed, are we not?'

'Yes.' She drew in a breath. 'It is only temporary.'

'Then you will wear the ring until we put a halt to it. It will look damnably odd if you do not. Hold out your hand.'

She did so. He took her slender hand in his own and slipped the ring on to her finger. He stared down at her hand now wearing the symbol of his family. He hadn't expected to feel anything, but the surge of possessive desire startled him.

She pulled her hand away. 'It is very lovely. I will take good care of it, your Grace.'

'Don't do that.'

She looked up at him. 'Don't do what?'

'Act as if we are strangers. No, worse, as if you can hardly stand to be in the same room with me.'

She lifted her chin. 'That is not true!'

'No? Ever since we have returned to Venice you have treated me with nothing but cold disdain.'

'I could accuse you of the same thing. You barely

speak to me except when necessary and after that day we bought the masks you have hardly been around!'

'Only because you have made it clear you do not want me around.'

'This conversation is pointless. You do not want me around and I do not want you around. It appears neither one of us is particularly fond of the other. I really think, your Grace, that perhaps we should end this betrothal now.' She started to tug the ring from her finger.

'If you do not want to marry me, then perhaps you will consider becoming my mistress.' He regretted the words as soon as they left his mouth.

Her head jerked up, the colour draining from her face. Her chin inched up a notch and she met his eyes. 'I would be most honoured to become your mistress.'

This time he was the one who started. 'You are bluffing, my sweet Cecily.'

'Only if you were bluffing when you asked me.' The little cool smile on her face did nothing to improve his temper.

'Not at all. I am leaving for the villa tomorrow. When I return we will negotiate the terms.' He had no idea what he was saying.

'You are leaving?' For a moment, her gaze faltered and then she recovered. 'I will look forward to discussing your terms.'

'Then let us seal our bargain. Properly.' He did not give her a chance to reply, instead he swept her into his arms and found her mouth. He finally lifted his head and released her. Her cheeks were flushed, her lips swollen, her breathing hard.

He stepped back, angry at his loss of control. 'You may slap me now if you'd like.'

'No. I do not think that will be necessary. The others are waiting for us. You are going to the masquerade, are you not?'

'Cecily.'

She swept from the room, leaving him staring after her.

He could no longer deny that he was falling in love with her.

Cecily stood with Bernardo and Eleanora in the salon of the huge palazzo leased by Sir Thomas and Lady Weston. Festoons of flowers and vines decorated the room and Chinese lanterns lent an exotic eastern aura.

'The musicians should arrive soon,' Eleanora remarked. She looked beautiful and quite intriguing in a flowing gown of dark blue silk.

'Then we should go to the *androne* now so we might have the best view.' The highlight of the evening was to be a barge of musicians arriving in front of the palazzo at midnight. Bernardo, dressed as Pantalone, held out one arm to Eleanora and the other to Cecily. Cecily smiled at him, determined she would not think about Nico. She had no idea where he was for Octavia had spirited him away shortly after they arrived.

Their parting before the masquerade had dashed any hopes she might have secretly entertained that something was possible between them. He'd asked her to become his mistress in anger and she had accepted in equal anger. She knew he regretted his words, the instant she saw his face after he'd kissed her. She was too numb to care, so when Bernardo appeared, a handsome troubadour, she found she had no trouble engaging in a mild flirtation with him. Perhaps her heart would not break after all.

Where was Cecily? Nico had lost sight of her among the crowd of masked guests. He finally spotted her with Bernardo and Eleanora heading towards the small hall that led to the stairs. He wanted to go after her, but he would hardly blame her if she refused to talk to him. Not after he'd insulted her. He felt a flicker of despair every time he thought of her face after he'd offered *carte blanche*.

'Severin, I must speak with you. In private.'

He turned and found a woman in a black half-mask and domino at his side. For a moment he thought he was staring at Barbarina Zanetti, then just as quickly recognised Thais Margate despite the black wig covering her curls. 'This hardly seems the time for a private conversation.'

'Please, I must talk to you before it is too late.'

She had an almost desperate note in her voice he had never heard before. 'What is it?'

'Not here. There is a room off the salon where we can go.' She placed her hand on his arm, her grip firm as if she had no intention of allowing him to get away.

Torn between curiosity and unease, he followed her across the crowded room and into one of the smaller rooms. Surprisingly enough, it was empty. She turned to face him, and even through the slits of her mask he felt the intensity of her gaze.

'What is wrong?' he asked.

'You cannot marry Cecily Renato. It is all wrong.'

'Why is it wrong?' he asked carefully.

'Because I love you. I always have.'

'Thais…' Shocked, he took a step back as she came towards him. He found himself backed up against a sofa.

'You must care for me at least a little.' She stood so close she was almost touching him.

Was she drunk? He caught her hand. 'Do not say anything more that you will later regret.'

She gave a peculiar little laugh. 'I only regret I did not tell you this when you were so determined to marry Angelina. Would it have changed your mind?'

He released her hand. 'I loved Angelina.'

'You could not have. Just as you do not love Cecily.'

'You are wrong. I love Cecily. I am going to marry her.'

She stared at him. 'I will never let that happen.' She spoke in a cold, controlled voice.

'What do you mean?'

'I mean that you will never marry her.' She whirled away from him and before he could stop her had run from the room. He dashed after her, but she slipped past a trio of harlequins. A feeling of dread washed over him and he knew he must find Cecily.

He started through the crowd. Many of the guests were gathered in front of the tall windows facing the grand canal. Others were leaving the salon and starting down the stairs to the *androne*. The barge of musicians must be coming. He vaguely remembered Eleanora mentioning they would watch the barge from the *androne*. He crossed the salon and out of the corner of his eye saw a short dark figure in a black cloak. The hair on the back of his neck prickled. He pushed his way through the crowd, ignoring the indignant mutters at his rudeness, and reached the stairs. For a moment, he could see nothing and then saw the black-cloak figure was already in the *androne*.

He ran down them, shoving past a quartet of youths who were idling on the stairs. He had nearly reached the bottom when he saw Eleanora and Bernardo. They were nearly at the gates leading from the palazzo to the dock on the canal. At first he did not see Cecily and then he caught a glimpse of her green mask. He heard someone call his name, but he paid no heed.

He jumped down the last step and began to run across the marble floor through the crowd.

Cecily stood next to Bernardo on the small dock in front of the palazzo. Sounds of a Vivaldi concerto drifting out over the water heralded the approach of the floating concert.

The crowd pushed forward, hoping to glimpse the barge. A large nun jostled her way in front of Cecily, who stumbled a little. She righted herself and found Bernardo was no longer next to her. The mass of guests seemed to close around her and a sliver of panic shot through her.

A hand closed around her arm. She attempted to draw her arm away and found herself looking at a dark shrouded figure. A prickle of fear shot down her back, for there was something sinister and familiar about the figure. 'I think, sir, that you have mistaken me for someone else.'

'Good evening, Cecily.'

She nearly sagged with relief. 'Thais. You frightened me.'

Her grip tightened around Cecily's wrist and she pulled something from the folds of her garment. 'You cannot marry him, you know.' With sick shock Cecily saw a flash of silver and realised she held a dagger. Thais raised it just as the musicians reached the palazzo, the strains of the concerto echoing all round.

'No!' Cecily pulled away with all of her strength and stumbled. At the same time another dark figure burst through the crowd and leaped towards Thais. They both tumbled into Cecily and all three of them fell into the cold, dark water.

She went under for a moment and then clawed her way up, gasping and terrified. Her heavy skirts wrapped around her legs and she fought to keep from slipping into the chilly depths. There was a splash next to her. Strong arms grasped her. She flailed out, fearing it was Thais who meant to drown her.

'Cecily.'

Nico. She had no idea how he came to be there. 'Thais, she...she tried to stab me.'

'Don't talk, sweetheart. I need to get you out.'

He helped her to the edge of the dock. He half-lifted

her as a man reached down and pulled her out. Her knees shook so hard she could barely stand and she was hardly aware of the voices and music around her. Someone draped a long cape over her shoulders. 'Come, *signora*, you must go inside.' She looked up and saw a man standing next to her.

'No. The…the others.' She realised Nico had not followed her out and in the dim light of the torches she thought she saw him swimming towards a black shape.

'Cecily. Thank God.'

Raf was suddenly at her side. 'Where is Nico?'

'In…in the water.'

He ran towards the dock just as Bernardo and Eleanora appeared. 'Cecily. Oh, dear lord, it was you.' Eleanora's face was pale. 'We must get you inside.'

'No. Wait.' For Raf had stooped to help another woman from the water. A woman whose hair was long and dark instead of blonde. He laid her on the dock and knelt beside her. Cecily ran towards her.

Cecily dropped down next to Raf. 'Barbarina!' Barbarina's eyes were closed, but she was breathing, thank God. She gripped Barbarina's hand. 'Barbarina, it is Cecily.'

Barbarina's eyes opened for a moment. 'You are safe. I tried to stop her…tried to warn you…warn him that she is wicked.'

'You must not talk.' She squeezed her hand and then quickly slipped the cape from her shoulders and covered Barbarina. 'She…she saved my life, Raf. We must take her inside. It is too cold.'

'I know.' He looked up and Cecily saw Nico standing next to them. Water dripped down his forehead and he was breathing heavily. 'How is she?'

'Alive,' Raf said. 'But barely. The other?'

'I could do nothing.'

Raf bent towards Barbarina. 'Barbarina. I will carry you inside.'

Her eyes fluttered open. 'No.' She looked past him to Nico. 'Must tell him…the Duke…' Her breathing was heavy. She closed her eyes.

'Nico?' Alarmed, Cecily looked up at him.

Nico dropped to the ground beside her. 'Signora Zanetti. Barbarina.'

With a great effort, she opened them. 'I saw her that day, when Angelina…'

'When Angelina what?'

'When she went to meet you. She followed… Angelina.' She paused, struggling for breath. 'She killed Angelina. I…I saw it in her eyes. At the fête, she…tried to kill Cecily. Because of you.' Her eyes closed and she drew in one last shuddering breath.

Horrified, Cecily stared at Barbarina and then at the others. 'Nico?' she whispered. He looked as if he'd turned to stone.

Chapter Twenty

Cecily set her book aside on the bench and waited for Nico to cross the *androne* to the courtyard where she sat. Two days had passed since Barbarina's funeral; nearly a week since the nightmarish masquerade. Her heart sank a little when she saw his face—he still wore the remote expression of a man who was utterly unreachable, buried away in his grief.

'I wanted to tell you that I am leaving Venice for a while,' he said.

'When will you go?'

'Today. In a few hours.'

She would not let him see her dismay. 'Where will you go?'

'To a small villa near Vicenza.'

She stood. He was polite, none of the arrogance she so associated with him present. If only he would attempt to ride roughshod over her. Or scold her. But he'd done nothing but shut himself away since that night. 'I am sorry.' She could think of nothing else.

If anything, his expression only shuttered more. 'Why? You almost lost your life because of me.'

'You are wrong. I almost lost my life because of Thais. You saved my life. You and Barbarina.'

He said nothing. A sort of angry despair washed over her. 'Thais deceived all of us, even me,' Cecily said. 'I do not want to spend the rest of my life thinking that you blame yourself for what happened to me. I could not bear it. So for my sake, I pray you will not.' She picked up her book. 'I will say goodbye to you now. As always, I wish you happiness.' She waited for him to speak and when he did not, she left him. She did not look back.

Raf called just before Nico was about to step into the gondola. 'What do you think you are doing?' he asked Nico without preamble.

'I am leaving Venice.'

'Why? Because you blame yourself for Angelina? For Cecily?'

'I am about to leave. I would prefer to continue this discussion later.' Or not at all.

'Damn you, Domenico. We will have this discussion now.'

Nico had rarely seen Raf so angry. He suspected that, if he were to step into the gondola, Raf would follow. 'We cannot talk here. Come into one of the offices.'

Inside the office, Raf glared at him. 'What is it? You

wish to take the guilt for Angelina's death upon your-self? You were not the one who pushed her that day.'

'No, but Barbarina spoke the truth; because of me Thais killed Angelina and tried to kill Cecily. I should have seen, should have known, what she was capable of doing.'

'None of us did. Do you think I have not blamed my-self for the very same things? Thais did everything pos-sible to convince me that Angelina was not happy with you—that Angelina loved me. I had some idea that Thais was jealous of Angelina, but it never occurred to me she would harm her. What of Barbarina? She sus-pected, but yet said nothing.'

'Thais did not have an obsession with you.'

'So that makes Angelina's death your fault? Did you encourage Thais?'

For the first time since that night, Nico felt a stirring of anger. 'No, damn it, but I should have made it clear I wanted nothing to do with her.'

'Do you think it would have mattered? She was not right; she was undoubtedly mad.' He looked at Nico. 'What of Cecily? You will leave her here by herself?'

'She is with my family. She has you if you are ever around.'

'She is betrothed to you, or perhaps you have forgot-ten that.'

'It is only temporary.'

'She loves you.'

He looked at Raf. 'Then she is a fool.'

Raf's fist balled. 'I should call you out for that,' he said softly.

'Choose your weapon.'

Raf stared at him for a moment. 'I am beginning to believe she is better off without you. She needs a man who will treasure her love, not trample it underfoot.' He strode to the door and then paused. 'Angelina is dead. And you have buried yourself with her.' He was gone.

Cecily looked around the bedchamber. The dressing table was bare; her fans and gloves neatly packed away in her bandbox. In another half an hour she would be leaving with Raf. She had decided she must return to Avezza. She had left a note for Nico with instructions it was to be given to him upon his return. She had left the ring with the Duchess.

'My dear, are you certain you want to leave us?' the Duchess asked. Cecily had not heard her enter the room. 'I do not like the thought of you returning to your home alone like this. You have been through a great deal in the past few weeks.'

'I will not be completely alone. Raf promised he will stay in Avezza for a few days.'

'Domenico needs you.'

She looked up at the Duchess. 'If anything, he has made it quite clear he does not. He would not allow me to give him anything. Not sympathy, not kindness. When I told him I was sorry he told me I did not need to be.' Just as Marco had refused to accept her comfort.

'My dear.'

'I can do nothing to help him,' Cecily whispered.

The Duchess was silent for a moment before speaking. 'He has not allowed any of us to help him, just as he did not before. In some way, for him, it is almost as if Angelina has died again. He blamed himself, you see, thirteen years ago, and I can only imagine how he must feel now. Not only about Angelina, but also about you. I have no doubt he feels he failed to protect you from Thais.'

'He is wrong. He did everything he could.'

'For him that was not enough,' she said gently. She took Cecily's hands. 'I cannot fault you for wanting to go, for you can do nothing for him unless he allows it. I only pray that he will open his heart before it is too late.' She bent forward and pressed a kiss on Cecily's cheek. 'It is time for you to go down.'

He had gone to the villa in the hills above Vicenza for a few days, but the solitude had brought him no relief. Instead his dreams had been restless and filled with imagies of Cecily and Angelina. He had given up and left for Treviso, the town where Angelina was buried.

Her grave was in the small cemetery near the villa that once belonged to her family. He found the marker easily enough, under the spreading shade of an old tree.

He thought of her dark laughing eyes set in an oval face, which she considered too long and which he found adorable, and her beautiful, curving body. She had enchanted him; he had wondered how any creature so exquisite and alive could adore him the way she had. He'd always had a sense she was not quite real; even their kisses tasted of magic, and he sometimes feared he would open his eyes and find she'd vanished like some enchanted creature.

In the end, she had vanished, leaving him bereft and empty-handed and wondering if his very attempts to capture her had somehow destroyed her.

In the end she had been destroyed because of him.

As Cecily had almost been.

Raf did not blame him. Nor did Cecily. He would never forget the look of despair on her face when she walked away from him, as if by holding himself responsible he was somehow hurting her as well.

Raf said Cecily loved him. He wondered if that was still true.

Raf was correct; he was not the same youth who fell in love with Angelina. *I wonder—if you were to meet her now for the first time, would you still want her? Or if you would discover it was Cecily you wanted after all?*

For despite the hours he and Angelina had spent together, talking and laughing, and flirting, he could not recall one time when he had told her anything of substance. He had not spoken to her of the sorrow he felt over his father's ailing health. Or the apprehension he felt at the prospect of becoming the next Duke and finding himself responsible for his family's vast holdings and wealth and all those, family and employees, who would be dependent upon his goodwill and judgement. The few times he had brought such things up, she would tease him for his seriousness. 'You will become dull, Nico, if you continue to speak of such solemn matters!'

He could imagine telling Cecily those things. Just as

he could imagine coming to her now when he needed her quiet understanding. Raf had asked him, if he met Angelina for the first time now, would he want her?

He had no idea if she would even want him, for he had changed just as Raf had said. He was no longer the young raffish marquis she had adored. He had a reputation for a cynical coolness she would undoubtedly find appalling and he spent more time on his estates than he did in London.

With cold clarity he suspected, if they met now, they might feel nothing more than a passing attraction for each other. If Cecily was with him, he doubted he would look at Angelina at all.

The realisation brought him no comfort. Tears sprang to his eyes. He bowed his head and for the first time since Angelina's death he was finally able to weep for her.

And allow her to rest in peace at last.

He decided to return to Venice that day. He must see Cecily. He had hurt her, trampled over her heart, just as Raf said he had. He had thought only of his own needs when he'd offered for her. He wanted her, but on his terms. He had not been prepared to give her all of himself, but he wanted all of her. He had not understood why, if she cared for him, she would refuse him.

He understood now. He would offer himself to her and pray she might forgive him.

Nico found his mother in the library. She was sitting on the sofa, a book open on her lap. She tore her gaze away at his approach. A warm smile lit her face when she saw him. 'Domenico. You are finally back.'

She set her book down on the sofa and rose. She held out her hands and searched his face. 'I think that you are better.'

'I am better. Much better.'

'I am glad.'

'So am I.' He pressed her hands. 'Where is Cecily?'

'She is not in Venice. She left for Avezza with Rafaele.'

He felt a stab of fear and then anger. 'Why? With Raf?'

She hesitated. 'She sent a note that she wished given to you when you returned.'

'Where is the note?'

'In your bedchamber.'

He released her hands. 'Then you will forgive me if I go to retrieve it now.'

'Of course.'

He found the note on the bureau. He broke the seal and quickly scanned the brief missive.

To His Grace the Duke of Severin,

I am most deeply grateful for your kindness in offering me the protection of your name so that I might be safe from the attentions of a man whom I find most repugnant. Under the circumstances I feel it is best that I return to Avezza and that we do not meet again.

As always, I wish you all happiness,
Cecily Renato

He cursed. What the devil did she mean by saying she felt it best they never meet again? He had intended to beg her for forgiveness and then insist she marry him. And why the hell was she with Raf? Common sense told him it was quite natural for Raf to escort her, but he remembered Raf's parting words—what if Raf had changed his mind and decided he wanted Cecily after all?

At the very least she could tell him face to face that she never wanted to see him again.

He went down the stairs and met his mother in the hall. 'I am leaving for Avezza,' he told her.

'What will you say to her?'

He stopped. 'I intend to ask her exactly why she found it necessary to leave Venice before I returned. I will also inform her that if she wishes to end our betrothal she must do it in person.'

'Perhaps she thinks it is you who wishes to end the betrothal.'

His brow snapped down. 'Why the devil would she think that?'

'What did you tell her when you left Venice?'

'I told her I was leaving for a few days. What else was I to tell her?'

'I do not suppose you told her that you love her?'

He could feel an unfamiliar heat rising to his cheeks. 'No.'

'Then I think you must.' She gave him a gentle smile. 'Go, then. I will inform Eleanora you needed to leave straight away. I have no doubt she will understand.'

* * *

Cecily found the leather-bound book under a pile of old shawls in Barbarina's room. She picked it up and saw it was a journal. How odd, for Barbarina did not seem the sort of person who would write down her innermost thoughts. She carefully opened it and saw the delicate, neat writing did not resemble Barbarina's spidery scrawl at all. The first page was dated 1 January 1803.

She rose and sat on the chair near Barbarina's bed. She turned to the last page: 15 August 1803. *I am going to meet Nico...*

Nearly an hour later, she slowly closed the book, tears streaming down her cheeks. Angelina had not believed Thais' lies; she had loved Nico up until the very end. She wanted to meet him that day, not to call off their betrothal, but to tell him she would marry him.

Barbarina must have read this as well; why had she allowed Nico to believe Angelina no longer wanted to marry him? But then Barbarina had done nothing to stop Thais; she had known about Thais' lies and had used them herself to attempt to drive a wedge between Nico and Angelina.

Because she hoped Angelina would marry Raf if Nico was gone. It was only after Angelina died that Barbarina realised how truly wicked Thais was.

She stood. Perhaps Nico wanted nothing from her, but she had one last thing she would give him before he returned to England. She had no doubt he would marry soon; most likely a proper English girl who would provide him with beautiful dark-eyed children…

How ridiculous. She could not think of such things. She would miss him. Terribly. She was grateful to him for so much. She had finally broken out of her self-imposed exile. She had written a letter to her grandmother and, for the first time in years, the burden of the anger she had carried towards her grandmother was now gone. She had even begun to think of visiting England.

She had loved again and, although he had not returned her love, it had not destroyed her.

Perhaps knowing that Angelina had loved him to the end would ease some of the pain he carried. She would give this to him, but it was not her gift…it was Angelina's.

Raf did not look surprised when she told him she planned to leave for Venice the next day or when she explained why. 'I will, of course, accompany you.'

'You do not need to.'

'It is what I wish. For you, for Nico and for Angelina.'

Chapter Twenty-One

They stopped at an inn the late afternoon of the following day. Cecily stepped down from her carriage and waited while Raf spoke with Figaro.

She started towards the inn and then her heart lurched when she saw the crest on one of the carriages standing near by.

It could not be. No, that was quite impossible. Perhaps she could inquire if an Englishman was staying at the inn. Then determine if he was dark and spoke fluent Italian and was a duke. If so, she would...

'Good evening, Cecily.'

She spun around, her hand going to her breast. The blood rushed to her head and for a dreadful moment she thought she would swoon.

He stood behind her, arms folded. He was hatless, the sun slanting through the trees onto his hair.

'I...I had no idea you were here,' she stammered.

'And if you had, you would have jumped back into

your carriage and driven away as quickly as possible?'

'I do not know.'

He smiled, although it was not pleasant. She knew, then, he had received her note. He was angry.

Part of her was relieved. If he could feel angry, then perhaps there was hope after all. His gaze fell on something behind her and then his brow snapped down. 'Vianoli. What the devil is he doing here?'

'He is escorting me to Venice.'

'The hell he is.' He strode past her to Raf.

'Nico! Stop!' He looked as if he planned to knock Raf down. She hurried after him and caught his sleeve just as he stopped in front of Raf.

'What are you doing with my fiancée?' he demanded.

Raf's brow shot up. 'Is she? I was under the impression that your betrothal was of a temporary nature.'

'You are wrong. At least until she tells me to my face that she will not marry me.'

Raf glanced at Cecily. 'Do you wish to tell him that?'

'I…' She took a deep breath. 'This is ridiculous. We cannot stand out here and discuss this.'

'Then we will go inside,' Nico said. He took her arm. 'Coming, Vianoli?'

'Of course.' If anything, Raf looked slightly amused.

She glanced up at Nico. 'You can release my arm. I do not plan to run away.'

'I beg your pardon.' He dropped his hand away. They went inside to one of the vacant public rooms.

'Where are you travelling to?' Raf asked politely.

'Avezza.'

'Ah.'

'And why are you and Cecily going to Venice?'

'That is for Cecily to tell you.'

Nico turned to her. 'Why?' he demanded.

In an inn with Nico glaring at both her and Raf was not how she'd envisioned telling him about the journal. She wondered why she had ever felt sorry for him, for he was in the stupid arrogant duke role that she detested. Why was it any of his business what she was doing with Raf? 'I would prefer to tell you at a time when you are not in such a disagreeable mood, your Grace. And when you speak to me in civil tones. For now I wish to go to my room.'

He stepped in front of her. 'At least tell me if you are in love with Raf.'

Her mouth fell open. She looked up into his dark eyes and the hard set of his jaw. 'At the moment, I do not think I am in love with anyone. Or ever want to be. Good evening, your Grace.' She swept past him with a feeling of satisfaction.

Nico turned on Raf as soon as she had left the room. 'Do you plan to let her walk away like that?'

'Do you?'

'She has made it clear she wants nothing to do with me.'

Raf merely looked at him. 'So why are you going to Avezza?'

'To see Cecily. To beg her to marry me. If it is not too late.' His gaze hardened a little. 'I will not let you have her without a fight if you have changed your mind about wanting her.'

'She is not in love with me. Nor am I in love with her. However, that does not mean I intend to let you have her. Not until I am assured that you will not walk all over her heart.'

'I love her,' he said quietly.

Raf eyed him for a moment. 'Then I suggest you tell her that.'

'If she will listen.'

'I will talk to her and ask her to dine with you. However, if she does not wish to hear you, I cannot force her.'

Hope was beginning to rise in his chest. 'I would not expect you to.' Not that he intended to allow her to refuse.

Raf smiled a little. 'One more thing—I would suggest you actually ask Cecily to marry you rather than telling her she will do so.'

Cecily gazed around the room. It was small but at least the bed linens appeared fresh and there were no unpleasant smells that would indicate a general lack of cleanliness. She sat down on the single chair in the room. She had no idea whether to laugh or to cry. Was it possible Nico was acting so oddly because he thought she was in love with Raf? That she and Raf were travelling together for some clandestine purpose? Just as Raf had accused her and Nico of the same thing?

They could be, at this very moment, fighting in the

public room downstairs for all she knew. Not that she particularly cared. Perhaps they would knock some sort of rational sense into each other. At any rate, she was quite weary of feeling responsible for everyone else.

She bent down and was about to unlace her half-boots when someone knocked on the door. She straightened, feeling slight trepidation. '*Sì?*' She prayed it was not Nico.

It was Raf. She walked to the door and opened it. 'I would like to speak to you for a moment,' he said.

'Come in.' She stepped aside and allowed him to pass her into the room. 'You have no bruises,' she told him.

'What?'

'It is nothing. What do you wish to say to me?'

'Nico would like you to dine with him tonight. In private.'

She frowned at him. 'I really do not feel inclined to do so.'

He sighed. 'I am rather weary of playing matchmaker for both of you. He cares for you. You care for him.'

She shook her head. 'He asked me why, if I cared for him, I could not marry him. I told him I could not live with another ghost.'

'Caterina.'

'I never made Marco really happy. He always mourned her.'

'Barbarina told you that, no? She did not want you taking Caterina's place, but more than that, because her husband did not love her, she did not want Marco to love you.'

'It was not just Barbarina. I saw it when he looked at me.'

He took her hand. 'Listen to me, Cecily. He mourned her, it is true, but he loved you as well. He knew he was ill almost as soon as he brought you to Italy, but he did not know how to tell you. He worried about you and did not want to burden you with the knowledge he would not live very long.'

Tears sprang to her eyes. 'I…I did not know. He never said anything to me.'

'It was not always easy for Marco to speak of his feelings. Nico is much like him in that regard.' He looked at her for a moment. 'I think you should at least hear what Nico has to say to you. You did wish to give him the journal, no?'

'You could give it to him.'

'It will mean more if you do.' He closed her hand over her palm. 'At this moment, you hold his happiness here, in your hand. It is only right that you let him know what you have decided.'

'What if I do not know?' she whispered.

He brushed a kiss across her knuckles. 'I think you do.'

Cecily stood in the doorway of the small salon for a moment. Nico stood near the window and turned immediately. He stared at her for a moment as if she was an apparition. 'You came,' he finally said.

'Yes. Raf said you wanted to see me.'

He moved towards her. 'Come in.'

She stepped into the room.

'You are only here because of Raf?' he asked.

Certainly he did not look as if she held his happiness or fate or whatever nonsense Raf had said in her hand. 'Is there something you wished to say to me?'

'Why are you travelling to Venice with Raf? Particularly since you so recently left it.'

'I was coming to see you. Raf insisted on escorting me.'

Surprise flickered across his features. 'Indeed. I rather thought from your polite note that you had no wish to see me again. Except in the capacity of a relation. So were you coming to see me as a relation?'

'I have something to give you.'

'Indeed. Then it is most convenient that we met here. You will not need to travel all the way to Venice after all. What is it you wished to give me? It cannot be the ring—you left it in Venice.'

He was still angry. Because she had hurt his pride? She was suddenly very tired.

She held out the journal. 'I found this among Barbarina's possessions. I wanted you to have it.'

He took it from her and then opened the book. He stared down at the page for a moment, then slowly looked up at her. 'It is Angelina's journal.'

'Yes.'

'Why did you bring it to me?'

'Because you loved her. And because, if you read her last entries, you will see that she loved you. She never had any intention of breaking off your betrothal.'

He looked back down at the book. She waited for a moment and then silently left the salon.

She had just reached the door of her room when she heard footsteps behind her. 'Cecily,' Nico said.

'What is it you want?'

He hesitated for a moment. 'I was going to Avezza to find you.'

She looked up. 'Why? To take me to task over the note I wrote? Or the ring? Perhaps I should have waited until you returned, but you were so distant and so cold that I did not think it mattered whether I was there or not. At any rate, I think we have said all that needs to be said between us.' She inserted the key into the lock, only to find his hand over hers.

'We haven't said all that needs to be said. At least, I have not,' he said quietly. 'Would you grant me a few moments at least? I vow I will not approach you again unless it is your wish.'

The arrogant duke had fallen away. Instead he looked almost desperate. 'Very well.'

'In your room or downstairs? I promise I want nothing more than to talk to you.'

Downstairs would be more circumspect, but she was too tired to think of going back down. 'My room, if you please.'

She managed to open the door despite her trembling hands and stepped into the room. He followed her and she moved as far away from him as she could. He shut the door and leaned against it. He had Angelina's journal in his hand.

She tried to keep her voice calm. 'What do you want to say to me?'

'When I read your note, I was angry. But more than that, I was afraid.' His dark eyes were fixed on her face. 'Afraid I would not see you again. Afraid you would never agree to marry me.'

'I thought we had agreed we were not going to marry.' She clasped her hands together to keep them from trembling.

'I've changed my mind. I want you to marry me.'

'I have no idea why.'

'I love you.'

Her head spun for a moment. 'You cannot,' she whispered.

'But I do. I came to ask you to forgive me for hurting you. For wanting all of you without offering you the same in return.' He took a step towards her and set the journal down on the dresser. 'I am offering you myself. All of me. With no ghosts between us.'

'Nico…'

He took another step towards her, his eyes never leaving her face. 'You said you cared for me. Is there any chance you still do?'

'Yes. I—'

'Good.' He moved towards her and she found herself backed up against the dresser. 'Because I intend to make you fall in love with me.' A touch of his usual arrogance had returned.

She drew in a shaky breath. 'You do not need to make me fall in love with you.'

His body was nearly touching hers. 'Yes, I do. I intend to begin now.'

'You…you said you only wanted to talk.'

'I have changed my mind about that as well.' The determined look in his eye made her legs tremble.

'Nico…wait, there is something I must tell you.'

'Later.' He caught her into his arms and pulled her against him. His mouth sought hers. She resisted for a moment, and then her body melded into his as she gave herself completely to him.

Nico opened his eyes. The soft, warm body against his filled him with a lazy, peaceful contentment. He shifted a little, moving his arm out from under her so that he could turn and pull her more fully against him. He felt the stirrings of arousal, but he would control his urge at least for now.

He could not keep from nuzzling her neck, however, revelling in her clean, sweet taste and the faint scent of lovemaking that clung to her. She had responded with the same passion as before. She would succumb soon enough. Before they returned to Venice he intended to first take her to the small villa he owned in the hills above Vicenza where he would thoroughly and enjoyably compromise her.

She stirred. His groin tightened and he could not resist planting another kiss on the back of her soft neck. She half-turned, her breast brushing his hand and he nearly groaned. Her eyes fluttered open. 'You are still here,' she whispered. 'I was not dreaming.'

'No, *cara*.' He brushed the hair from her forehead.

'Nor were you dreaming when I told you that you are going to marry me.'

A half-smile touched her lips. 'You could ask me, you know.'

'You might say no. I would rather you had no choice.'

'I might say yes.'

His pulse quickened. 'Would you?'

'Yes. Yes, I think I would.'

'Only think? I want you to be certain.'

'But are you?'

He saw the doubt in her eyes. His first impulse was to kiss all her reservations away, but something in her expression stopped him. 'Why would you think I am not?'

She sat up. 'Where did you go after you left Venice?

He sat up as well, the cover falling from his chest. 'I needed to tell Angelina goodbye.' He looked away for a moment. 'For the first time since her death I felt she was finally at peace. I knew she was finally gone.' He glanced down at Cecily. 'I left that day to return to you. I wanted to see you, beg your forgiveness. But you were gone.'

She caught his hand. 'I am so sorry. I did not think you needed me. Or wanted me. So I…I left. But then Raf came. He insisted that I return to you because you needed me. And because he needed a happy ending.'

'Raf is very wise.' He drew her against his chest. 'Promise me you will not run away again.'

'No. Yes, I promise I will not.'

He drew her against him. 'So, if I ask you to marry me, will you say "yes"?'

'Yes.'

His arm tightened around her. 'Will you marry me, Cecily?'

'Yes.'

'As soon as I procure the licence.'

'In the family chapel?'

He laughed and dropped a kiss on her forehead. 'No. Here. First, I've no intention of giving you time to change your mind. We can have a second ceremony when we return to England. We will spend as much time in Italy as you wish.'

'I think I would like to become reacquainted with England. I finally wrote to my grandmother.'

'Good. We will invite her to our wedding.' Although he was not paying much attention. The quilt had fallen away to reveal one pink-tipped breast and he could think of nothing but loving her again. He slid down and pulled her on top of him. 'But for now, I have other business to attend to. Such as making you fall in love with me.'

His hand cupped one of her rounded breasts, his finger and thumb tracing leisurely circles around the sensitive, hardened nipple.

Her little moan made him smile. 'In fact, I am considering holding you prisoner until you do.'

'Nico…' She gasped as his hand drifted down her stomach to the juncture of her thighs. 'Please…wait. I must tell you something.'

'Not now.' He had no intention of allowing her to change her mind. His mouth found hers, stifling any protest.

* * *

A fortnight later Cecily and Nico stood in the garden of the Villa. Their wedding had taken place that morning, a quiet ceremony that was attended only by their families. Raf had come as he promised, although he did not stay long. After the ceremony and the breakfast, Nico brought her outside to the garden.

He took her hand and she glanced at him, her heart swelling with tenderness and love. His face, which had always seemed so harsh, was now familiar, the hardness no longer quite so visible, particularly when he turned to smile at her as he did now. He looked happy and she was still amazed that she had that effect on him. She returned his smile and then took a breath.

'I have something I have wanted to say to you since we met at the inn.' For some odd reason, her hand was shaking.

His smile faded and he dropped her hand. 'It is rather late if you have suddenly changed your mind about wedding me.'

'Oh, no.' She caught his hand to hold it again. 'It is not that at all. I wanted to tell you that I...I love you.'

He looked rather stunned. 'You love me?'

'I tried to tell you at the inn. That you did not need to make me fall in love with you because I was already in love with you. You would not give me a chance to tell you.'

His laugh was shaky. 'I promise from now on I will give you as many chances as you want. I cannot think of a better wedding gift from you.'

She wrapped her arms around his neck and drew him to her. Their kiss was tender and unhurried, a kiss full of promise and, most of all, a kiss full of hope.

* * * * *